Suddenly the Splendid Samaritan was looking at a gun pointed at his head.

"This," the cleaning woman said, " in case you don't recognize it, is a .22-caliber pistol, fully loaded. Not a large gun, but quite effective. I can put six bullets in your head before you can do anything else foolish. Now sit down."

Trent collapsed in his chair shaking.

"What do you want?" he managed to ask in a quivering voice.

"All will be revealed in good time," the cleaning lady replied. "Now, Mr. Splendid Samaritan, please put your elbows on the desk and place your hands together as if you are praying. You do know how to assume the attitude of prayer, don't you? After all, you are a great Christian leader."

REVEREND RANDOLLPH AND THE SPLENDID SAMARITAN

Charles Merrill Smith

IVY BOOKS • NEW YORK

Ivy Books
Published by Ballantine Books
Copyright © 1986 by Charles Merrill Smith

Library of Congress Catalog Card Number: 85-30132

ISBN 0-8041-0141-8

This edition published by arrangement with G. P. Putnam's Sons, a division of The Putnam Publishing Group, Inc.

Manufactured in the United States of America

First Ivy Books Edition: August 1987

To Betty with love: wife, mother, grandmother, whole person

Foreword

Concerning the Reverend "Con" Randollph
and Charles Merrill Smith

At this point in history the public is seldom impressed by overly sanctimonious people, no matter what their particular persuasion may be. Claiming to be "holier than thou" is no longer a popular attitude. At times one wonders how much better off we might be if the Puritans had never landed here with their banners, their arrogance, and their virulent prejudices.

As we have progressed in medicine, other sciences, and the arts, we have found more of what is expected of us and how we are supposed to live. We have learned, for example, that we are not to hold our fellow men in bondage, although we still do in some parts of the world, or put them to the torture to force them to profess an official faith, whether they believe in it or not. But despite this, the whole religious establishment has maintained a certain mustiness about it and a strongly ingrained reluctance toward any material changes.

Then in 1965, a clergyman, Dr. Charles Merrill Smith, published a book called *How to Become a Bishop Without Being Religious* and blew a stream of welcome fresh air through the whole ecclesiastical structure. The book became a runaway best seller and Dr. Smith an overnight celebrity. Bishops of the stature of James A. Pike and Gerald Kennedy praised his work.

Next came *When the Saints Go Marching Out*, a work that kept the light burning brightly in homes and parsonages far into the night. Not everyone in church work was delighted, but no one could deny the brilliant mind and keen wit that were awakening such a fresh interest in church affairs and doctrines.

Well warmed up, Charles Merrill Smith next produced *The Pearly Gates Syndicate, or How to Sell Real Estate in Heaven*, a delightful and entertaining history of the Christian Church with sidelights on "How to Convert Pagans at the Lowest Possible Cost" and other fascinating topics.

Pyramid climbing in the social sense received the Merrill Treatment in *Instant Status, or How to Become a Pillar of the Upper Middle Class*.

Then came Reverend Randollph. In a striking departure from his previous form, Dr. Smith undertook the exacting and sometimes intricate format of the classical detective story and scored heavily the first time out with *Reverend Randollph and the Wages of Sin*. After that he was "in" as a top flight mystery writer with an engaging new detective and a remarkably deft hand at devising ingenious plots for him to unravel.

The Reverend "Con" Randollph is the temporary pastor of a very affluent Chicago congregation that owns a skyscraper in the Loop. The church occupies the bottom floors, the rest are rented out at ascending rates to other tenants. All but the penthouse, which is the parsonage. Con (for confidence man) Randollph is a retired quarterback of the Los Angeles Rams professional football team. He earned his nickname when an opposing player remarked on his signal calling, "He keeps selling us the Brooklyn Bridge and we keep buying it."

Con Randollph is a very good minister, not too overlaid with piety, who has an engaging wife and a decided talent for detective work. Take it from there. Every one of the Reverend Randollph books is a gem and they are all wonderfully entertaining.

It was at the 1984 Bouchercon mystery convention in Chicago that I met Dr. Smith. As it happened, I was on a panel charged with discussing the most promising new talents in the crime writing field. It fell to me to mention him before any of the others did. At that point our chairman announced that Dr. Smith was present in the audience. Far in the back a quiet gentleman stood up and received the applause of his peers. It was the first time he had appeared at a mystery convention.

Later we lunched together. Mrs. Smith was most patient while we discussed many aspects of crime writing, religion, and various other matters. He told me that the church he had created for Reverend Randollph had an actual prototype in the city, and that there *was* a seminary known as East Jesus Tech. It was a memorable occasion and I am eternally grateful that I was there to enjoy it.

Not long after that I learned that he had passed away. It was then that I fully realized the depth of the friendship that had been formed in so brief a time. His son, who is also a notable and gifted author, has finished the last few pages of this work in accordance with his father's intentions. He was the ideal man for the job. And if he chooses to continue the saga of Reverend Randollph, I suspect he will have some fine guidance from a very high plain indeed.

John Ball

Prologue

The squat frame building would have been vastly improved by a coat of white paint to cover the sickly green that Fanny Evans had chosen for her husband's office. The dull green was already peeling. Huddled in the dusty parking area this August evening were two abused-looking pickup trucks, a middle-aged Buick, and a Ford losing its life to rust. A new Chrysler New Yorker also cockily flaunted its two-toned tail fins. The hot, heavy air distributed, as always, the smell of oil refineries.

The sign on the door of the building stated that it housed C. Albert Evans, Attorney at Law.

Inside there was a small room furnished with five plain chairs, upholstered in green plastic, for the convenience, if not the comfort, of clients wishing the counsel of Mr. Evans. It also contained a gray metal desk with a typewriter and a plaque announcing that Bobbie Belle Parker was a Notary Public.

The remainder of the building was divided into Mr. Evans' office, a file and storage room, and what the gilt lettering on the door said was the conference room.

In the conference room, three men and one woman were seated at a long metal table painted to look like wood. Another man was moving from person to person designating where they should sign a document of several legal-size pages. Like the others in the room, he was young, probably little more than thirty. But his brown hair was already thin. He was a large man, something over six feet, and had a belly and jowls that predicted that before long he would be not merely corpulent, but genuinely fat.

Two of the men and the woman signed the document without looking at it. One man said, "Hey, Big Al, this just say what we all agreed to?"

"Just like we agreed, Everett. Phrased in proper legal language, of course."

"Good enough," Everett replied and signed.

"Your turn, Norbert. Seein' as how you're the big cheese in this here enterprise, we accord you the honor of puttin' the last touch, so to speak, on it. Here's where you sign." Big Al pointed with a finger fat as a sausage.

Norbert, though, picked up the document and began to read it. He was a tall man, slender, but not skinny. His mop of blonde hair needed trimming, and his white shirt, though clean, was frayed at the collar. He might have been handsome but for a mouth too small for his face, which gave an impression of weakness. Had he been a man sensitive to people's moods, he would have noticed the tension among his associates around the table as he read.

"The important part, it's over here on page six," Big Al said hastily. Without taking the document, he flipped the pages. "See here, Norbert, it says plain out—plain out as a lawyer can be—" he laughed, a snort that said we're all good friends here, nothing to worry about "—that you, bein' the inventor of this oil drillin' tool which we believe will revolutionize the industry, that you are awarded forty percent of the stock, controllin' interest. The rest is split up even among the rest of us. That's our compensation for puttin' up the money you needed to finish your invention." Big Al paused to let this sink in, then continued.

"'Course, you could back out. All we got is a verbal agreement between friends. Be like welshin' on a bet, something no honorable man would do. But you could." Big Al let the words hang there in the silence.

After a moment, Norbert smiled, and the others almost visibly relaxed. He took the pen Big Al was holding out to him, scratched his signature at the bottom of the page, and said, "I don't understand business and law and all that. I'm an engineer and I like to invent things, improve things."

Big Al patted him on the back. "That's why you need us, boy." He turned to the woman. "Now Bobbie Belle, if you'll be so kind as to notarize this here document, Acme Enterprises will be in business."

When the document had been notarized, one of the men spoke up, apparently hesitantly. "Uh, Big Al, hadn't we ought to have a meeting of the company, sort of get organized? Got to have a secretary, anyway, to take minutes of our meetings."

"Guess we should, Tim." Big Al spoke hastily, like the lead in the senior class play who was afraid if he didn't blurt out his lines he would forget them.

"Then I nominate Bobbie Belle Parker be our secretary."

Another man said, "Tim, you gotta have a chairman to preside over this meetin'. That right, Big Al?"

"The proper legal way to do it, Ev, would be to name a chairman pro tem."

"What's that mean?"

"It means a temporary chairman who will act until a permanent chairman is chosen."

The man named Tim looked annoyed with himself. "Guess I forgot that. Big Al, why don't you be chairman whatever you said? Unless anyone disagrees."

No one disagreed.

"Glad to," Big Al said. "Now Tim, your nomination of Bobbie Belle for secretary is in order."

"So move," Tim said.

"Second? Everett seconds. Any other nominations? Hearing none, those who agree to the nomination of Bob-

3

bie Belle Parker as secretary of Acme Enterprises say aye. Opposed no. The ayes have it. Bobbie Belle, did you get all that?"

"Sure, Al."

"You're now the secretary. Is there any other business needs tendin' to tonight?"

"Uh, Big Al—I mean Mr. Chairman, there is one little matter I'd like to bring up."

"Yes, Tim, what's that?" Big Al tried to look surprised.

"Uh, this item, uh—" he flipped the pages of the document, of which they all had copies "—page nine, paragraph 4A states that Acme Enterprises is authorized to issue ten thousand shares of stock."

"That's right, Tim."

"Par value one dollar per share."

"Right."

"And Norbert gets four thousand shares considering his invention, and the rest of us get a thousand shares each considering our financing the project up to this point."

"Well, mine is in return for doing all the legal work without charge."

"Right. Makes no difference. Now paragraph 4B states that any time, by a majority vote of the stockholders, Acme Enterprises can buy out the stock of any stockholder?"

Norbert, who had been slouching in his chair bored by the business discussion, suddenly sat upright. "I don't remember anything in our verbal agreement about that kind of provision."

"Just a legal thing, Norbert." Big Al spoke soothingly. "It's, uh, customary to include such a clause in this kind of contract." He didn't sound very convincing.

There was a nervous shuffling of feet and clearing of throats around the table. Tim decided he'd better get on with it before some of the group lost its nerve.

"I move, Mr. Chairman, that Acme Enterprises purchase the four thousand shares awarded to Mr. Norbert Palmquist at par value as provided by paragraph 4B, et cetera—you can get the details down right, can't you, Bobbie Belle?"

"Sure," Bobbie Belle said.

"Hear a second to the motion?" Big Al said.

"Second." The voice was almost a whisper.

"Speak up, Ev," Big Al instructed.

"Second." This time louder.

Norbert Palmquist looked stunned. "You can't do this, you can't," he finally managed to say. "It's my invention. It's worth millions."

"We don't know that," Tim said. "It has possibilities of being profitable." He turned to Big Al. "Mr. Chairman, I call for the secretary to poll each of us on this question."

Bobbie Belle said, "I vote aye." She then queried each of the men, leaving Norbert Palmquist till last. "Norbert?" she asked. He didn't answer.

"Seein' as how the vote is unanimous except for Norbert, record him as not votin', Bobbie Belle, I declare the motion carried."

Tim stood up. "In accordance with the provisions of the Acme Enterprises rules of incorporation and this vote, I now present a certified check for four thousand dollars to Norbert Palmquist to buy his shares in this corporation at the stipulated par value." He walked around to Palmquist and laid the check on the table in front of him.

This seemed to rouse Palmquist from his stupor. He looked at each of his erstwhile business partners in turn. Some of them avoided his gaze. He spoke with no anger, only despair.

"You were my friends," he said slowly. "I trusted you. I usually trust people, but especially my friends. My invention would have made us all rich. It will make you all rich. But not me." He paused. "I don't long to be rich and live in fancy houses and drive big cars. I just wanted to provide for my family and have enough money to spend all my time inventing things. But you cheated me. My friends. You're all crooks."

"We aren't crooks, Norbert," Tim spoke smoothly. "Just

5

businessmen—and women, a businesswoman. There's nothing crooked about it. You didn't have to sign the papers. In business, if it's legal, it's honest. Isn't that right, Big Al?"

"Yeah." Big Al didn't sound very sure about it.

"Now, since you're no longer a stockholder and we have some further business to transact," Tim continued smoothly, "we'll excuse you, Norbert."

Norbert Palmquist rose wearily from his chair, shuffled slowly to the door. He turned around, looked at each person in the room as if searching for someone to come to his rescue. Then he left, closing the door softly.

After Palmquist had left, Tim said, "Mr. Chairman, I move that Norbert's shares in Acme Enterprises be distributed as follows: twenty-five hundred shares to me because I have put together the financing to get this company started. None of us has the money to do it, none of us has any real money—but I know where to get it, and I'm the only one of us who can. The remainder of Norbert's shares are to be divided among the rest of you. And I'll include in the motion that I be named president of the company. That, by the way," he added, "is a condition stipulated by the financial backers I've lined up."

The motion passed.

"Can Norbert cause us any trouble?" Everett Stagg asked. "Could he sue?"

"Anybody can sue," Big Al answered.

But he won't," Tim assured them. "I know people. Norbert's brilliant, but he's weak. Now, if you'll excuse me, there's a lady I promised to take for a ride in my new Chrysler."

The next morning Tim, trailing a stream of dust, zipped his New Yorker into the parking area next to the law office of C. Albert Evans and docked it with a flourish near the building's door. It was too early for the sun to have gotten down to its serious business of making the day hot, humid, and miserable. The stench from the oil refineries was not yet the suffocating miasma it would become later in the day.

Tim went up the steps of the porch fronting the Evans building with the vigor of a man who had a busy day ahead and was looking forward to it. He went through the reception room and entered Albert Evans' office without knocking.

"Mornin', Big Al," he said to the large tubby lawyer sitting at his desk and staring moodily at the dry and desolate landscape outside the window. "Well, we did it, by God, we did it! Hey, how come you look so glum? Happy days are here again! You're going to be a rich man."

"Guess you haven't heard the news, Tim," Big Al said, still staring out the window.

"What news you talkin' about? By the looks of you anyone'd think they'd just announced that the Russkis had pushed the button and the big one was already on its way."

"Norbert Palmquist went home last night and shot himself," Big Al said.

Tim selected the most comfortable chair in the office and took his time settling into it. He had a fast, clear mind that was able to reduce problems, even complex problems that require immediate solution, to their essentials. He saw immediately that Norbert Palmquist's suicide was a lucky break for Acme Enterprises. It removed the possibility, however remote, that Norbert could make trouble over the way he had been swindled out of his invention.

On the other hand, he knew that Big Al, like most people who are not above a bit of chicanery if the prize to be won is large enough, cherished a vision of himself as honorable, or at least reasonably honest. They were able to delude themselves unless something happened to one of their schemes so shocking, so unexpected, that self-deception was no longer possible for them. Big Al, he knew, was suffering from feelings of guilt, which he believed came from his contribution to the suicide of his quondam partner and friend, but which Tim knew actually stemmed from

7

Big Al's inability to continue regarding himself as an upright, decent chap.

"Left a wife and three kids," Big Al said to the window.

Tim knew that Big Al could indulge in a little crookedness and rationalize it as sharp but legitimate business practice, leaving his self-image intact. But believing he had a hand in another man's death was just too much for him. Tim saw that the first order of business was damage control, and that he'd better not waste any time. First, placate Big Al.

"Al," he said in a solemn voice, "that's sad news, real sad. I knew, I told you that Norbert was weak. We all knew that. The financial backers I got lined up knew it too. They wanted him out, they were afraid of how he might gum up the works, him having effective majority control. They just didn't want any part of a business with Norbert Palmquist in it." Tim did not consider it relevant to mention that he'd been the one to suggest to the money men that Norbert Palmquist could become a problem for the business.

"I s'pose you're right," Al Evans answered. Tim could see, though, that Big Al was not convinced.

"Look at it this way, Al"—Tim was pleading now—"Norbert had to be, uh, a little off center to do what he did. Nobody with all his marbles kills himself. Oh, people with incurable cancer, maybe. That I can understand. But Norbert was young and healthy and had everything to live for. But, first little problem, first little setback he has, he kills himself. Now I ask you, is that the act of a sane man? Did you advise him to do it? Did I put the idea in his head? No, we didn't. There's nothing we did, nothing anybody did to make him do a damn fool thing like shooting himself. Just keep reminding yourself that you aren't, we aren't responsible for what Norbert did."

Big Al brightened considerably. He was convinced, or at least half-believed, that he wasn't really a bad fellow after all, because he so desperately needed to be convinced.

"You're right, Tim. It certainly isn't our fault."

8

"That's the way to think, Al."

"He didn't do it last night, he probably would have done it next year or sometime," Big Al erected this additional rafter in the self-image he was rebuilding. He paused, then frowned at something he'd just thought of and wished he hadn't. "They were sayin' at Mabel's restaurant—I always eat breakfast there, get the latest gossip that way—that Norbert left a letter to his wife explainin' why he did it."

"A letter can't hurt us," Tim said quickly. This was a good opening for the next step in his damage control program. "We'd better all have the same story about what happened, though."

"Like what?"

Tim thought a minute. "Let's say that Norbert disagreed with policies the rest of us agreed on, and he got mad and said, OK, then buy him out. And that's what we did. And that's all we're going to say about it, period. We stick together, who's to deny our story?"

"Yeah, who could deny it?" This was the kind of minor cheating that Big Al understood and with which he was comfortable.

Tim got up to leave. "I've got to get crackin', get the business underway. You have Bobbie Belle, when she comes in, get hold of Everett and tell him what our story is, and that not one of us is to say any more than that."

"I'll take care of it, Tim."

"And if he gives her any trouble about it, well, I'll be in touch later and handle it. OK?"

"OK," Big Al said.

I

Randollph was bored and irritated. He wished he were somewhere else, almost anywhere else. He'd attended more than his quota of prayer breakfasts and felt that a benevolent Providence should spare him this one. As a matter of fact, he'd ducked numerous invitations to invoke the blessing of Almighty God on the monthly prayer breakfast of Business Executives for Christ (Chicago chapter) through either a fortuitous or a contrived conflict of schedule. But James T. Trent, founder and national president of the organization, was a member of the Church of the Good Shepherd, of which Randollph was senior pastor. The Reverend Mr. Hamilton Haynes Reynolds III, national chaplain of the organization, also occasionally attended his church. It had been at Reynolds' vigorous insistence that Randollph had reluctantly consented to be here today. It was like going to the dentist. You kept putting it off until the pain of not going was greater than the pain of getting it over with.

Chaplain Reynolds, an earnest, attractive young man,

had given Randollph the kind of introduction he got all too often, and which he despised.

"We're especially honored to have with us today the Reverend Dr. C. P. Randollph. He's probably best known to most of you as Con Randollph, the former great quarterback of the Los Angeles Rams." Chaplain Reynolds then went ahead to recite some of the impressive statistics Randollph had piled up as a professional football player, ending with, "But now he's throwing those touchdowns for Christ. Dr. Randollph will now say grace."

There was a spotlight focused on the podium. As Randollph approached it to tell the Lord how much they appreciated the food they were about to receive, Chaplain Reynolds darted to the end of the table, quickly checked a videotape camera set on a tripod. Satisfied that it was correctly aimed at Randollph, he started it going, then—still standing—bowed his head for prayer.

As soon as Randollph said "amen," the waiters began pushing carts of covered plates among the tables, whipping off the covers with a practiced speed, placing a plate in front of each Business Executive for Christ. Most of them dug in immediately to the grayish-yellow scrambled eggs and links of sausages resembling miniature brown hot dogs. Clearly, Randollph thought, it was not the quality of the cuisine that had drawn more than two hundred prosperous-looking men to the hotel's banquet room this morning.

Randollph was meditating on the appeal the Business Executives for Christ prayer breakfasts apparently had for these men and thousands like them meeting all over the nation, eating similar unappetizing food and listening to a gospel that preached that following Christ guaranteed success in business. He hadn't come up with an answer when Chaplain Reynolds sat down beside him.

"I hope you didn't mind the camera running while you were praying," he said. "It does make a little noise, not much, but some."

"I didn't mind," Randollph assured him, "as I expect

11

God could hear me above whatever noise the camera made."

Chaplain Reynolds looked taken aback, then smiled. "I expect He could."

"Why did you make the tape?" Randollph asked, more to make conversation than to satisfy any curiosity he had about it.

"It was the Splendid Samaritan's idea. One of my responsibilities as chaplain is to organize new chapters of BEFC, and the SS thought the best way was to go into a town where some interest had been shown, hold a dinner for the top businessmen in the area, and show them an actual meeting. And I like to do it. I'm afraid I'm a video nut."

"Will you use that shot of me saying grace in one of your, er, promotional films?"

Chaplain Reynolds replied with enthusiasm, "Bet your life! Everyone from Florida to Alaska knows who you are —the men, anyway."

Randollph felt a fresh surge of irritation and started to say: "I refuse to be used to encourage people to join Business Executives for Christ. I will not put my imprimatur on your organization's silly theology, which—so far as I can tell—has no real connection with the Christian faith."

But he checked himself. It would be rude to browbeat this zealous young man who probably believed fervently in what he was doing.

When the Business Executives for Christ had cleaned up the indifferently prepared breakfast that Randollph had blessed, and waiters had refilled coffee cups, a tall, thin man with graying hair approached the podium and adjusted the microphone.

"That's Warren Helperin," Chaplain Reynolds whispered to Randollph. "He's president of our Chicago chapter and national board chairman. Very successful lawyer. Going to run for governor. He's only forty. Looks older." Helperin cleared his throat and called for silence. The noise

12

of conversation died a slow death, and Helperin helped kill it with a sharp rap of his gavel.

"Quiet down," he ordered. "We don't want to waste any time because we have a special treat today. Our founder and president of our national organization is our speaker today. He's one of us, of course, ours is the original chapter of BEFC, and he's a resident of our community. But he's on the road all the time speaking and promoting our great organization, so we don't see enough of him. But he's here today. Let's welcome Jim Trent, the Splendid Samaritan!"

The Business Executives for Christ were on their feet cheering, whistling, shouting as if Warren Helperin had just announced that the Cubs had won the World Series or the second coming of Christ would occur in the next minute or two.

Randollph had met James Trent, but didn't really know him. He hardly ever came to church because he was somewhere every weekend spreading the gospel that Christ could help you beat the competition in the strenuous world of modern business. About all Randollph knew about him was that he was very rich, that he made large and well-publicized gifts to many Chicago institutions, and that the news media always referred to him as the Splendid Samaritan. Randollph wondered if this appellation had been invented by a clever press agent or if James Trent had thought it up himself, then decided he was being cynical.

The Splendid Samaritan advanced briskly to the podium, leaned toward the microphone, and said, "Thank you, thank you, my friends. Please be seated!" He was not an impressive figure, but Randollph recognized "pulpit presence" when he saw it. James Trent, he knew, was about sixty years old, though a full head of thick black hair that a sharp eye could detect as a very expensive toupee helped—from a distance anyway—to make him look younger. He was not six feet tall, and not heavy. But he projected a personality that was accustomed to running things, giving orders and expecting to be obeyed.

13

Randollph wasn't much interested in Jim Trent's message. He could guess what it would be. There were other preachers of the doctrine of secular success flowing from religious faith. Most people sort of hoped and even expected to arrive safely in Paradise when they shuffled off this mortal coil. But they weren't in any hurry about it. As a sales pitch for espousing Christianity, it was not a powerful persuader. But religion as the path to getting a generous slice of this world's good things always got an enthusiastic reception.

But, Randollph had to admit, however dubious Jim Trent's theology, the Splendid Samaritan was a splendid speaker. He began with a low-key delivery, which he increased in power and persuasiveness. He related how he'd started life as a poor boy. But he read his Bible and studied the life of Christ. He'd learned that Christ had a clear goal and superb organizing ability, had mastered the art of influencing others, and worked hard. He'd followed Christ's principles in his own business career, and they worked. He gave all the credit to Christ.

By the time he finished, he had the crowd on its feet, cheering. Randollph reluctantly admired the skill with which Trent had excited his audience.

The prayer breakfast broke up after the Splendid Samaritan's speech. A cluster of Business Executives for Christ formed around Trent. Most of the men, though, hurried out, no doubt anxious to be about the business of getting to be top dog by employing Christ's principles of success. Reynolds thanked Randollph for coming. It occurred to Randollph that his brief blessing had been the only prayer uttered at this prayer breakfast.

Randollph had only to go out the front door of the hotel and then into the front door of the Church of the Good Shepherd. This unusual juxtaposition of hostelry and holy place had been created by the last of the church's series of incarnations.

The Church of the Good Shepherd had been established

when Chicago was an infant, little more than a trading post. Its inhabitants were mostly a rough lot, more interested in the sins of the flesh than Christian piety. No records exist as to the success of the little frontier mission in turning drunks, brawlers, prostitutes, and thieves from their ungodly ways and into exemplary Christian citizens. But as an institution, it prospered. As the city grew, the little mission transformed itself into a genuine church. And, by the time Chicago had become hog butcher to the world, with a significant entrepreneurial class, the Church of the Good Shepherd perceived that the Lord wanted it to minister to a more genteel class of sinners. It managed to corner the market in what passed for an upper class in this rowdy young city, discarding several modest buildings when they became inadequate and raising successively larger and more pretentious houses of worship to accommodate its rapidly increasing clientele.

But socially conscious sinners always want to worship the Lord in an edifice that not only testifies to the glory of God, but also reflects favorably on their station in life. So, at outrageous expense, the church built a large, ponderous-looking Romanesque house of God. Some people thought it a mite gloomy, but all agreed that it was imposing. And the trustees assured them it would last for at least two hundred years.

Unfortunately, the trustees had failed to anticipate the rapid growth of Chicago's business district and the spectacular increase in real estate values accompanying it. Suddenly, it seemed, the Church of the Good Shepherd was occupying a large plot of the most expensive real estate in the city. Almost every day the trustees received offers from the real estate developers to buy the church for ridiculously high prices. This was the occasion for much pain among the trustees and other businessmen in the congregation who knew and fully appreciated the value of a dollar. There developed a strong sentiment among them to sell out and relocate the church in some affluent suburb.

Then one trustee said, "Why don't we tear down the

15

church, then build our office building and hotel with the church inside it?" Some members thought this mixing of commerce and Christianity sounded sacrilegious until it was explained to them that the plan would lift an increasingly onerous financial burden from the backs of the membership, since the income from rents and leases, rather than personal contributions, would provide most of the money the church needed for operating expenses. This explanation enabled the doubters to see that the Lord was leading them to keep their church downtown.

"But we've got to do something to make it look like a church," some of them insisted. So when the office-cum-hotel building was up, it was topped off with a giant ecclesiastical tower tapering into the city's sky and resembling a huge inverted funnel decorated with gargoyles and other carvings appropriate to medieval ecclesiastical architecture, thus stamping a divine blessing on this wedding of faith and Mammon.

The street door of the church didn't open on the nave. It admitted Randollph to a busy lobby with banks of elevators on each side. This lobby was always crowded during business hours with businessmen, secretaries, and customers either being disgorged from the down cars or waiting for transport upward. Randollph decided to take the stairs to the third floor where the church's offices and his study were located. He needed the exercise.

As he climbed the steps he knew that Miss Windfall would be waiting with a list of his duties for the day. He had inherited Adelaide Windfall along with the job. She was the kind of secretary who had secretaries. Her long tenure had made her privy to a vast amount of information about members of Good Shepherd, both those present and those who had long since been assigned their niche in the next life. Randollph doubted that Miss Windfall ever included Christian commitment, moral merit, or upright living in calculating the worth of any member of Good Shepherd. Were she God, Randollph was certain, Miss Windfall would have dispatched members of Good Shepherd to heaven, hell, or purgatory on the basis of how many generations of their family had been connected with the church.

Miss Windfall had established a ritual of trailing the pastor into his study laden with correspondence to be signed, memos of what she and Good Shepherd expected him to accomplish this day, and other matters that Randollph classed as trivia, but that Miss Windfall considered the essential oil that kept the machinery of the church operating efficiently. Before she could begin her recital, Randollph asked: "Miss Windfall, what can you tell me about James Trent? I know he's a member of the church, and that he's wealthy—and, of course, that he's very generous with his gifts to charities. But that's about all I know about him."

Miss Windfall placed her pile of papers on the corner of Randollph's desk. "Mr. Trent is a member of Good Shepherd because, after he moved to Chicago, he married the widow of Martin Augustus Jackson. Her maiden name was Elva Cooper. Both the Jackson family and the Cooper family have been members of Good Shepherd for generations. Mr. Trent is a member here because he married Elva Cooper Jackson." Miss Windfall didn't actually sniff when mentioning Trent's name, but by her tone, she dismissed him as of no consequence. No matter that he was rich and generous. No matter that he was "a truly good man," as an editorial in some paper or other had recently said. No matter that he was known as the Splendid Samaritan. By Miss Windfall's standards, Trent's entry into Good Shepherd was recent and through the back door. He was, in her opinion, unworthy.

Randollph sighed and wondered idly where Miss Windfall was able to purchase a foundation garment of the size and strength needed to contain her formidable bulk.

"Do the Trents have any children?" he asked her.

"No, Elva Jackson—Elva Trent was unable to have children. She and her first husband adopted a boy and a girl—both grown now."

17

"I see," Randollph said.

Miss Windfall picked up the sheaf of papers she had brought to Randollph's desk. She put several letters in front of him. "Please sign these in time for the ten o'clock mail pickup. This is Mr. Smelser's monthly financial report, which he is anxious to have you read today. This afternoon is your scheduled day for hospital calling. I've listed on separate cards each patient's name, condition, and hospital, as usual. Then—"

Miss Windfall placed prodding pastors into doing their clear and current duties high on the list of her job responsibilities. They were, in her experience, shameless procrastinators.

II

Big Al Evans had mixed feelings about late-night appointments with prospective clients. On the one hand, they interfered with his drinking. He spent almost every evening hoisting a few with his buddies at one of several exclusive clubs. On the other hand, a late-night appointment with a client who wished to remain anonymous usually meant the client needed to be extricated from some mess, probably crooked, that he'd gotten himself into. And that, in turn, meant fat fees for a lawyer who could enable the client to escape the consequences of his folly.

The sign on the door read Evans, Kimball, and Turnbull, Attorneys at Law. He'd come a long way since he'd moved to Houston. The office was in one of the most prestigious and expensive buildings in the city. Kimball was a specialist in the oil business. Turnbull was a whiz at managing trusts and estates and added a touch of class to the firm's reputation.

Big Al liked to say, "I ain't got any specialty. I'm just an' ole country lawyer, do anything the young fellers don't want to do." As a matter of fact, he conducted the most specialized practice in the firm. Big Al was a fixer. He knew how to bribe a judge. He could suborn jurors without getting caught at it. On occasion he employed professional muscle to intimidate hostile witnesses. He was especially good at the use of discreet blackmail against officials of the Internal Revenue Service to insure that a client in tax trouble would get a favorable ruling.

Naturally, he couldn't advertise his legal specialty, but he didn't need to. Everyone in Houston knew that if you had legal problems with dim prospects of solving them in any orthodox manner, Big Al Evans was the man to see. This specialty commanded the highest lawyer's fees, and he wasn't bashful about charging them. Anyway, his clients usually thought of the cost as a bargain and were grateful to him.

He left the door to the office suite unlocked, as he'd told his anonymous client he would. He passed quickly through the large reception room that had been furnished by Houston's best-known interior decorators. To the critical eye it looked antiseptically expensive, but Big Al thought it elegant. His own large office, as costly and tasteless as the reception room, was behind the first door off the hall that gave access to the equally spacious accommodations of his partners and the offices, considerably smaller and plainer, of several attorneys who were not partners but employees.

Big Al turned on the bronze chandelier that looked like something twisted and bent without forethought or design and left the door open so his client could find him easily. He settled himself in the oversized chair behind the monstrous slab of marble perched on teakwood legs as large as tree trunks. The chair as well as the desk had been custom made. Big Al liked large things, and it pleased him to know that there wasn't another chair or desk like these in the whole world. It also pleased him that the ridiculously high price of such items was a deductible business expense, which was almost like getting them for nothing.

Big Al had just gotten settled behind his desk when he heard the door to the outer office open and close. At least the client was on time. There was a knock on Big Al's partially opened door. Big Al heaved himself to his feet and said, "Do come in." His first look at prospective clients who made such late-night appointments was always interesting. Sometimes they almost smelled of money. But other times they didn't. One of the largest fees he'd ever received had come from a client who looked as if he'd assembled his wardrobe at a secondhand clothing store, and who stunk as if he hadn't had a bath in a year.

"Mr. C. Albert Evans?"

"Yes, indeed. Here, take the chair near the desk." This client didn't look rich and didn't look poor. The client was carrying two rather large, square leather-covered cases. This was a good sign. Big Al made a bet with himself that those cases contained files filled with tax records. Tax problems, which he could usually fix, merited the largest fees.

The client didn't say anything. This made Big Al uncomfortable. Late-night clients usually were so anxiety-ridden that they began babbling before they even sat down. Sometimes he had to interrupt them, slow them down, cajole them into talking coherently.

"You have a problem?" Big Al was impatient, but did not permit this to alter the friendly I'm-just-here-to-help-you tone of voice.

The client said, "Yes," then laid a sheet of paper on the slab of marble in front of the lawyer. "I need the addresses of the people on this list—except for the first name on the list. That one I already have."

"I don't see—"

"You will. Look at the list. You recognize the names, don't you?"

Big Al quickly scanned the list and suddenly felt weak. "Who are you?" he managed to ask.

"Look at me carefully," the client replied. "Think back twenty-five years or so. Do I look like someone you knew then? Someone who thought you were his good friend?"

Big Al was genuinely scared now. He couldn't remember when his heart had pounded so. His doctor had warned him to lose weight. He was asking too much of his heart, the doctor had said, and sooner or later it would refuse to work hard enough to pump blood through the massive blubber he'd accumulated with a diet of sixteen-ounce sirloins and heaping plates of Texas barbecue, all sloshed down with copious tumblers of sour mash whiskey.

"I see that you recognize me," the client said. "Yes, I'm who you think I am. Now write out the addresses of those names on the list. You were easy enough to find. And so was the first name on the list. But I haven't been able to locate the other two. I'm sure you'll help me."

Big Al decided to bluster his way out. "Who says I'll give you these addresses?" he demanded belligerently.

"This," the client said. Big Al was suddenly looking at a gun in the client's hand. His heart took another jump.

"But perhaps you want to remain stubborn," the client spoke pleasantly. "So let's do a couple of things to aid your memory."

"You can't get away with this, there's laws against it!" Big Al was almost shouting now, his voice pushed up several decibels by the fear that was clutching at him.

"You ought to know," the client said. "You've been breaking most of the laws of God and man for a long time."

The client opened one of his leather cases. "We need a little equipment to do this properly," he said. He took a small coil of thin wire from the case. "Put your hands in front of you, palms together, like you were praying. You a praying man, Mr. Evans?"

Big Al tried to answer, but no words came.

"You might want to try it," the client said. "Do as I tell you."

Big Al placed his elbows on the marble desk top and put his palms together. The client quickly wrapped several strands of the thin wire around Big Al's wrists. "That won't be too uncomfortable if you don't move your hands," he assured the lawyer, "but if you make any sudden movement, try to free your hands, it'll hurt worse than anything you've ever felt, not to mention making hamburger out of your wrists. Now let's see. I have a little equipment to set up. Hmm. Ah yes, I can clamp this light to the back of this chair, just so. We'll do this interrogation just like you see the police do it in the television movies. I shine this bright light in your face, turn out the lights, and then ask you questions. Just one other little thing to do first, then we'll be ready."

The room darkened except for the high-intensity light that framed Big Al like a portrait of a man saying his prayers. Even his eyes were closed.

The client found a straight-backed chair, reversed it and sat down straddling it. "Now for the questions. Your name is C. Albert Evans?"

"Y-y-yes." It came out as a croak.

"Commonly called Big Al?"

"Y-y-yes." Another croak.

"You originally practiced law in a little town named Hollyhock Hills, a few miles from here?"

"Yes." Big Al was recovering his wits. Play this madman along, maybe he'd get out of it after all.

"You were one of the founders of Acme Enterprises?"

"Yes."

"And your partners were the names on that list I showed you?"

"Yes."

"Plus a man named Norbert Palmquist, who'd invented an oil-drilling tool that promised to revolutionize the industry?"

"Well, yes." Big Al's voice was stronger now. "We thought it had promise of being profitable, but it was a gamble, you see—"

The client cut him off. "Now you're lying to me." The client stood up and reached for a cloisonné box on the desk. Big Al thought that with a sudden lunge he could bring his bound hands down on the client's neck and knock him out.

23

"Don't even think about it," the client said. "You can't see it in the dark, but I've got the gun on you." He flipped the box open. "I see that you smoke cigarettes. Foreign brand, too. Nasty habit. Bad for your health. Don't use them myself. Don't like the taste." He picked a cigarette out of the box and Big Al saw a flame in the darkness. He decided to try a little friendly conversation. It might help.

"Thought you didn't smoke," he said with all the geniality he could muster.

"There are occasions when it is necessary," the client answered. He moved around behind Big Al. "Now you and your partners have made millions out of Palmquist's invention, right?"

"It turned out better than we had hoped or expected."

"You're being evasive." Suddenly the client jabbed the burning end of the cigarette against Big Al's cheek. Big Al screamed and involuntarily jerked his manacled hands up to knock the cigarette away. The thin wire bit cruelly into the flesh of his wrists. He yelled again.

"I told you you'd hurt yourself if you moved your hands," the client spoke pleasantly. Then, shifting to a hard voice, "Now maybe you'll be more cooperative. Acme Enterprises made millions out of Palmquist's invention, but he didn't, did he?"

"No."

"Why?"

"He sold his interest," Big Al said in an anguished voice.

"Why would he do that?"

"Differences of opinion over policy."

The client took another drag on his cigarette, then suddenly pressed the tip against Big Al's forehead. Again Big Al screamed and jerked his wire-bound wrists upward.

"You cut yourself that time," the client said solicitously. "You're bleeding all over that fancy desk. I'll bet it hurts. Now, why did Palmquist sell his interest? You tricked him, didn't you? You cheated him out of it, didn't you?"

"It was done legal," Big Al whimpered.

"And whatever's legal is moral? Is that what you're telling me? You didn't do anything wrong when you tricked, cheated Palmquist out of his invention?"

"It was Timmy's idea. He set the whole thing up."

"But you all went along with it. You were all greedy. You could have said no."

"You don't know Timmy. He made it sound like a good idea, just good business."

"And what happened to Palmquist?"

Big Al didn't say anything.

"I'm taking another drag on this nasty cigarette so it will be nice and hot, red hot, then I'm going to—"

"No!" Big Al shouted in terror. "He, Palmquist, he killed himself."

"So you and your partners are not only swindlers, but murderers as well?"

"Yes. No. Swindlers maybe, but not murderers. He killed hisself."

"No, you're murderers, all of you. Not legally, but morally." The client sighed. "But I suppose you wouldn't understand that, morally, you all pulled the trigger. Since you have no morals, no ethical sensibilities, I can't expect you to grasp this." The client paused for a moment. "But I can persuade you that it is your moral responsibility to provide me with the present addresses of your partners. I'll just take another drag on this cigarette and—"

"No! No!" Big Al yelled. "I know where they all are. I II tell you, I'll—"

Suddenly the worst pain he'd ever felt lanced across Big Al's chest. He couldn't scream. He couldn't breathe. He knew, in this last moment of his life, that his heart had finally rebelled, as his doctor had warned him that it would. His head fell forward, making a loud thump as it crashed against the marble top of his desk.

The client saw immediately what had happened, then checked to be certain that C. Albert Evans hadn't just fainted from fear but was now standing before a judge he could not bribe. Satisfied that Big Al was dead, the client

25

uttered a string of expletives in sheer frustration. The client hadn't gotten the information so vital to his plans. But one name could be crossed off the list. From the moment Big Al had made that late-night appointment with an anonymous client he was a dead man. The attorney's heart attack had only obviated the client's opportunity to shoot him.

Well, there was still a little work to be done. The client straightened Big Al in the oversized desk chair. Fortunately it had wings on it against which to prop his head. It took a little doing to get Big Al's bound hands on the desk in the attitude of prayer, but finally it was done. The client then took a hundred-dollar bill, swiped it through the blood that had dripped on the desk from the cuts on Big Al's wrists, and inserted it between the dead man's praying hands. Big Al's last client then closed the drapes on the expanse of glass behind the marble desk and adjusted the high-intensity light a bit so that the person who found C. Albert Evans would get a vivid picture of the gross old crook at prayer clutching a bloody piece of currency.

III

"The bishop is here to see you," Miss Windfall informed Randollph over the crackle of the imperfectly wired intercom on Randollph's desk. She would have asked if he had time to see the mayor, or a senator, or perhaps even the President of the United States. Miss Windfall knew that her job included the protection of the pastor from casual callers, no matter their prestige. But bishops were different. They occupied the pinnacle of power in the denomination, they were the boss of bosses. Therefore, the bishop had immediate access to the pastor apart from what Miss Windfall or the pastor wished. Miss Windfall had a thorough grasp of how a bureaucracy worked.

Randollph said, "Welcome, Freddie," to his old friend. "To what do I owe the honor of this visit?"

"I ought to say something like I had a sudden craving for your company. The truth is that I'm using your office as a refuge from a visitor I wish to avoid. I often give thanks for the fact that episcopal headquarters is located in Good Shepherd's office building. Makes it easy for me to escape when the occasion calls for it."

"My, my, Freddie, you are devious."

The bishop settled himself in one of the slightly scruffy leather chairs, which matched the slightly scruffy long leather sofa with which the Reverend Dr. Arthur Hartshorne, Randollph's predecessor, had furnished his spacious study. He crossed his short, oxford-gray-sheathed legs, folded his hands over his plump belly, and said: "I prefer to think of my hasty retreat as discreet rather than devious. Am I interrupting you in the midst of some important task?"

"I should say that yes, you are," Randollph replied. "The truth is, though, that I was just woolgathering."

"Since we're just killing time, entertain me with the products of your woolgathering."

Randollph tilted back in his desk chair, which was extra-large so that it had comfortably accommodated Dr. Arthur Hartshorne's generous gluteus maximus, clasped his hands behind his head, and said: "I guess I started thinking about the open house for the congregation we're having at the parsonage this evening. You and Violet have promised to come, you remember?"

"We're looking forward to it."

"It was Samantha's idea. Do you know Good Shepherd's never had an open house at the parsonage?"

"Matilda Hartshorne was not a very friendly woman. Quite different from your Samantha."

"Well, anyway, that led me to thinking about the strange directions my life has taken, which led to the thought that you, Freddie, have influenced or been the cause of all those twists and turns more than any other single factor."

"Well, I must say I'm flattered. But you're giving me too much credit. I just pointed out some possible directions to you, set some things in motion."

"When I applied for admission to seminary you asked me to drop by your office. Does the dean personally interview every student who applies for admission?"

"Well, no," the bishop admitted. "Mind you, when I was dean I enjoyed getting to know the students. In all honesty, I was curious about you. It isn't often that a famous and highly paid professional athlete suddenly retires at the peak of his career and enters the seminary. I wondered what motivated you."

"There were questions I had about life to which I didn't have the answers, and for some reason I couldn't explain I thought I might find them in a seminary. Do you know that when I told you all this I expected you to reject my application for admission? After all, your job was to turn out professional pastors, not to deal with some muddlehead's attempt to make some sense out of life. Why ever did you accept me?"

"Now you're not giving me enough credit." It was almost a reprimand. "After that interview I hadn't the faintest idea how or where you'd come out. But you had a good mind, I saw that. I know at the time I thought it would be wonderful if more of our students came to us with the combination of a good mind and a hunger for answers."

Randollph stood up and stretched. He paced over to the wall opposite the desk, inspected and straightened an excellent copy of El Greco's *View of Toledo*.

Randollph resumed his seat behind a desk massive enough for the president of a top-five hundred corporation.

"During my woolgathering I also wondered if you are clairvoyant, Freddie."

"Oh? I've been accused of many things. Bishops often are. Just or unjust, we make good targets. But I can't recall that anyone ever said I was clairvoyant. What gave rise to that random thought?"

"You encouraged me to get my doctorate in church history and join the faculty of the seminary. And I did, and I was happy as a teacher. How did you know it would turn out that way?"

"Not hard to explain, C. P. Just observation. It was no trouble to discover that history fascinated you. And you have the ability to communicate verbally. Perhaps that's a legacy from your days as a quarterback. I don't know

29

much about football, but I understand that the quarterback tells the other players what to do."

"He does when the coach lets him call his own signals —which mine did. The language of communication in the huddle, though, bears little resemblance to the language a professor in a school of divinity uses in the classroom. For a long time I had to watch myself carefully when irritated by a dull or smart-aleck student."

The bishop laughed, a merry rumble that seemed to start in his plump belly. "You never confessed that to me. No matter. You were a splendid teacher, and happy at it, were you not?"

"Very happy. But I've always wondered why you insisted I be ordained. Did you look into your crystal ball, see that you would be elected bishop of Chicago, and lure me from my contented existence in the groves of academe and make me pastor of this church? You knew I had no intention of ever becoming a parish pastor."

The bishop inspected his highly polished pebble-grain black oxfords.

"No, nothing of the kind. I insisted you be ordained, first, because it is some advantage to a seminary professor if he's had episcopal hands laid on him. My main reason, though, was to give you an extra option. Administrators are fond of all the options they can get—or give. Do you regret it?"

"No, you know I don't. I like what I'm doing. My woolgathering included an unspoken prayer of gratitude for all you've done for me. After all, if you hadn't brought me here, persuaded me to come, I'd never have met Samantha."

The bishop seemed genuinely touched. "Thank you, C.P. I'm glad for you." Then, abruptly changing the subject, he said: "I understand you attended one of Jim Trent's prayer breakfasts recently. What did you think of it?"

"Have you been to one, Freddie?"

"Yes, I got roped in. Trent and I are board members of several charitable organizations. He gives them money, and

I give them episcopal dignity. He's a member of Good Shepherd, is he not?"

"Yes, but I hardly know him. What do you make of him?"

The bishop scratched his ear as he pondered the question. "Everything I know about him is positive. He is personally charming. And who can speak any ill of one who is so generous with his money? I've persuaded him to help some of our causes that have been languishing for want of adequate funding." The bishop's voice trailed off.

"You sound as if you have reservations about him, Freddie."

"I'm afraid the right name for it is prejudice, C.P."

"A prejudice, Freddie?" Randollph prompted him.

"Over the years I have developed distaste for those who see to it that they extract the maximum publicity for their generosity to worthy causes. I always wonder what they're buying, or trying to buy."

"You take their money."

"Oh, yes," the bishop replied cheerfully. "It's not for me to judge them. Trent's money will accomplish good works just as well as alms given in secret." He paused and thought for a minute. "I expect that it's that name, the Splendid Samaritan, and the fact that he apparently glories in it that bothers me. But I'm being morally picky. Trent is apparently a worthy citizen with a generous heart. Do you have an outside line that doesn't go through Miss Windfall?"

"Certainly." Randollph pushed one of the plastic buttons on his phone and handed the receiver to the bishop. "You want to call your office to see if the coast is clear. I'll dial it for you."

The bishop took the receiver, muttered a question, then handed it back to Randollph. "He left fifteen minutes ago under the impression that I wouldn't be back today. Unless he's lurking in the hallway, I'm rid of him. Thank you for the sanctuary, C.P. I'll see you this evening."

31

The Church of the Good Shepherd was an inappropriate bucolic name for an institution that was totally metropolitan in character and mission, Randollph often thought. Most of its members had seldom, if ever, seen a sheep. On the other hand, the name probably appealed to some of every Sunday's congregation. That the church was packed every Lord's Day morning was due not to the extraordinary faithfulness of its members, but to the visitors attending the scores of conventions held each week in nearby hotels. Dr. Arthur Hartshorne had perceived early on that this was the way to fill the pews, and had succeeded in making attendance at Good Shepherd a traditional item on the itinerary of Rotarians from Butte, Montana, or Kiwanians from Cheyenne, Wyoming, who had presumably seen a lot of sheep and even understood what a shepherd did.

Dr. Hartshorne maintained his farm-boy folksiness throughout his incumbency. But Matilda Hartshorne's tastes were neither simple nor rural. So she pointed out to her husband that the enormous amount of empty space in the church's Gothic tower could be converted into a penthouse parsonage suitable for people of their prominence and station in life. She directed her husband to point this out to the trustees of the church. Dr. Hartshorne was wise enough to stress the economy of utilizing wasted space, and the advantages of having the pastor so near the church in persuading the trustees to adopt the plan. Thus, Randollph lived in one of the most luxurious and spectacular penthouses in Chicago. His conscience often pricked him when he remembered that Jesus usually slept in some primitive hut or in the open, and that Saint Paul not infrequently spent the night in the slammer. But the enjoyment of living there usually chased away these attacks of puritan guilt.

Access to the penthouse was provided by elevator from the hotel. Randollph left the office early to get ready for the open house, scheduled to begin at seven-thirty. "Clarence will have a quick, simple meal for us," Samantha had told him. "It's almost against his religion for people to eat in a hurry, but he's got plenty to do looking after the refreshment table. Including baking all the pastries himself."

He took the only elevator that went up to the penthouse level, climbed three steps, and unlocked the heavy, supposedly burglar-proof door. Sammy was in the foyer arranging flowers on the table where the guests would register and have name tags stuck on them. She was already dressed for the evening in a long daffodil-colored dress simply but artfully draped to emphasize her slender, obviously feminine figure. It contrasted nicely with her bright red hair.

"You're beautiful," Randollph said. She kissed him. "I love you," she said. "You need a shave."

Randollph rubbed his face. "So I do. Five o'clock shadow. The curse of dark-haired men."

"Snap to it, then. Shave and shower in half an hour. Hey, that's a poem. Also an order. The maid Clarence has hired for the evening has to have that bathroom spotless in time for the first visitor."

"On my way." He sprinted up the stairs thinking it was about the only exercise he'd had today. He wondered what the members of Good Shepherd would think of the master suite. The big bedroom's wall-to-wall carpeting was thick, soft, and golden. There was an oversize bed with a headboard containing books, a small radio, and an alarm clock. A moss-green sofa was fronted by a long coffee table. Two easy chairs upholstered in a white fabric laced with gold and green threads completed the furniture, except for a television set with a twenty-five-inch screen.

The bathroom, slightly smaller than a handball court, was done in blue and white tile. It contained a large sunken tub, a glassed-in shower stall, two sinks with ample counter space, a stool and a bidet in separate cubicles. Randollph wondered how many of this evening's visitors had ever seen a bidet, let alone used one. He doubted that Saint Simeon Stylites would have considered a bidet as essential to holy living.

Ablutions completed, he dressed hastily in lightweight gray flannels, a navy blue single-breasted jacket, and a white shirt with broad blue stripes. He chose a blue raw silk tie with one diagonal stripe in crimson. Miss Windfall, who'd be taking a turn at pouring tea this evening, would —Randollph was certain—think this outfit too snappy for the pastor of Good Shepherd.

"You look spiffy," Samantha said. "We re eating in the kitchen. I've invited Dan. He's going to be one of the tour guides, you know."

"I must warn him not to tell our guests that the master bedroom looks like a high-class whorehouse. That's how he described it to me when he showed me the place my first night at Good Shepherd."

"Well, so long as he makes it clear that the resident lady of the evening has only one customer, I don't mind."

Randollph thought again of the circuitous route that had led him to this church, this penthouse, this woman. The seminary, teaching, the bishop's invitation to pastor Good Shepherd. All this had included inheriting as associate pastor Dan Gantry, who had in turn introduced him to Samantha, hostess of the city's most popular television talk show, *Sam Stack's Chicago,* who had invited him to be a guest on her show. He remembered well that first meeting. This tall, slender, beautifully groomed redhead had announced almost immediately that she was an atheist. She'd wanted to shock him, so he shocked her.

"An atheist isn't a bad thing to be, Miss Stack—or is it Mrs. Stack?"

"It's Mrs. Stack. I'm a one-time loser. He was a lush. Call me Sam. But you're supposed to be against atheists, aren't you? How can you say—"

He'd interrupted her. "An atheist originally was someone who refused to worship the popular gods of current culture. Many of the early Christians were condemned and executed on the charge that they were atheists."

"Is that right?" she'd appealed to Dan Gantry.

"Beats me," Dan had replied. "But he ought to know— he's a professor of church history."

"Oh, hell, that takes all the fun out of being an atheist."

"You'll just have to settle for being an agnostic," Randollph had told her.

She was so totally different from the kind of woman he'd preferred, was drawn to, and occasionally considered marrying, that he'd been amazed when he discovered, eventually, that this was the only woman in the world he wanted to be his for a lifetime.

Sam Stack, in turn, had found Clarence Higbee, a diminutive Englishman whose skills qualified him to be a chef in the finest restaurants, but who refused to work for anyone he didn't like. He liked Randollph and Samantha.

So here I am, Randollph thought, preaching the gospel in a fashionable church, living in a luxurious penthouse parsonage, married to the world's most desirable woman, who is an agnostic, and served by a chef who would have no trouble finding employment at the Ritz or the Savoy. The incongruities inherent in his present life were obvious. He often felt that the lines had fallen unto him in such pleasant places that there had to be a catch to it.

Dan Gantry was already seated in the kitchen's breakfast alcove, which was seldom used except by Clarence.

"Evening, boss," he said. "Hi, Sam. You look like a gorgeous flower, a red rose with a yellow stem, if there is such a thing. Nice stem, too."

"Why, thank you, Danny boy. You look like a banker in that dark three-piece suit."

"It's a disguise. Conservative types take me for one of their own. They can't believe that beneath this vest beats the heart of a social reformer. Confuses the bastards."

"Food will be ready in a moment," Clarence announced from the stove. Randollph saw that he was wearing his customary black double-breasted jacket, striped gray trousers, and bat-wing collar. That meant Clarence considered this evening's occasion informal. A proper major domo, by Clarence's standards, only wore tailcoat and white tie for formal dinners.

"I understand this is to be a boozeless evening," Dan remarked.

"Right, Danny boy," Sam replied. "It wouldn't be proper. And someone'd be bound to get squiffed. We'll have enough problems without that."

"I've had a hard day organizing a nuclear freeze march. Would it be possible, Clarence my dear friend, to have a quick snort, a little something to pick me up?"

"Make it vodka," Sam instructed. "I don't want you conducting tours smelling like a distillery."

"Not as good as Scotch, but better than nothing. You got some, Clarence?"

"I have a bottle of Stolichnaya in the freezer," Clarence said. He placed the bottle and a two-ounce glass in front of Dan. "The Russians say to toss it down in one gulp," he commented.

Dan did. "Wow!" he said. "It doesn't taste like much, but it lets you know it's going down. Thanks, Clarence."

"I'm serving you hamburgers," Clarence informed them. "A plebeian dish, best suited for al fresco dining. But time is limited, as you know. And they're on rolls I baked."

"Suits me," Dan said. "I'm a big guy, so I hope you fixed two for me. The boss is a big guy, too."

"I've anticipated your needs, Mr. Gantry."

"He can have my extra one. I'm a big girl, and I don't want to get any bigger."

"Where's the mustard?" Dan asked.

"I can, of course, supply mustard, Mr. Gantry. But try a bite first. I've prepared these hamburgers with ingredients that are savory enough to require no condiments."

Dan bit a chunk out of his sandwich, chewed for a moment, then said: "Cancel the mustard. My God, I never tasted a burger like this. What's in it?"

"I mix the ground sirloin with red wine, butter, a bit of chopped onion and garlic, lemon juice, and minced parsley. And broil them, of course." He served second sandwiches to Dan and Randollph.

"Munch them in a hurry," Sam instructed them. "Clarence has more important responsibilities this evening than stuffing you two."

The bishop and his wife, Violet, were the first to arrive. The bishop wore a black suit with clerical collar and episcopal purple rabat.

"I thought I'd make myself easily identifiable," he explained to Randollph. "Most of these people have never seen me, don't know me. One of the penalties of my office is that I have so little contact with the laity. I miss it."

"You'd better get a name tag, too," Randollph suggested. "Most of these people won't know that a purple rabat is a symbol of your office."

Sammy had enlisted Good Shepherd's Women's Guild to help with the name tags, conduct tours of the penthouse, pour coffee and tea or ladle punch, and serve the pastries. The church membership had been divided alphabetically with time of invitation separated so that everyone wouldn't arrive at once. Not every member of the church would come, but the curiosity factor was certain to bring in a lot of people. It wasn't long before the place was crowded. Randollph was ashamed that he had to read the name tags to identify most of the guests. A pastor ought to know his flock, he believed. But many of them seldom came to church, and most of them lived in the suburbs. He had yet to devise a method for getting acquainted with all the sheep for whom he was the spiritual shepherd.

Toward the end of the evening, when people with surnames beginning with S through the remainder of the alphabet were scheduled, Randollph was certain that he had a glazed look and a limp handshake. He was, he feared, just repeating banalities and forcing an air of welcome and friendship. He therefore had to look twice to identify a man who came up to him and said, "Mrs. Trent sends her apologies, but she didn't feel well this evening. And I apologize for failing to thank you for your prayer at our recent breakfast." Clearly the Splendid Samaritan expected Randollph to recognize him immediately. He wasn't wearing a name tag.

"Oh, er, ah, yes, yes, of course. Happy you could be here, Mr. Trent. And I was honored to be invited to participate in the prayer breakfast." Randollph had discovered that he frequently was forced to tell small lies like this for the greater good of the Kingdom.

"My greatest satisfaction in life comes from helping others," the Splendid Samaritan continued. The words themselves, Randollph thought, were self-righteous and pharisaical. But they didn't sound that way. Once again he was impressed by the power, the magnetism of the man's personality.

Trent was eating one of Clarence's pastries. "This is the best cake I've tasted in years. Mostly the kind of stuff you're served on occasions like this is so bad it's hard to choke down."

"Glad you like it. Our chef—"

"Been planning to ask your advice about a project I'm considering," Trent interrupted. "As you know, only business executives are eligible for membership in Business Executives for Christ. Even Ham Reynolds—you know him, our chaplain—doesn't qualify for membership. Don't know what I'd do without him."

"He seems an exemplary young man," Randollph replied lamely.

"Lovely wife, too. I hadn't thought of having a chaplain, but after I met him—well, we just took to one another. Anyway, Ham thinks it would be a good idea to start a prayer breakfast organization for the clergy dedicated to the creed and principles of Business Executives for Christ. What do you think?"

Randollph was appalled. He saw the bishop passing by and surreptitiously signaled him for help.

"You could hardly call it Clergymen for Christ," Randollph replied. "That would be redundant, wouldn't it?"

"Oh, I don't know. The way some preachers talk today they should be called Clergymen for Marx."

The bishop rescued Randollph. "Ah, Mr. Trent, I've been wanting to speak to you about this committee meeting we have next week." He led the Splendid Samaritan away.

Sam kicked off her shoes, moaned, "Oh my poor feet," then did a little dance between the bed and the sofa.

"If your feet hurt, then why are you dancing?" Randollph asked as he shucked out of his jacket and tie.

"Because I'm happy."

"You usually are."

"I know. It's one of my endearing qualities. But I'm happy the evening's over. And I'm happy it went so well. Everyone seemed so pleased."

"No problems?"

"Well, one snooty type lady asked how we could afford our own chef."

"And you said?"

"I get asked that every now and then. I gave her my stock answer."

"Which is?"

"I told her we took in washing."

Randollph winced.

"And another one, a pious type, I expect, do we have any of those?"

"A few."

"She asked why would a preacher marry a girl who professes to be an atheist."

"And?"

"I told her that I was actually an agnostic. She probably didn't know the difference. Anyway, I said I'd raised the question with you when you proposed, and you said you weren't marrying me for my theology."

Randollph unbuttoned his shirt. Sam watched him, then said, "Tell you what. Since Dan says this looks like the bedroom in a high-class whorehouse, let's turn it into one. You pretend I'm an expensive hooker, and I'll pretend you're a rich businessman out on the town."

"I feel certain, Samantha, that were you a professional

39

hooker you'd command top dollar. But I supposed you'd be too tired tonight."

"I'm still on an emotional high. A good screwing will bring me down. I'll do a strip tease while you get out of your pants."

"I'd never thought of sex as a sedative, but you never know."

He never did know, Randollph mused, whether it would be the bawdy Samantha or the tender, romantic Samantha with whom he'd be going to bed. All he knew was that whichever Samantha it was, their ecstatic couplings were based on a deep and enduring love. He'd had enough experience during his football days with impersonal recreational sex to know that it was love that made the difference. Sex with Samantha was a better proof of God's existence than all the dogmas thought up by the theologians. The fact that it was accomplished by what appeared to the objective eye as a ridiculous wrestling and undignified positionings of the body indicated to Randollph that God did indeed have a sense of humor.

When it was over, Samantha said: "I hope you're a satisfied customer."

"You're the best little hooker in Chicago."

"Leave the money on the dresser before you go, buster." She yawned, turned on her side, and was asleep in less than a minute.

When James Trent left the parsonage penthouse, he glanced at his watch. Still plenty of time. During the elevator ride to the lobby of the hotel he debated the advisability of walking to his office building. It wasn't far. It was a pleasant evening. He'd find it invigorating. On the other hand, downtown Chicago wasn't always a safe place to walk at that hour of the night. Muggers lurked in dark alleys. Some of them were bold enough to knock you down on a lighted street and rob you if there weren't too many people about. City people, the muggers knew, preferred not to get involved. They could do their work unmolested.

40

He always carried three or four thousand dollars in cash. Trent had an obsessive affection for cash. It gave him a feeling of security. Also, there were certain business deals best conducted quickly and on a cash basis. He kept plenty of cash readily accessible in his office. It would take the most expert of professional burglars to crack his safe, even if he knew where to find it. He liked just knowing the money was handy.

He decided he'd be wise to take a cab. It was a short ride, so he tipped the cabbie generously. Entering the building, a new high-rise that he owned, he said, "Evening, Jack," to the night guard, and signed the book on the guard's desk.

"Evening, Mr. Trent," the guard spoke deferentially. "Working late?"

"Having a number of business interests is like having a bear by the tail, Jack. You can't let go or he'll turn around and eat you."

"'Spect that's true. I ain't seen any bears around tonight, just the cleanin' ladies. And they'll all be gone 'fore long." Jack liked and admired Mr. Trent. He was always friendly. Not snappish and uppity, which many of the tenants were. James Trent, in his opinion, was a genuinely good man.

Trent got on one of the elevators and pushed the button for the top floor. As the elevator rushed silently upward, Trent thought about the evening ahead and felt a pleasant tingling in his groin. He'd worked on this one a long time, and had been consistently rebuffed. But he'd finally succeeded. The effort he'd put in to change a no into a yes only made the anticipation keener. How sweet it is, he thought, as the elevator stopped. The entire floor was occupied by his various companies. His office was at the end of a long hall. He whistled as he walked toward it. He was happy. He'd been disturbed by that newspaper clipping that had come several days ago in an envelope with no return address. Disturbed and confused. But he'd finally put it down as the work of some crank. He'd all but forgotten it.

The pleasant prospects for this evening had blotted it from his mind.

He unlocked the door to his office and switched on the overhead light. He enjoyed looking at his office. There was something reassuring about the mahogany, the leather, the enormous Chinese carpet, blue with unostentatious accents in red. An expensively furnished room, but understated, conventional. Class. Some people had class because it was bred into them. It was like a genetic inheritance. Those not so fortunate had to learn it and earn it. Well, he'd had to learn it and earn it, but he was satisfied in his soul that he'd done it. He was the Splendid Samaritan.

He glanced at his watch, a Piaget that had cost more than ten thousand dollars. But it, too, was an artifact of understated elegance. Simple design. Even the diamonds marking the hours, though flawless and perfectly matched, were small. Class. Well, it wouldn't be long now. He settled in the chair behind his desk. It was nice to have a moment to anticipate what was to come. It helped his performance, and heightened his pleasure.

He didn't have to wait long. There was a discreet knock on the door.

"Come in, my dear," he said in what he imagined was a seductive voice.

The door was pushed wide and a cart used by the cleaning ladies to carry their supplies was pushed in. Pushing it was an old woman in a long, dirty brown skirt, a stained tan sweater, and a large multicolored bandana wrapped around but not entirely concealing grayish and unkempt hair.

James Trent was so startled that he came up out of his chair. Then his shock turned to a flaming anger.

"What the hell are you doing here?" he shouted at the old woman.

"You were expecting maybe Bo Derek?" the old woman answered in an unnaturally high-pitched voice.

"Don't get smart with me, you miserable old bitch," he yelled at her.

42

"My, my, what vulgar language. And you being such a good Christian. Are you forgetting you're the Splendid Samaritan?"

Trent felt tiny tendrils of fear reaching his heart.

"You, you're not a cleaning lady," he sputtered.

"You guessed it."

Trent was not a coward. He felt his anger returning, pumping the adrenaline of courage into his spirit. He quickly seized a heavy antique inkwell from his desk and flung it at the cleaning lady. She ducked, and the inkwell hit the wall behind her with a loud thunk.

Suddenly the Splendid Samaritan was looking at a gun pointed at his head.

"This," the cleaning woman said, "in case you don't recognize it, is a .22-caliber pistol, fully loaded. Not a large gun, but quite effective. I can put six bullets in your head before you can do anything else foolish. Now sit down."

Trent collapsed in his chair, shaking.

"What do you want?" he managed to ask in a quivering voice.

"All will be revealed in good time," the cleaning lady replied. "First, I need a little time to set up some equipment." She reached for a case on her cart, never taking her eyes off Trent or lowering the gun. "Now, Mr. Splendid Samaritan, please put your elbows on the desk and place your hands together as if you are praying. You do know how to assume the attitude of prayer, don't you? After all, you are a great Christian leader."

IV

Randollph heard a ringing noise, distant and, his sleep-fogged brain told him, just something he dreamed or imagined. But the ringing persisted, prodding him into semiwakefulness. It was, he dimly realized, the telephone. He glanced at the bedside clock, which informed him that it was six-thirty. He reached for the phone, missed it, then grasped it on his second try.

"Randollph residence," he mumbled.

"Sorry to wake you, doctor."

Randollph recognized the voice. "Oh, good morning, Lieutenant." He couldn't imagine why Lieutenant Michael Casey, homicide, would be calling him at this ungodly hour.

"James Trent was a member of your church, wasn't he? I seem to remember you mentioning it."

"Yes, but you've got your tense wrong. He is a member. I saw him last evening."

"Sorry to inform you that the past tense is correct. I'm in his office now, looking at him. He's in his desk chair with a bullet through his head."

Randollph, his wits still not warmed up, had to take a moment to absorb this information.

"I've got to tell his widow before she hears it on the morning news. Thought as her pastor you might like to go with me."

What Casey meant, Randollph realized, was that Randollph could do the actual dirty work of informing Mrs. Trent that her husband had been murdered. This duty was part of a pastor's responsibility. Even in his short tenure as pastor of Good Shepherd, Randollph had, several times, had to inform a family of the impending or actual demise of a loved one. But he'd never before faced a situation that called for him to tell a spouse that her husband had been murdered.

"Yes, that's something I ought to do," he told Casey. "I appreciate your calling me."

"Pick you up in fifteen minutes, OK?"

"I won't have time to shave." Randollph realized this was a silly remark as soon as he'd made it.

"Use powder," Casey said. "They—she lives in Lake Forest. Quite a trip, and I want to get there quick. Fifteen minutes." He hung up.

Randollph found the slacks and shirt he'd worn last night on the floor. This was uncharacteristic. He was usually neat, never left clothes lying around. Then he remembered the urgency with which he'd discarded them. He'd done that before, but always put everything in its proper place afterward. Maybe Samantha was right. Sex was a powerful sedative.

He decided that under the pressure of time he'd use last night's wardrobe. He managed to scramble into his clothes in seven minutes. Hastily descending the graceful curved free-hanging stairway, he went immediately to the kitchen, where Clarence was already busy with preparations for breakfast. Clarence, dressed in his daily uniform of gray-and-black-striped trousers, black jacket, and bat-wing collar with black tie, said, "Good morning, sir. You're a bit early, but I'll have your breakfast ready shortly. Baked

45

eggs in tomato shells on English muffins. And that superior bacon I have cured to my specifications."

"I'll have to postpone it, Clarence," Randollph said, thinking how ridiculous it was to be suddenly hungry and wish he could eat right now. He wondered what the early Christian martyrs had for breakfast just before they were fed to the lions. He told Clarence quickly what had happened, eliciting from the little Englishman a "How dreadful! Such a good man, by all reports."

"Please tell Mrs. Randollph that I'm going to Lake Forest with Lieutenant Casey. She's still asleep."

"I'll inform the madam, sir, and also call Miss Windfall." Randollph had completely forgotten about Miss Windfall. It wouldn't do to leave her stewing about his absence from the office. He was grateful that Clarence remembered. Clarence, Randollph suspected, did not entirely approve of Miss Windfall. He guessed that Clarence thought the old girl assumed airs and authority beyond her proper station. Clarence was, in his way, a snob. He believed that people should remain within the boundaries that life and occupation had drawn for them. But Miss Windfall, whatever her shortcomings in his eyes, was entitled to be informed of Randollph's whereabouts, and it was his duty to inform her.

Casey was pulling up in front of the hotel in an unmarked blue police Pontiac just as Randollph emerged. As soon as Randollph was in the car, Casey made the tires squeal, cutting off an enraged truck driver who shouted an obscenity. Casey, Randollph noticed, was not his usual stylish self. Normally he was indistinguishable from the prosperous young attorneys and stockbrokers who thronged Chicago's downtown streets at lunchtime. But this morning his blue button-down shirt was rumpled, and his tan jacket had a couple of stains on it. He also had probably dressed in a hurry, too bleary-eyed to take his customary care before presenting himself to the world.

Randollph asked himself if his and Casey's concern with clothes was a bond between them. They had a rather peculiar relationship. He'd met Casey shortly after coming to Chicago. When Samantha had consented to become Mrs. Randollph, he'd discovered that Casey was the nearest thing he had to a male friend other than the bishop in the city. Randollph's contemporaries and peers were mostly teachers at the seminary in California, and too impecunious to afford a trip to Chicago. So he'd asked Casey to be his best man. They were friends, mixed socially on occasion, yet still addressed each other by their titles rather than their given names.

"Tell me about it, Lieutenant."

Casey, heading the Pontiac north on Michigan Avenue, ran a yellow light.

"You ever been in Trent's office?"

"No." Randollph had thought of a program to visit all members of Good Shepherd who had downtown offices, but hadn't gotten around to it.

"Very fancy. Well, he came to his office last night. Logged in about ten, signed the book for anyone who comes in after lockup. The guard knew him, of course."

"He must have gone there right after leaving our place."

"What was he doing at your place?"

"Samantha was having an open house for all members of the church. Hardly any of them had ever seen the parsonage."

"Seems funny to call that fancy penthouse a parsonage."

"Yes."

Casey, on the Lakeshore Drive now, swore at a blockade set up for construction crews already breaking up concrete with their noisy power hammers. He signaled to the policeman controlling traffic who identified the unmarked sedan with a glance and stopped enough cars to let Casey slide around the obstruction. Casey waved a thank you to the cop, then asked, "Did Trent have his wife with him?"

"No. Made apologies for her. Said she wasn't feeling well."

"Anyway " Casey continued, "the night man said it

wasn't unusual for Trent to come in after hours, sometimes quite late, stay awhile, then check out."

"But not last night?"

"No. Jack—that's the night man's name—got worried, oh, along about four o'clock, nearly as he can remember. He liked Trent. They were kind of friendly. So he calls Trent's office and doesn't get any answer. Thinks maybe Trent's sick or had a heart attack or something. So he takes the elevator to Trent's floor. Isn't supposed to leave his post, but everyone's out of the building, all accounted for." Casey broke up a clot of traffic with a touch of the siren button, then quickly got the car back up to seventy.

"And?"

"Jack finds the door to Trent's office open. The overhead light was off, but a high-intensity light was clamped to the back of a chair and focused on Trent's face and hands, the part of him you could see above the desk."

"That's a bit weird, isn't it?"

"Wait till you hear the rest of it. His hands were wired together like he was praying—thin wire. And he'd been tortured."

"Tortured? How?"

"Cigarette burns on his face and the back of the neck. And a pretty savage stab wound on one of his arms."

"These aren't pretty things to think about before breakfast," Randollph said. He felt slightly nauseated.

"No, they aren't. And you haven't heard it all yet."

"Go on."

"He's got a hundred-dollar bill clasped in his hands. A bloody hundred-dollar bill. We figure that's what the stab wound was for. A bill soaked in his own blood."

"And that's it?" Randollph thought it was surely enough, too much. How could you tell the widow all these gory details. He had a vague picture in his mind of Mrs. Trent. A slight, dark-haired woman, as he remembered. He'd no more than spoken to her after church services. Again, he decided he'd have to do a better job of getting acquainted with Good Shepherd's members, even if they lived in far-flung suburbs.

"That's not quite it," Casey said, squirting through a tight space between a Jaguar sedan and a Buick Park Lane with the negligent ease of an expert driver. "Trent had a safe in his office. It was well-concealed behind the wood paneling. You had to know just where to press to make the panel slide back. It was open and empty.

"Burglary? Is it your theory that he was tortured to get him to open the safe?"

"Could be. Jack—when he finally quit shaking and could talk coherently—told us he'd heard rumors that Trent kept a lot of cash handy. Have to check it out. I'd like to think it was burglary. We'd probably clean that up in a hurry."

"Oh? How?"

"Snitches. Professional snitches. You'd be surprised how many cases, especially burglaries, are solved through information we get from our—well, sources outside the law."

"But you aren't convinced?"

"That it's burglary? I would be if it weren't for the other stuff. A burglar might tie up a victim and torture him to get the combination to a safe—and in this case its location. But why the funny stuff with the light and the hundred-dollar bill, blood-soaked yet? No professional burglar I've ever met would waste a hundred dollars. I don't get it." Casey sighed as if the bad guys shouldn't complicate a simple, standard crime with a lot of unnecessary trimmings.

Lake Forest is the preferred suburb for those who have made it to the top, or for those whose progenitors had made it to the top and left an estate sufficient to maintain large houses and stock them with servants.

The Trent home was on the lakefront, probably with riparian rights. It was a large and sprawling half-timbered structure that managed to look weathered and ancient yet

49

well cared for. It was fronted by an immense lawn liberally dotted with flower beds.

"Place would need one guy full-time just to look after the lawn," Casey remarked as he parked on the regularly raked gravel drive that looped in front of the house before continuing to a garage large enough to stable six cars. They walked up the steps to the arched wooden door. "You do the talking, introduce us," Casey instructed Randollph. "Less of a shock to meet a pastor than a policeman this early in the morning."

The door had a prominent brass knocker, brightly polished. But Randollph spotted a button set in the doorframe, a small concession to modernity and convenience. He pressed it. They waited. He pressed it again. After an interval the door opened. A stocky woman in a maid's uniform gazed at them.

"If yer sellin' somethin', we ain't buyin'," she said truculently. "What you botherin' us for this hour of the day?"

"Permit me to present myself," Randollph said soothingly. "I'm C. P. Randollph, Mrs. Trent's pastor. It is urgent that I see Mrs. Trent immediately."

"She'll be just gettin' up," the maid said, but her attitude had softened considerably. She looked at Casey. "Who's he?"

"Lieutenant Michael Casey, Chicago police," Randollph answered.

"What's a preacher and a policeman want with the lady?"

"We need to discuss that with her privately," Randollph said, he hoped without betraying the irritation he felt with this stubborn domestic.

"Well, you might as well come in, then." The maid said it grudgingly, but she knew when she was overmatched.

They entered a large central hall. "Wait in there," the maid indicated a door. "I'll tell the lady you're here." She disappeared.

"A rather snippy type for a maid," Randollph said as they went into what people in Lake Forest probably called

50

the drawing room. The carpets were oriental. The furniture, dark and heavy, looked like it had been around a long time. It would have been a gloomy room except for French doors that would bring in sunlight as soon as the sun decided to get up and about its business. And there was Lake Michigan, which appeared to begin just outside the doors.

"I can tell you why the maid was snippy," Casey said.

"I'd be interested to know."

"I'll bet you she's been with Mrs. Trent for years. What you might call an old family retainer. She feels her first obligation is to protect her mistress. Mixture of affection and duty. She's a type I've run into before. Not all of them are that rude, though."

Randollph supposed Casey was right. Casey was the man in homicide always sent to deal with cases involving the powerful and the wealthy. He had the look and manner of one of them. He knew how to handle people who believed their wealth and social position conferred on them the right to be difficult. Randollph knew that this talent accounted for Casey's rapid rise to the rank of lieutenant, and marked him as a "comer" in the Chicago police hierarchy.

Casey and Randollph were both admiring the view of the lake and didn't notice that Mrs. Trent had joined them. She was standing in the door, the maid directly behind her like a guard against unexpected dangers, when she said: "You are always welcome in this house, Dr. Randollph, though I hardly expected a visit from my pastor so early in the morning." Then, turning to the maid, she said, "Dora, I'm sure these gentlemen would appreciate a cup of coffee. I know I would."

"I've got it made," Dora said and disappeared.

Mrs. Trent was wearing a long blue silk dressing gown with a wide sash resembling an obi, which, with her dark hair and slightly slanted eyes, gave her a faintly Oriental look. He could see that she had once been a beautiful woman. She would be yet, he thought, except that something was missing. She was well-groomed. Her face was smooth and obviously cared for. Why wasn't she beautiful, or at least handsome? Because, he decided, she had no inner spark. Had she ever had it? he wondered. She was gracious and correct, but spiritless. It was as if that inner glow which gives vitality to the personality had been snuffed out. The spirit had been squeezed out of her.

Dora was back almost immediately with a fragile-looking antique pot, cups and saucers, cream and sugar, on a beautiful silver tray that one of the Georges might once have owned.

"Thank you, Dora. I'll pour." It was a kind way of dismissing the maid.

"Cream and sugar, gentlemen?"

"Black." The delightful aroma of coffee freshly brewed from an expensive blend came drifting across the room.

"Black," Casey said.

"Oh, I'm sorry. I've been remiss in failing to introduce Lieutenant Michael Casey of the Chicago police."

"Dora told me you had a policeman with you," Mrs. Trent said. Her voice was listless. She showed no curiosity concerning the purpose of their visit.

"I fear we have some unpleasant news for you, Mrs. Trent," Randollph said.

"Oh?"

The time had come. He had to say it.

"Your husband, it grieves me to tell you, is dead."

Randollph, prepared for hysterics, shock, violent upheaval, could discern no reaction whatever to his announcement. The silence hung in the room, a palpable if unseen presence. Randollph searched his mind for a euphemism for murder but could find none.

"I also regret to tell you that Mr. Trent was murdered."

Elva Cooper Jackson Trent sipped daintily from her exquisitely designed cup. "That's terrible." She spoke with no more emotion than if she were commenting on the reported passing of someone she'd never met.

Casey cleared his throat. "Ah, Mrs. Trent, there are

certain regulations required, stipulated, in a death by homicide. I regret to bring them up now, but—"

"That's all right."

"There's formal identification of the body. You can have another member of the family or a friend do it if you wish."

"I'll do it."

"And an autopsy will be necessary."

"I understand."

"Could I ask you one question now?" Casey said gently, but implying that there would be more questions later.

"Of course."

"Mr. Trent was, er, found in his office. His safe had been opened and was empty." Casey paused to let this sink in. "We have heard unconfirmed rumors that he always kept a considerable amount of money in his safe. Would you know about that?"

"More coffee, gentlemen?" She topped up their cups. "No, I wouldn't know. My husband never discussed his business with me."

"Thank you." Casey abandoned the field to Randollph.

"May I call at a time convenient to you to discuss funeral arrangements?" Randolph asked.

"I can tell you right now," Mrs. Trent said. "He was a member of Good Shepherd, so I shall appreciate it if you will conduct the service, Dr. Randollph."

"Of course. In the church, I take it?"

"No, it will be held at the funeral home." Mrs. Trent sounded more positive about this than anything she had said this morning. "And, Dr. Randollph, I hope you will not be offended if Hamilton, Chaplain Hamilton Reynolds, delivers the eulogy."

Randollph tried to conceal the relief he felt. He'd been wondering how he was going to heap the praise the mourners and the public would expect on a man he hardly knew and who espoused a version of the Christian faith Randollph found false and distasteful. He silently wafted a

53

prayer of thanksgiving toward heaven for getting him off the hook.

"I'm surely not offended, Mrs. Trent. The choice of Chaplain Reynolds is most appropriate. I'll get in touch with him immediately and relay your request."

Casey and Randollph didn't speak until the Trent house was well behind them and they were headed back to the city.

Casey said, "What do you make of her, Doctor?"

"What do you?"

"Damned if I know. A normal reaction would have been for her to go into shock, or have a screaming fit. But what does she do when you tell her her husband's been murdered? She goes right on pouring coffee." Casey shook his head as if offended by Mrs. Trent's failure to react in a proper manner to distressing news. He drove a few blocks, then said, "Is she one of those types who keep themselves under control no matter what happens?"

Randollph pondered the question, then said: "I hardly know her, so I can't tell you what type she is. I'm just guessing. But from observing her this morning, I'd be more inclined to say that she would have reacted in much the same way if I'd told her we were there to announce that nuclear warheads aimed for Chicago would be arriving shortly."

"I don't get it." Casey sounded puzzled.

"I think she's not much interested, no matter what happens."

"Why?"

"I have no idea."

"She sure wasn't interested in her husband's murder. Does that mean she didn't much care for him, good man that he was supposed to be?"

"That's a possibility, I suppose. It's a second marriage for her, though that doesn't mean it wasn't happy." Randollph thought of Samantha, who'd announced early in

54

their acquaintance that she was a one-time loser in the marital arena. She'd been wary of marriage until Randollph came along.

Casey, absorbed in his driving and his thoughts, was silent for a while. Then he said, "Did you know Trent wore a wig?"

"I guessed it. A very well-made and expensive hairpiece. Why?"

"Whoever shot him took it off him and put it on the desk in front of him. Also, his wallet was empty—he's supposed to have carried quite a lot of cash on him—but the burglar didn't bother to take his watch. It's a very expensive watch. That's another reason I can't figure this for a simple burglary with a murder thrown in.'"

When Randollph finally got to his office he found, instead of a crisp, efficient Miss Windfall prepared to lay out his duties for the day, a strangely subdued secretary waiting for his instructions. This only happened, Randollph recalled, when some tragedy befell one of Good Shepherd's prominent families. Randollph couldn't imagine that Miss Windfall had any particular affection for Mrs. Trent, and he already knew that the secretary thought Mr. Trent was not a bona fide member of the church. Anyway, affection —to all appearances—was a quality of personality the Good Lord had neglected to include when he created Miss Windfall. Randollph supposed it was a protectiveness, almost an identification with the institution of Good Shepherd that depressed her when some unanticipated ugliness threatened to stain the church.

"Your man called," she said, with a nearly undetectable trace of venom in her tone. Miss Windfall's regard for Clarence matched Clarence's reservations about Miss Windfall. "There are a number of phone calls for you," she added. "I've marked the ones that are urgent." She was beginning to sound normal.

"First," Randollph instructed her, "it is imperative that I get in touch with Chaplain Reynolds—that's Hamilton

Haynes Reynolds. I suppose the Business Executives for Christ has an office. Would you call it, and if he isn't in ask them where I can locate him. Stress the urgency if you will, please." Randollph tried never to issue an order to a subordinate unless it was framed as a request. It had been a difficult habit to acquire after years of playing quarterback. Quarterbacks never made requests, and their orders were often embroidered with language he'd had to discard. He went into his study and shut the door.

When the intercom crackled Miss Windfall said in a voice distorted by the ancient speaker, "Chaplain Reynolds is in Sacramento, California. I have the name of his hotel. Do you wish me to ring him?"

"Yes, please do." He settled back in his chair thinking of how he would break the news to Reynolds. It wasn't long before the voice of Miss Windfall informed him that Reynolds was on line one. Randollph pushed the lighted plastic button and said, "Mr. Reynolds?"

"Yes. You just caught me as I was leaving. I'm out here organizing new chapters for BEFC. I'm glad to hear from you, Dr. Randollph, but curious."

"I'm afraid I have some distressing news, Mr. Reynolds." Might as well make it brief and to the point.

"There's nothing happened, nothing wrong with my wife, is there?" His voice was apprehensive.

"No, so far as I know she's fine. It's Mr. Trent. He's dead."

There was a silence, then, "Oh, my God!" Another silence, then, "Why, I just talked to him yesterday. He sounded fine. Was it his heart?"

"No," Randollph answered, "he was shot, sometime late last night in his office." He could almost hear Reynolds struggling to get control of himself.

"Who? Why? Why would anyone want to kill the Splendid Samaritan?"

"There is some evidence that it might have been a burglar or burglars." Randollph saw no point in further explanations, which would only upset the young chaplain the more. "I've seen Mrs. Trent. She has requested that you deliver the eulogy at the funeral. May I suggest you return to Chicago as quickly as possible?"

"I don't know whether I can do it," Reynolds said. "I just don't know whether I can do it."

"You mean you can't return immediately?" Was the young man obtuse?

"No, oh, no. I'll be back as quickly as I can. I mean I don't know whether I can do a eulogy for the Splendid Samaritan without breaking down. He was like, well, like a father to me." Randollph thought he heard a stifled sob.

"We'll talk about it when you get back," Randollph said briskly. But Reynolds had already hung up.

Randollph summoned Miss Windfall, who came in bearing a sheaf of telephone messages and other papers. Before she could begin the ritual of instructing him about duties he'd rather dodge, he said, "Would you sit down for a moment, Miss Windfall."

Miss Windfall, looking faintly surprised, sat down.

"You've known Mrs. Trent for many years, I take it?" Randollph asked.

"Yes, since she was a girl." Then she added, "Of course, I didn't, don't move in the Jackson and Cooper social circles." Randollph thought Clarence would approve of that.

"What was she like as a person?" he asked.

"Oh, full of pep, mischievous, not wild, but liked a good time. A very popular girl, and a very popular young matron when she was Mrs. Jackson."

"Have you noticed any, ah, change in her personality in recent years?" Randollph was inviting Miss Windfall to gossip, a despicable enterprise, he supposed, especially from a man of the cloth.

Miss Windfall, he knew, was not averse to gossiping.

"Yes. In recent years she's given up entertaining—she used to love entertaining—and going to parties."

"I got the impression this morning that she was, ah, well, a spiritless sort of person," Randollph explained lamely.

"She changed not long after her marriage to James Trent."

"You're telling me it wasn't a happy marriage?"

"There are rumors," Miss Windfall said darkly. "She had to marry him, you know."

Randollph looked startled.

"Oh, no, no, that's not what I mean." Miss Windfall actually blushed. For some reason, probably ignoble, he suspected, Randollph was pleased to see Miss Windfall flustered.

"What I mean is Martin Jackson was a fine man, but not a very good businessman. He inherited the family business, a good business. But when he died—he was still a young man—it turned out that the business was practically bankrupt. Some men just aren't cut out for business," she said, implying that this was no scar on the family escutcheon if the family itself were acceptable. "So there she was with that big house she'd inherited, and two children to educate, and no money. So she needed a husband with money. It was her only way out."

"And what did Trent get out of the deal?" Randollph asked.

Miss Windfall looked at him as if she were surprised that he'd failed to grasp the obvious.

"Why, immediate introduction into Chicago's best social circles. Instant respectability."

"I'd have thought that his money would have insured that," Randollph said.

Miss Windfall sniffed. "There are some things money can't buy—even in Chicago," she pronounced.

"She was most positive about holding the funeral not in the church but in the funeral home. That puzzled me."

Miss Windfall tilted the corners of her mouth upward in as near to a smile as she ever came.

"Generations of Coopers have been baptized, married, and buried from the Church of the Good Shepherd," she announced without hesitation. "This is her way of telling the world that James Trent was not really one of the family."

V

Randollph appraised the young man across a desk, broad as a boardroom table, that had buttressed the Reverend Dr. Arthur Hartshorne against countless visitors.

He hadn't looked forward to this session with Chaplain Reynolds; the young man looked glum and hollow-eyed.

"I still don't know whether I can do it," he told Randollph. "I'm honored, of course, that Mrs. Trent requested it. But it's going to be a tough job for me."

"You can do it," Randollph reassured him. "You're still in shock, but you'll pull yourself together." If Reynolds chickened out now, Randollph thought, he'd be drafted for the job. He didn't want that to happen.

"You're a professional clergyman," Randollph said in what he hoped was a spine-stiffening tone of voice.

"Yes, but I've never taken part in a funeral. I've never had a parish. This is my first job." He paused, inspected his shoes as if some revitalizing ray might be hidden there just waiting to shine on him from their well-buffed surface. "I don't know what I'll do now."

"You mean the Business Executives for Christ will fold up without the Splendid—without Mr. Trent?"

"It might. He was the soul of it. He funded it."

This was a good sign that Reynolds was getting over his shock, Randollph decided. Self-interest was now mingling with sorrow in the young chaplain's breast.

"You could always take a parish," Randollph suggested.

"I don t think I'd care for that."

"Why not?"

Reynolds thought about this, then said, "I don't think I'm cut out for it. I'm afraid I'd find it boring after the excitement of this job, the travel, the fun of doing something you believe in passionately. And I'm sure my wife wouldn't care for it."

"Oh?"

"She has her own career, you know—or did you?"

"No, I didn't."

"She's a buyer of women's clothing for a chain of department stores—the Save-A-Lot stores. It's a discount chain, and she takes great pride in getting quality merchandise for bottom dollar. She's very good at her job."

"I'm sure she is."

"She travels, too," Reynolds volunteered. "Sometimes we don't see each other for two or three weeks at a time. That's the worst part of being married to a career woman."

"I'm married to a career woman," Randollph said, "but her work is here in Chicago."

"That's nice."

Randollph could see that he was slowly coaxing Chaplain Reynolds out of his state of depression and anxiety by getting him to talk about himself.

"Where did you do your seminary work?" Randollph asked.

"Harvard."

"Fine school." Reynolds didn't comment.

Randollph tried another tack. "Am I correct that there were no black businessmen at the breakfast I attended?"

This seemed to surprise Reynolds. "Well, you see, that

is, we have no black members, because, well . . ." He didn't seem to know how to finish the sentence.

"You surely don't have a policy excluding black members?"

"No, not that. It's just that, well, the Splendid Samaritan, well, had what you might call some old-fashioned ideas." Reynolds was careful in choosing his words. "He believed—I'm not saying I agree—that blacks, well, don't make very good businessmen."

"Then," Randollph said, "you must see the irony in his nickname the Splendid Samaritan."

Reynolds looked blank. Randollph wondered what kind of courses they were teaching in New Testament exegesis at Harvard these days. Or maybe Reynolds was just one of those people who didn't understand irony. It wasn't that they were stupid. It was more like they had a gland missing.

"The Parable of the Good Samaritan gets its extra power," he explained, "from the fact that two professional religious men refused to help the injured traveler, but a Samaritan did. The Samaritans, as you of course know, were looked on by the orthodox religious community as an inferior people, not worthy of association with good people—meaning themselves. Your Splendid Samaritan, who was apparently proud to be called that, excluded from your organization people he considered inferior."

Reynolds looked genuinely distressed. Maybe he had gone too far, Randollph thought. Maybe he'd let himself be carried away. Maybe, probably, this hadn't been the time to make such an observation. He quickly changed the subject.

"You could put together a eulogy from all the laudatory editorials, letters to the editor, even the stories in some national magazines praising the good works and high moral character of Mr. Trent," Randollph suggested. "Most of them pose the question why does something like this happen to a good man and exemplary citizen instead of the more than ample supply of crooks and thugs whose passing would improve society."

"I've read most of them," Reynolds said. "And don't think I haven't asked myself that question. Why the Splendid Samaritan? Why did it happen to him? How could God let it happen to him?"

Randollph's opinion of the biblical instruction at Harvard Divinity went down another notch. Or maybe Reynolds was one of those students who slid through courses that didn't much interest them. He'd had plenty of the type in his classes during his teaching career.

"You could make that question the theme of your funeral discourse," Randollph suggested. "You could use as a text Jesus' words in the Sermon on the Mount. Let's see, where is it?" He picked up the Bible that was always on his desk and began leafing through it. "I never can remember exact chapter and verse. Ah, here it is. Matthew 5:45 b. 'For he makes his sun rise on the evil and the good, and sends rain on the just and the unjust.'"

Reynolds pondered this suggestion. "Of course," Randollph added, "you would have to wrench the text out of context to make your point." Randollph admitted to himself that he wasn't above a bit of exegetical fudging now and then to make a point.

"I think I'll just stick to talking about all the good that he—that the Splendid Samaritan did," Reynolds decided.

The Alton and Kirk Memorial Home, Randollph thought, could, quite appropriately, have tasteful signs on its hearses and limousines reading: "Purveyors of last rites to their majesties the carriage trade of Chicago and affluent suburbs." No one, he suspected, was ever launched on the final voyage from this emporium of macabre good taste if the family or the deceased had a shaky credit rating. The chapel was a large room with an arched ceiling that looked a little like a church but was not cluttered with religious emblems identifying it with a particular faith. This, Randollph supposed, enabled Alton and Kirk to dispatch Christians, Jews, atheists, or that considerable fraction of the wealthy whose ties to religion were so tenuous as to make a service in a house of faith a final hypocrisy. The chapel even had a small but genuine pipe organ casting a layer of melancholy music over the whispering, shuffling of feet, and suppressed coughing characteristic of a large crowd waiting for the show to begin.

Two somber minions of the funeral establishment dressed in black tail coats, striped trousers, and gray gloves glided forward and closed the casket with unobtrusive movements. Except for the gloves, their costumes were almost identical with what Clarence Higbee always wore when serving a formal dinner. Randollph doubted that Clarence would appreciate the comparison.

The organist let the last lugubrious tune fade away and die. On the lectern a small red light that only Randollph could see flashed on, signaling him to get going. He stood behind the lectern, opened his little black book to the Order of the Service for the Burial of the Dead, and read the prayers and scriptures he'd chosen for the occasion. It didn't take long. He sat down. Now it was Chaplain Reynolds' turn. Randollph was apprehensive about Reynolds' getting through his part, but the young chaplain apparently had pumped himself up and was off the mark at once reciting the Splendid Samaritan's victories and virtues. This was going to take some time, Randollph could see. And it was going to be boring. He relaxed and let his mind wander. He'd had a look at the Splendid Samaritan before the service. They'd either rescued his hairpiece from the police or had a duplicate made in a hurry. And he was unable to detect any signs of the cigarette burns or the gunshot wound on the face, a tribute to the skill of Alton and Kirk's cosmeticians.

Tiring of this, he inspected the crowd. Mrs. Hamilton Haynes Reynolds III was prominent among the chief mourners, but she wasn't mourning. She was smiling sweetly at her husband. She was a good-looking girl. Her name, Randollph remembered, was Teresa. Her husband called her Tess. She was wearing a simple black dress that Randollph would bet hadn't been selected off the rack at one of the Save-A-Lot stores she worked for. He also would bet that she knew she looked good in black. It emphasized her blonde hair.

Mrs. Trent, he saw, was apparently listening to Chaplain Reynolds monotonously blathering on about the goodness of the Splendid Samaritan. At least she was looking at Reynolds. But Randollph doubted if much of what the chaplain said was registering with her. She had that spiritless, uninterested demeanor she'd demonstrated that day he and Casey had gone to her house to tell her her husband was dead.

She was flanked by her two children. The girl was as blonde as Teresa Reynolds, but with her hair cut short. She wasn't bad-looking, but she wasn't beautiful either. She wore a blue suit that seemed to be saying, "To hell with the convention that says I have to wear black." She wasn't mourning, either. She was looking grim. Randollph knew she was some kind of career woman, but couldn't recall exactly what she did. He guessed she'd be active in the feminist movement.

The boy, on the other hand, was trying to look interested in Chaplain Reynolds' eulogy, but couldn't conceal his boredom. Not much past thirty, he was already growing bald. He compensated for it with a heavy guardsman's mustache. Randollph remembered that the boy was a lawyer, head of his own small firm. He wondered if Trent money and Trent business had set the young man up.

Sitting in the row directly behind the family was a man Randollph recognized, but for a moment couldn't place. Oh yes, the chap who'd introduced the Splendid Samaritan at the prayer breakfast for which Randollph had blessed the food. What was his name? Helperin, Warren Helperin. President of the Chicago chapter of Business Executives for Christ. Randollph remembered that Chaplain Reynolds had said Helperin wasn't as old as his graying hair intimated, and that he was planning to run for governor of Illinois. Looking older than he was might be a political asset, Randollph supposed. Randollph reflected ruefully on the specks of gray popping up here and there in his own dark hair. They were reminders that springtime was past, and that the brief summer of life turned to autumn all too soon. Well, he'd had an interesting and rewarding springtime, sown a few wild oats better left unsown, he supposed. And he was having a glorious summer. He hoped the autumn and winter days would, in their ways, be as good to him.

He wondered what Warren Helperin was thinking. He appeared to the casual glance properly solemn. But it was obvious to Randollph that the man wasn't crushed or taking refuge in the deep caves of sorrow. Perhaps he was estimating how many votes were in this crowd, or planning the place and occasion on which to announce his candidacy.

The crowd was getting restless. Reynolds was going on too long. These people, presumably here out of respect or affection for James Trent, were being drenched with the details of Trent's righteous deeds. The young chaplain, who had thought he couldn't do the eulogy, was now overdoing it. A surfeit of goodness, while morally commendable, could also become boring.

Some alteration in Reynolds' voice brought Randollph's reveries to an abrupt end. Reynolds was at last coming in for a landing. Randollph's work wasn't finished. He had to do the final prayers and benediction. He was grateful that he didn't have to go to the cemetery. The Splendid Samaritan was to be cremated. This, Miss Windfall had opined, was to insure that Trent, an imposter, would not rest in peace awaiting the day of resurrection planted among the Coopers. Randollph had offered to conduct a committal service at the crematorium, but Mrs. Trent had told him that wouldn't be necessary.

When Randollph got back to his office, Miss Windfall informed him that Lieutenant Casey was waiting to see him. Miss Windfall had admitted Casey to Randollph's study. She would have kept the commissioner of police or the president of a university twiddling their thumbs in the outer office. But she knew Casey was on the short list of people Randollph was always willing to see, and that he was to be accorded every courtesy. Casey was also on the short list of people Miss Windfall liked. Randollph had never been able to figure out why Miss Windfall chose to bestow her approval on some people and withhold it from others. Logically she should have disapproved of Dan Gantry. He wasn't at all like Dr. Arthur Hartshorne, in her opinion the mold in which all true clergymen should be cast. Dan was breezy, irreverent, called her Addie, and often got his name in the paper as spokesman for some cause Miss Windfall thought it inappropriate for a representative of Good Shepherd to be allied with. But she found no fault in him. This enigma served to remind Randollph that you couldn't safely categorize people, that even those who were as predictable as Miss Windfall exhibited inconsistencies of character and behavior.

Michael Casey was stretched out on the scruffy leather sofa that matched the scruffy leather chairs in Randollph's study. Samantha had wanted to redecorate the study, but Randollph liked the old leather furniture. It gave the room the feel of an English gentleman's club. Casey sat up. He was holding an unlighted cigarette.

"I thought you were quitting," Randollph said as he searched in his desk for an ashtray.

"I'm down to three a day, most days," Casey said. "Sometimes when I'm frustrated I cheat. I'm deciding whether I'm frustrated enough to cheat on this one."

"I don't wish to be an occasion for sin," Randollph said as he placed an ashtray on the coffee table in front of Casey, "but you'll probably be easier to talk with if you go ahead. You can put it on the list for your next confession."

"Oh, what the hell," Casey said, and lit the cigarette.

"What's got you so frustrated?"

"This damned Trent murder. The commissioner wants it solved yesterday, Trent being such a prominent and admired citizen, and I haven't even started."

"Why not?"

"Because nothing about it makes sense. Most of the murders I deal with fall into patterns. You learn to recognize which pattern it is, then it's usually just a matter of figuring out who had the motive to execute the pattern. There's no consistent pattern to this one. And that's why I'm frustrated."

"No rumors among—what did you call them, your snitches—about a burglary?"

"Not a one. And we've got some snitches who usually hear about it when that kind of burglary goes down."

"So what's next?"

Casey took a deep drag on his cigarette, inspected it, and decided there was another puff or two in it. "That's why I'm here. I think you might be able to help me."

Randollph was surprised. "I can't imagine how."

"How did the widow seem at the funeral today?"

"About the same as she seemed when we took her the news that her husband was dead."

"Not broken up?"

"No. Why?"

"What I want to know is something about the—about how she and Trent actually got on, some details on the status of their relationship. I figure some of the people in your church would, well, people who moved in the Trents' social circle, would know about that."

"Why me?" Randollph said. "If you want to know, why don't you ask them?"

"Because the police brass doesn't want us snooping around important citizens trying to get them to gossip."

"But it's OK for their pastor to snoop around trying to get them to gossip," Randollph said, thinking that was exactly what he'd done when encouraging Miss Windfall to dish any dirt she knew about the Trent marriage.

"No, I suppose it isn't," Casey said gloomily. "I'm just trying to get a foothold. I'm going back to basics. It's a rule that the most likely suspect in a murder of this kind is the surviving spouse. So I'm going to go after Mrs. Trent

68

first. It would help a lot if I knew there was a reason she had it in for her husband."

Randollph was astonished. "You can't seriously believe she killed him."

"Why not?"

Randollph searched for a defense of Elva Trent. "I doubt she's strong enough physically, for one thing."

"Doesn't take much strength to pull a trigger."

"No, I suppose not," Randollph conceded. "But why the burglary?"

"To divert suspicion."

"And why the bloody hundred-dollar bill?"

"I haven't figured that out. Probably only the killer knows why. It's trying to make some kind of statement about Trent, I'd guess. Trying to say something nasty about him, though I don't know just what. It's the kind of thing someone that hated the guy would do. That's why I need to know if she hated the guy, if she had a strong motive to knock him off. Of course, she'll be a very rich woman now, and that's always a good motive. But I suppose she has enough of her own, so I guess we can't count on that as a motive."

"As a matter of fact, she doesn't have any money of her own. "

"Well, I'll be damned," Casey said, looking more cheerful. "That is a motive, then. How do you know?"

"Miss Windfall told me. She's an inexhaustible well of information about the lives of our members—those from old established families that have been members of Good Shepherd for a long time, anyway. How she picks up all this personal stuff about so many people I don't know. She even knew that Mrs. Trent was infertile."

"But she has children."

"Adopted. When she was Mrs. Jackson."

Randollph hesitated, then said, "I suppose I should tell you all I know. I can answer your question about the relationship between Trent and his wife. Miss Windfall informed me that it was not a close relationship, that it wasn't a happy marriage—at least for Mrs. Trent."

"Well, well," Casey said, rubbing his hands together. "A place to start. I'm glad I came."

"I still can't picture her as a murderer."

"She might have hired someone to do it," Casey said. "That would explain the burglary. You can hire a killer in this town for a lot less than Trent probably had in his safe."

"But she didn't know about the safe."

"So she says. That doesn't make it so. I like it. It fits a familiar pattern. Spouse hates spouse, wants him out of her life, and at the same time gets her hands on an enormous fortune by knocking him off." Casey was as enthusiastic as a theologian whose views on dogma had been reinforced by an unexpected bit of evidence.

The intercom squawked. "Mr. Gantry is calling you on line two," Miss Windfall reported. "He insists that it is urgent."

Randollph punched the button for line two. "Yes, Dan, what's the problem?"

"Boss, I'm in the pokey."

"What?" Randollph was startled.

"I'm in jail, or about to be. They're booking me now."

"Whatever for?"

"Well, it's like this," Dan said. "I was leading this march of the Nuclear Freeze Movement, down State Street. We had a city permit, all legal and OK. All of a sudden this big guy in the crowd yells 'you Commie pinko bastards!' Then he charges into the street, and since I was the nearest marcher to him, he grabs the sign I was carrying and starts beating me with it."

"Then why are you in jail?"

"Well, boss, this guy isn't in too good shape at the moment." Dan hesitated, then went on. "They took him to the hospital and they say his jaw is broken."

"And how did his jaw get broken?"

"Uh, you see, I sort of had to protect myself."

"You mean you hit him?"

"Yeah, you could say that. It was, well, I guess, kind of instinctive. He comes at me like he wanted to kill me or something, and I guess you could call it a reflex action on my part."

"Hold the line a second," Randollph said. He quickly told Casey what had happened. Casey took the phone from Randollph's hand. "Dan," he said, "let me talk to the watch commander." There was a pause, then Casey said, "Captain, this is Lieutenant Michael Casey of Homicide. In the case of the Reverend Mr. Daniel Gantry, don't do anything until I get there. It won't take me long. What's that? Of course I know I have no jurisdiction over you. I'm offering you a piece of excellent advice. There are cases, as you well know, when hasty action gets us in a lot of hot water. In my judgment, this is one of them. I'll be glad to explain it to you when I get there. None of us wants an unnecessary black mark. It nearly always hurts our careers. You'll wait for me? Thank you, Captain." He handed the phone back to Randollph and said, "Let's go."

"Shouldn't I get in touch with a lawyer?" Randollph asked.

"Won't be necessary."

When Randollph and Casey got to the precinct station where Dan was being held, they found him in a waiting room with miscreants of one kind and another being booked before they were put in a cell, or holding pen, as the cops called it. Dan was handcuffed. Sitting beside him was a huge uniformed policeman with thick red hair. Casey introduced himself politely and asked where the captain was.

"He's in a meeting. Left word he can't be disturbed," the officer answered truculently. "Told me to handle it." Randollph, knowing something about how bureaucracies worked, interpreted this to mean that the captain had sensed he'd be better off keeping clear of this one.

"What's your name?" Casey asked the big red-headed policeman.

71

"Officer Rafferty."

"You the arresting officer?"

"Yes."

"Tell me what happened."

Rafferty scratched his nose. "I see this punk—" he nodded at Dan "—he's one of these antinuke crazies, he's attacking this guy—"

Casey spoke quietly. "Back up, Rafferty. Are you telling me that this punk, who is the Reverend Mr. Daniel Gantry, one of the pastors of the Church of the Good Shepherd, and, incidentally, a very good friend of mine..." he paused long enough for Rafferty to grasp all this, "... are you telling me he left his place as leader of a legitimate parade, charged into the crowd, and attacked someone?"

Dan started to speak, but Casey motioned him to silence.

"What actually happened, Rafferty?"

Rafferty scratched his belly before answering. "Uh, maybe I wasn't looking when it began."

"Was Reverend Gantry—" Casey emphasized Reverend "—was he on the sidewalk attacking this fellow, or was the fellow out in the street attacking Reverend Gantry?"

Rafferty let his anger flare up again. "With all them bastards milling around, who can tell?"

Casey still didn't raise his voice. "Now listen to me, Rafferty, and listen carefully. I have a report on what happened. I'm informed that this guy who got hurt charged Gantry, who was leading a peaceful and legal parade, grabbed this sign he was carrying, and started beating him with it while cursing him."

"You got no right—"

"Shut up, Rafferty, I'm not through talking to you. You're the arresting officer. You have to write up a report on what happened. Now you'd better be certain you get it exactly right, just the way it happened."

"You got no jurisdiction over me," Rafferty muttered.

"No, I haven't," Casey said pleasantly. "But I'm taking a personal interest in this case. If you fake your report, I'll

72

have your ass. You'll never make sergeant, and you could be walking a beat in no-man's land. Now I suggest you release Reverend Gantry, since he's committed no crime. That way you won't even have to write a report."

Rafferty had one more feeble protest in him. "This fellow Gantry hit wants to sue him for assault and battery. He got his jaw broke, maybe some other stuff, too."

"Fine," Casey said, "we'll get word to him that we'll charge him with assault and battery, inciting a riot, interfering with a legal parade, and a half dozen other things we can think up. His legal bills will be astronomical. Now will you release Reverend Gantry, or does Dr. Randollph here have to go to the trouble of getting a lawyer down here to bail him out and make a court case out of it?"

"I'll release him," Rafferty said, deciding that protecting his own hide was more important than the satisfaction of making trouble.

"Let's go, then," Casey said.

Rafferty looked at Dan Gantry with grudging admiration. "I will say this preacher's got one hell of a good left hook."

On the way back to the church, Dan said, "Thanks, Mike. I appreciate that. I'll remember to include you in my prayers tonight—or does a Protestant prayer count in a Catholic heaven?"

"I'm glad to get any kind of help I can," Casey answered. "My pastor at St. Aloysius probably thinks God doesn't bother to hear Protestant prayers. But then, as my wife often says, he's an old poop."

"I must say, Lieutenant, I was impressed by your performance."

"Thanks, Doctor." Casey was pleased by the compliment from Randollph, and pleased with himself. "I was glad to help Dan. And I detest cops like Rafferty. He's the kind that gives the police a bad name. And, I'm sorry to say, there's more than one Rafferty on the force."

"Could you do all that stuff you threatened him with?" Dan asked.

"Sure. And he knew it. I don't often throw my weight around. It's a temptation for a cop to use—abuse his authority. But there are times that it's the only way to do it." He appealed to Randollph. "Isn't there something in the Bible about when your cow falls into a ditch or something on the Sabbath it's OK to break your own rule and pull it out?"

"An ox in the pit is the way the Scriptures put it," Randollph said. "I think the more appropriate biblical injunction here is to be as wise as a serpent and harmless as a dove."

"Rafferty may agree that I was pretty sneaky smart," Casey answered, "but he might take exception to the part about me being harmless as a dove." Casey grinned. "At least I did some harm to his pride. And I intended to."

"I'll add an extra line or two in my prayers for you," Dan said.

"Speaking of the Scriptures, Dan," Casey said, "I know they say that when someone treats us badly we're supposed to turn the other cheek. Don't you believe that?"

"Yeah," Dan said. "I believe it. But when some big bum comes after me, I forget it until after I've socked him."

"Then I'd better include you in *my* prayers," Casey said.

"Won't do any harm," Dan answered. "And by the way, boss, I don't think we've heard the last of this."

"Oh? Why?"

"Because we've got some members on our church governing board who feel about the antinuclear movement about the same as that guy who attacked me. They may raise a stink."

Randollph hadn't thought of that. Dan was probably right. One more problem to cope with.

"Let's wait for the explosion, no pun intended," he counseled Dan.

VI

Lieutenant Michael Casey had plenty of time to think as he drove once more to Lake Forest. Not about his driving. Through long experience driving in Chicago's unpredictable and often fierce traffic, he'd learned how to be aware of what was happening all around him while devoting his mind to the problems of his current homicide investigation. He knew that this habit worried his wife, Liz, who was convinced that all Chicago drivers were maniacs. But she was cheerful about it, even when making horrendous predictions about what was going to happen if he didn't concentrate more on his driving. Liz was cheerful about most things. Maybe this was what had attracted him. No, he admitted to himself, he'd been attracted to her—first, anyway—by carnal desire. He had lusted after her shapely body. Sex appeal, though, was more than a seductive figure. Her—what was the word for her? The best he could come up with was "aliveness." She had a zest for life. He knew he was sometimes given to gloomy moods, especially when his work wasn't going well. And a Homicide detective sees too much of life's dark underside not to give way, sometimes at least, to a jaundiced view of the human species. But on his worst days he knew that, once home, Liz would light up the world for him.

Casey often pondered what made a good marriage. In a society that dissolved thousands of marriage bonds daily, was one just lucky if his marriage worked so well? Or had the mysterious ways of Divine Providence labored to bring Liz into his life?

He decided he'd ask Randollph about it. He couldn't imagine two more different personalities than Randollph and Sammy. Randollph was a man with strong Christian convictions. Casey knew this because he and Randollph had enjoyed many theological discussions and debates. Casey considered himself an enlightened Roman Catholic. He didn't buy what he had been taught in parochial school, that outside the one true church there was no salvation. If there was a heaven, he was certain Randollph would be there. But Sammy was an agnostic. It didn't make sense for a clergyman to marry an agnostic.

Also, Randollph was—well, not an introvert. Reserved might be a better description. He spoke with an almost professional care and dignity. Sammy, on the other hand, was the state-of-the-art extrovert. Some people called her a tough and brassy broad. What had attracted them to each other? And what spiritual glue held them together in what was obviously a gloriously happy marriage? Their union, he decided, was an argument in favor of a capricious and even whimsical Divine Providence.

Casey supposed he was thinking about the nature of marriage because he was on his way to investigate one. Was a bad marriage the motive for the murder of James Trent? Casey had investigated enough homicides to know that one spouse's desire to be rid of a hated mate was a common enough reason for murder. People usually solved this kind of problem through divorce. So there had to be some added incentive to murder one's mate rather than adopt the simpler solution of the divorce courts. He'd had cases where the hatred was so strong that nothing less than killing could assuage the anger.

Without interrupting his train of thought, he pressed the button for the siren to warn of a blue Porsche that was trying to cut into a narrow space between the unmarked police car and a wildly decorated van. The startled driver of the Porsche went scurrying toward an inside lane. It was a beautiful April day, sunlight glittering on the lake and dancing on the brightly painted hulls of sailboats keeled over taking advantage of a stiff breeze. But Casey didn't notice. Did Mrs. Trent kill her husband because she hated him? Possible. His information, admittedly gossip, indicated an unhappy marriage. Perhaps Trent had fought the idea of divorce because it would damage his image as the Splendid Samaritan. Perhaps Mrs. Trent couldn't face the publicity of a divorce. But all this seemed unlikely to Casey. If she were guilty, it was probably a coupling of distaste for her husband with the inheritance of a very large fortune. It was a neat, tidy theory. It fit a familiar pattern. At first he'd welcomed it eagerly. On reflection, he still liked it, except—except what? That Mrs. Trent didn't seem to be the kind of person who'd resort to murder? No, he'd had a hand in running down too many killers who just weren't the kind of people who killed other people. One of the most sadistic murderers he'd ever caught was, by manner and appearance, a sweet little old lady who could have been sent by central casting to play the role of a favorite aunt. Casey had to fight against the conviction that anyone and everyone was a potential murderer.

Except what, then? Not the burglary of Trent's office. That didn't fracture the pattern. Rather, it reinforced it. If Elva Cooper Trent cared enough about money to murder her husband, she'd likely lift the reportedly large amount of cash from his safe. If she'd thought through her plan for murder—and whoever had done in Trent had planned carefully—she'd have known that robbing the safe and the dead man's wallet would confuse the police. It could have been a burglary.

Casey knew he wanted Mrs. Trent to be the guilty party. It would simplify his life by quickly wrapping up a case he was under pressure from his superiors to dispose of in a hurry.

Except.

He couldn't account for the wire-bound hands of the victim grasping a bloody hundred-dollar bill. Or the high-intensity light left shining on the body. They didn't make sense. Why go to all this seemingly unnecessary trouble? Casey's experience had taught him that you couldn't ignore incongruous details like this in a homicide investigation.

When he arrived at the large old house by the lake, Casey had to park behind a maroon Mercedes sedan. It looked new, though you couldn't tell for certain. A four-year-old Mercedes, its paint burnished to a high gloss, was nearly indistinguishable from a new one.

He thought how pleasant it must be to go through life rich and socially prominent. If Mrs. Trent had been a waitress or a stenographer, she likely would have been brought to Homicide headquarters and been interrogated by a crude cop like Sergeant Garboski. But the upper classes would receive a visit in their homes and at their convenience. And the visit would be from Lieutenant Michael Casey, such a polite young man, my dear, so well dressed, such excellent manners, why he wasn't at all like a policeman, he was more like one of us. Casey knew he was a good detective. But there were plenty of good detectives in Homicide who hadn't made lieutenant yet. He was aware that the police brass valued him not for his brains, but for his ability to deal with the rich and prominent who believed their importance in the scheme of things entitled them to deference and special treatment not necessary when dealing with peasants. His conscience nagged him that this wasn't fair. But his experience answered his conscience that, hey, this is the way the world is, buddy. Why not go along with it and let it work for you?

Dora answered his ring, and while she didn't radiate good will and pleasure at seeing him, she had discarded the hostility with which she had treated him and Randollph on the former visit.

"Come in, Lieutenant," she said. "The lady is expecting you." She led him into the parlor or drawing room or whatever it was called, and announced, "Lieutenant Michael Casey to see you, ma'am."

Casey, expecting the spiritless and disinterested person he'd met on his first visit, saw immediately that this Mrs. Trent was an entirely different woman.

She rose from the sofa, approached him with a warm smile and extended hand.

"How nice of you to come all the way out here to talk to me, Lieutenant," she said. She was wearing a bright red dress trimmed with black velvet. Like the Mercedes in the driveway, it looked new. No widow's weeds for her, Casey thought, unless you counted the minimal amount of black trim on her dress. The main difference in her, he thought, was that sparkle had been added to her personality. Also, Casey noticed that she had a less severe hair style than when he had last seen her. She looked, he thought, about ten years younger today than on that morning when he and Randollph had called to tell her that the Splendid Samaritan was dead.

"Please sit down, Lieutenant. Dora, would you bring us some tea? I do enjoy a cup of tea this time of day, don't you, Lieutenant?" Without waiting for an answer, she went on. "And Dora, do you have any of those scones you make?"

"Just about to take some out of the oven," Dora answered. "I'll bring 'em."

"How nice. I'm sure the lieutenant will enjoy them. Now," she said, turning to Casey, "I know that you have a job to do. I just adore mystery stories. I read two or three a week. I'll wager the first question you want to ask to me is where I was on the night my husband was murdered."

Casey felt as if he was an actor in a drawing-room comedy, but he quickly collected his wits. He smiled at her and said, "Yes, that is one question it is necessary to ask."

"Just routine, ma'am. Isn't that what the gruff but decent detective always says in the stories?"

Casey kept the smile pasted on his face. "We do have a routine."

"Do you think I need an alibi?" She was almost teasing him.

"We don't think anything until we have collected all available facts," Casey lied.

"Your job must be exciting," Mrs. Trent said irrelevantly.

"Not as much as you might think. Most crimes are solved by hard, plodding investigation. It can be pretty boring at times."

Elva Trent made a face. "You disillusion me. I think it's terribly exciting when Nero Wolfe asks those brilliant, penetrating questions and reveals the murderer without ever leaving his house."

"But don't forget," Casey told her, "that he has Archie Goodwin and Saul Pauzer out doing the hard work of collecting information for him, and which provides him the raw material from which he finds the answer." How in the world had he been maneuvered into discussing detective fiction with her? He struggled to regain control of the interview. "So you won't mind telling me where you were the night your husband was murdered?"

"No, of course not. I was right here. I went to bed early—with a new mystery novel. Dora will confirm it. Don't you want to write this down?"

"I have a good memory," Casey said. "Now Mrs. Trent, the routine we mentioned sometimes requires us to ask questions of a personal nature, questions we'd really rather not ask because to some people they seem offensive. I hope you'll bear with me."

"I have nothing to hide," she answered. But Casey could sense that her mood had changed from the impish to a slight but detectible wariness.

"That's good. It will make this so much easier." He paused, then asked, "Would you say that your relationship

80

with your late husband was warm and emotionally reward-ing?" Casey guessed she'd been expecting a question of this sort, but he could see her become tense. She didn't answer for a moment, then said: "Lieutenant Casey, are you married?"

"Yes." Her question had surprised him.

"Do you love your wife?"

"Very, very much."

"You adore her?"

"'Adore' is hardly a strong enough word to describe my feeling for her. But yes, I adore her." Where was this con-versation leading, he wondered.

"Now, Lieutenant, imagine that she died. I know it's an unpleasant thought, but try. Do you think you would, in time, remarry?"

Casey was shocked. "I can't imagine being married to anyone else," he said lamely.

"You cannot believe you could ever feel the way you feel about her for anyone else?"

"That's true."

"You are wrong, and you are right," Mrs. Trent said.

Who's conducting this interview, anyway? Casey thought. He was mortified to have let her steal the initiative from him.

"Let me explain," Mrs. Trent continued. "I was deeply in love with my first husband. You knew I'd been married before, didn't you?"

"Yes, I knew that."

"I felt about him the way you feel about your wife. He was the only man in the world for me. When he died—he was a young man when he died—I knew there would never be anyone who could replace him." She paused, as if to measure out a new portion of words. "But in time, when the pain of my loss had dulled, I became increasingly lonely. I made a—I guess you'd call it a rational decision —that I didn't want to spend the rest of my life a widow, alone." She stopped talking and gazed—sadly, Casey

81

thought—at the lake lapping the seawall almost outside the glass doors of the room.

"Oh, don't think I was willing to settle for just anyone," she said. "But I was willing to settle for someone who was pleasant, attractive, and companionable. I wasn't going to demand or expect the kind of feeling I had for my first husband. I knew that only happened once. Did you know Mr. Trent?"

"Slightly."

"What was your impression of him?"

Casey had the feeling that he was again losing the initiative. "I thought he was a man with an extraordinarily strong personality."

"So he was. He was an attractive man. He was interesting, and, well, a good companion. He liked to attend social events of the sort one finds in my circles. That was part of the agree—that was part of his attraction. He was the answer to my loneliness, my need for companionship. And that's why I married him." She sank back in her chair as if exhausted by this recital.

"I can understand what you have told me," Casey said gently. "But it still doesn't answer my question."

She didn't answer immediately. Finally, she said, "The adjustment was more difficult than I'd thought it would be. I suppose—" she sighed and then continued "—I suppose I was still grieving for Martin, my first husband. I probably, well, in my mind I knew it would never be the same. But in my heart I cherished the romantic dream that at least some spark of what I had with Martin would be rekindled into a small flame at least."

"And that didn't happen?"

"No."

"But you had the companionship you sought." Casey put it more like a question that a statement.

"Not as much as I'd expected."

"Oh?"

"You see, Mr. Trent had wide business interests. And of course his Business Executives for Christ. He traveled a great deal. And when he was home, he had meetings most nights. I was alone much of the time."

Casey knew he'd been had. Elva Cooper Trent had evaded saying her marriage was unhappy. She must have guessed that Casey would have picked up the rumors that her union with the Splendid Samaritan hadn't exactly been made in heaven. She was smart enough not to paint a picture of marital bliss, and wise enough to offer him an involved but credible story to account for the rumors. He knew she was lying, or evading the question. Or maybe she'd told the truth but by no means the whole truth. But, he knew, this was all he was going to get. Elva Trent was a very clever woman.

He tried another tack.

"Could you tell me something about the relationship between your children and Mr. Trent?"

It was apparent to Casey that she'd anticipated this question, too.

"Actually, Lieutenant, they never felt very close to Mr. Trent. Let me explain. They both went off to college not long after I married Mr. Trent. There is only two years' difference in their ages, you know. And what with him being gone so much, they hardly had the opportunity to know him well."

"They had no hostile feelings toward him?"

"Oh, at first, a little. They loved Martin—Mr. Jackson —very much. It was only natural that they would resent someone they saw as taking his place."

"But they got over it?"

"Hostility, like affection, needs an opportunity to grow, Lieutenant. As their contacts with Mr. Trent diminished, so did their hostility. They've seen very little of him for several years now."

It sounded to Casey like a speech she had memorized.

"And you can't think of any enemies, anyone who had it in for him, Mr. Trent, that is?"

"No. As I told you before, I knew very little about his affairs—his business affairs, that is. I don't even know

83

much about his early life. He wasn't a very communicative man about things like that. I suppose all very successful men make some enemies along the way. But he never mentioned any to me. In the end, I expect you'll discover it was a burglary." She smiled at Casey, the tension gone. "You see, I've tried to treat it like a mystery story. And the clues add up to burglary."

"But that doesn't account for the bound hands, the bloody bill, and the light." Might as well go along with her, Casey thought.

"No, no it doesn't. That's a puzzle. But I'm working on it. Ah, here's Dora with the tea and scones."

The trip wasn't a total loss, Casey decided. The scones were delicious.

VII

Clarence Higbee set a silver bowl filled with shaved ice banking a glass of orange juice in front of Randollph, and another at a place as yet unoccupied.

"May I inquire, sir, if you expect the madam soon?"

"Madam is already here," Sam said from the doorway. "Good morning, Clarence. Good morning, master of the house." She kissed Randollph on the cheek. "Well, how do you like it?" She pirouetted for his inspection.

"How do I like what? Oh, the outfit." He inspected her avocado-colored pants suit. "New, isn't it?"

"Of course it's new. Cost a packet, too. You'd better like it."

"If I may say so, madam, it is most becoming."

"Why, thank you, Clarence." She dropped him a curtsy.

"If you will excuse me, I'll prepare breakfast." Clarence disappeared.

"I like you in outfits that don't conceal your lovely legs. But I agree with Clarence. And the way it fits doesn't conceal your gender."

"Now that's nice, Randollph. I don't wish to conceal

my gender." She sipped at her orange juice, then continued. "I'm interviewing an alderman this morning who has a reputation as a feeler."

"A what?"

"Feeler. He gets a girl alone in his office, and—first thing you know—he's got his hand on her knee and just keeps going. In a pants suit, he can look, but it doesn't do him any good to touch. Also it helps to keep the lechers at the station at arm's length."

"I'd think," Randollph said, "that they'd know you're married and give up."

Sam giggled. "A lot of guys operate on the law of averages theory."

"I fail to make the connection."

"Why, they figure they're going to get the brushoff a certain number of times. But they keep trying. You can't score, they say, unless you try. And if at first you don't succeed, try, try again."

"Oh."

Clarence arrived pushing a serving cart. He turned up a flame, set an omelet pan over it, waited a moment. Then he tossed some butter into the pan, listened to it sizzle, and poured four eggs from a bowl on the cart. He beat the eggs briskly, all the time shaking the pan. In no time at all, or so it seemed to Randollph, Clarence poured the contents of another bowl into the center of the omelet, folded it over the filling, and divided it in two. Pulling two plates from the warming section of the serving cart, he deftly flipped an omelet onto each plate and placed them before Randollph and Sam.

"Chipped beef omelet," Clarence announced. "We English have a fondness for chipped beef. I mix it with butter and heavy cream to make the filling for the omelet. I don't recall that I've ever served it to you before. I trust you will find it tasty."

"If we failed to find your cuisine tasty, it would be a first," Randollph said. How nice it was, he thought, to offer a compliment and not have to prevaricate.

"Thank you, Dr. Randollph." Clarence reached into the warmer again and produced a napkin-covered dish. "Those are my own recipe corn sticks baked this morning. And you will notice an assortment of jams and jellies in the server here—including gooseberry jam, your favorite."

Sam whacked off a section of her omelet, forked it into her mouth, and murmured, "Mmm, heavenly. You spoil us, Clarence.

"No, madam, I don't spoil you. I try to provide wholesome, nourishing food prepared in as palatable a manner as possible. If I did less, I would be failing not only you, but also myself."

"That is the philosophy of a conscientious craftsman," Randollph said. "Do you not also think of yourself as an artist?"

"If I may be presumptuous," Clarence said, "I approach my task of preparing food with much the same attitude you bring to the preparation of your sermons, Dr. Randollph. You have mastered the craft of constructing a sermon. You know the ingredients of a good sermon, the content, must be sound. It is important that they be put together in the proper order if the final product is to be worthy of an honest workman. I also hope, through inspiration or insight gained from experience, to raise the product of my labors to the level of artistry. One has to be a craftsman first, though, if one hopes to be an artist. The craftsman can take legitimate pride in his craftsmanship. If he reaches the level of artistry, then the proper emotion is joy."

Randollph was amazed. "Clarence, you have articulated the best philosophy of sermon preparation I've ever heard. Yes, that's the way I try to go about it, though I'd never thought of it the way you put it. You should be lecturing on homiletics in some seminary. I'll wager you'd turn out better preachers."

"Oh, no sir, I'm not a learned man."

"Neither was Saint Peter, but he drew good crowds if the New Testament estimates are correct."

Randollph thought about how Clarence Higbee had come into his life.

When Clarence had presented himself for an interview, Randollph thought he'd never seen anyone like him. Clarence was under five and a half feet tall. He was completely bald. His skin, burned by countless suns and lashed by wind and rain off the world's various seas, had the appearance of old, mellow leather.

Clarence had begun the interview by stating, "The employment agency informed me that you are in need of a cook, sir." He'd spoken in a clipped, correct accent. Not quite Oxbridge, but with none of the nuances peculiar to what the British referred to as the serving classes.

Clarence had recounted his credentials. They were impressive. Randollph had said that perhaps he hadn't the palate to appreciate Clarence's culinary skills.

Clarence, Randollph remembered, had smiled at this. "If the situation is congenial, sir, palates can be educated."

Randollph remembered the relief he had felt when Clarence apparently had accepted the job. But Clarence had another question.

"Perhaps I should explain that I was an orphan," he'd told Randollph. "I was born a Cockney, within the sound of Bow Bells, so to speak. At an early age I was put into a Church of England orphanage. It was strict, but the fathers were kind. When I expressed an interest in becoming a chef, they saw to it that I received the basic training. They'd already seen to it that I'd received some education. They taught me the manners and accent of the upper classes. Accent is very important in England. You can see, sir, that I owe my chance in life to the Church of England. My loyalty to it is most intense." Then, plainly embarrassed, he'd asked if, as an employee of a gentleman of the cloth, he'd be expected to attend the gentleman's church.

Randollph had almost laughed. He assured Clarence that his denominational affiliation had nothing to do with the position of major domo in Good Shepherd's parsonage.

Clarence then accepted the job. As he'd left, Randollph

remembered, Clarence had said, "I regard the Church of England as the one true church, sir. But I wish you to know that I hold no prejudice against those who do not adhere to it."

Clarence, Randollph thought, was a living example of what Christian concern could accomplish when it put its mind—and resources—to it.

"May I inquire as to the time your guests will arrive for lunch?" Clarence asked Randollph.

"I should think about twelve-fifteen."

"Guests for lunch?" Sammy inquired. "Who? No beautiful females, I hope."

"No, it's an all-male occasion," Randollph told her. "Dan Gantry and the bishop. We've a problem to discuss."

"The antinuclear thing? Is Dan in trouble?"

"There are rumblings from a few members of the congregation. Freddie's picked them up, and he wants us to be prepared."

"Church politics!" Sam exclaimed. "I think it's disgusting! One good reason for being an agnostic."

"I admit that church politics can be, and often are, petty and even nasty. On the other hand, they are an inevitable concomitant to the faith—any organized faith—and often a sign of health and vitality."

"Methinks great white father speak in riddles." Sam was unconvinced.

"Not really. Saint Paul had to do some politicking to persuade the early Christians that Jesus was for all people, not just for the Jews. That was a crucial decision, a major turning point in the history of the Christian Church."

"What's that got to do with Dan and the fuss over his problem with the people who don't like his being involved in an antinuclear demonstration?"

Randollph smeared gooseberry jam on one of Clarence's freshly baked corn sticks before replying. "Because there is a division of opinion among Americans, and among Christians, as to whether it is moral or immoral to continue the buildup of nuclear weapons. Dan believes it is immoral.

Some of our congregation believe it is moral. Here at Good Shepherd the issue as to whether Dan is right or wrong will be decided by a political process."

"I don't see how that proves the church, Good Shepherd, is healthy."

"I can see why you feel that way, but if a church goes on placidly, never a controversy rippling the waters of the faith, then it is not a vital organism. It is moribund. It should at least be able to work up a sweat over the major moral issues of the day. Dan's participating in that antinuclear demonstration has stimulated Good Shepherd to work up a sweat over the proliferation of nuclear armaments. It may cause us some unpleasant moments, but in the long run, it will promote the health of the institution." Randollph helped himself to more gooseberry jam.

"I'll have to think about what you've said. Maybe you're right about a little controversy pepping up a congregation. But I don't want Dan to get into any trouble."

"He'll survive."

Samantha got up to go. "Well, I'm off to interview my horny alderman."

"If he gets fresh," Randollph advised her, "tell him you find his concupiscence offensive."

"Hah! You don't know much about him. He wouldn't know the word. He might even think I was paying him a compliment." She kissed Randollph. "As all the clerks and salesgirls say, 'Have a nice day.' See you at dinner."

When Randollph got to the church offices, he noticed that there was something not quite as it should be in the outer room, where secretaries typed and filed, visitors seeking audience with the pastor awaited his pleasure, and Miss Windfall presided. Ah! That was it. There was no Miss Windfall in her large swivel secretary's chair, which Dan Gantry called the throne. "Addie thinks she's the queen around here," Dan had told Randollph, "and, come to think of it, she probably is."

Helen, a pretty dark-haired girl, hastily got up from her

chair, and said, "Miss Windfall is not feeling well this morning, touch of flu, she thinks, she'll be staying home today, she phoned in her instructions for our work." Helen blurted out her message as if she feared Randollph would hold her responsible for Miss Windfall's absence.

Randollph could not recall any other occasion when Miss Windfall had missed a minute's time at her post. He was amazed that a flu bug would have the temerity to attack her. He was sorry she was sick, but it was proof that she was human after all.

"Tell you what, Helen. There's a florist in the next block where I have an account. Would you run down there and order a nice bouquet—what kind of flowers does she like, do you know?"

"Roses."

"A dozen long-stemmed roses, then. Be sure they'll be delivered this afternoon. Select a nice get-well card and put all our names on it, including Mr. Gantry and Mr. Smelser. Charge it to my account."

Helen and the other girls in the office were obviously impressed by this gesture. For a moment Randollph was impressed with it himself. Then he wondered why he had done it. It wasn't as if Miss Windfall were mortally ill. She'd be back at her post tomorrow. Perhaps it was just an impulse generated by his kindly nature. Maybe some imp inside him had said, "Here's your chance to confuse the old girl. It will be unexpected, and when she finds out it was your idea, she'll not know how to handle it. It will put you one up." The good and the not so good often got tangled together. Was the Splendid Samaritan motivated to give generously of his wealth because he wanted to do good works? Or because he believed a responsible citizen should do what he could to improve his community? Or because he wished to be perceived as a good person? Or because he liked favorable publicity, and anyway his gifts were deductible from his taxes? Often hidden were the ways of the human heart. He sighed and went on in to his study, uncomfortably aware that he was followed by admiring glances from the girls in the office.

As he went to his desk, he failed to suppress what he regarded as an uncharitable thought. Because Miss Windfall was indisposed she wouldn't be around to pester him with paperwork, and he could get on with writing his sermon for Sunday. But he quickly discovered his mistake. Neatly typed, probably by Helen, was a list of duties and obligations Miss Windfall had laid on him for the day.

He shuffled through his mail, which consisted mostly of some company wanting to sell him, or the church, something; pleas for his donation to a dozen or so presumably worthy causes; and the promotional material from several denominational boards and agencies touting their indispensable contributions to the Kingdom of God. One envelope with only a logo that failed to disclose the nature of its contents caught his eye. It looked like a personal letter. The address was neatly typed. It was addressed to the Reverend C. P. Randolph. This told him that it was a cleverly disguised attempt to persuade the recipient to open it rather than just throw it away. "Dear Reverend Randolph," it began, "We know that as a busy pastor with never enough time to carry out all your heavy responsibilities you often have difficulty finding the hours to prepare your sermons." Well, that's true enough, Randollph thought. "So," the letter continued, "we want to help. We are, therefore, offering you our Sermon Service at the special introductory price of $49.95. For this you will receive, every three months, complete sermons for all the Sundays in the next quarter of the year. These sermons are prepared by a committee of distinguished preachers. They contain humor, illustrations bound to tug at your congregation's heartstrings. They are positive, uplifting messages that will inspire your people. They avoid any subject that could possibly cause controversy among your people, who after all come to church to be cheered up, not irritated. In addition, we will . . ." Randollph threw the letter into the wastebasket.

He thought of Clarence's definition of craftsmanship.

Clarence would consider these packaged sermons the equivalent of frozen television dinners. Just thaw and preach, no preparation necessary. They probably sold well, these instant sermons, he thought gloomily. Until he'd come to Good Shepherd, he'd never had to face the task of preparing a sermon every Sunday. He'd discovered that it wasn't as easy to prepare a weekly homily as he'd imagined, and—he supposed—most laymen thought it was, if they thought about it at all. Sometimes he wondered if all the labor he put into the preparation of his sermons was worth it. They were preached and done with. Did they change any lives, any attitudes? Did they lodge in the hearts of those who heard them? Only God knew for certain, probably. But the preacher knew if he'd been an honest craftsman or not. Clarence considered that fundamental to his work. That there were those who did not have the palate to appreciate the food he prepared and served was less important than that he'd been an honest craftsman in his appointed task.

And, Randollph admitted, preaching was at the same time frustrating and satisfying. Which reminded him, he'd better get cracking and finish his sermon for Sunday while there was no Miss Windfall hovering over him with paperwork she insisted needed doing.

Clarence deftly removed three plates from the portable warmer and placed them in front of the bishop, Randollph, and Dan Gantry.

"Marinated lamb chops, m'lord," he told the bishop. "I use a marinade of olive oil and dry white wine, flavored with a garlic clove and bay leaf. They are accompanied by broiled mushrooms. I think you will find the flavor interesting."

"Thank you for telling me, Clarence. It just saved me the trouble of asking."

"I am aware of your interest in the dishes I serve, m'lord. Needless to say, it pleases me."

Dan was the first to cut a bite of the chops. "Uh, Clarence, these are—what's a stronger word than delicious? But they are kind of small."

Clarence smiled. "I've anticipated your needs, Mr. Gantry. I'll have another chop ready in no time."

"Better make that two," Dan said. "I'm a big guy, have an active life, and need plenty of nourishment."

When Clarence had gone, the bishop said, "Speaking of the active life you lead, Dan, we might as well discuss the possible consequences of your latest activity."

"Is that big bum I socked trying to make trouble?"

"No," the bishop replied. "I understand Michael Casey explained to him the inconveniences he would undergo if he wished to pursue the matter. The trouble will come from the congregation of Good Shepherd."

"How many?" Randollph asked.

"Perhaps not many. I've had a few phone calls, some letters. But a handful of determined people can stir up a major fuss."

"So what are your thoughts about the matter, Freddie?"

The bishop speared a plump brown mushroom, chewed, swallowed, and said, "Superb. But then, everything Clarence fixes is superb."

"I don't mean what do you think about the mushrooms, Freddie. What about the trouble from the congregation you think may be imminent?"

The bishop put down his fork, dabbed his mouth with his napkin, and made a steeple of his hands.

"My feelings are mixed, C.P., as they always are when my role as administrator crashes head on with my role as defender of the faith."

"That statement could stand a bit of expansion, Freddie."

Clarence returned with two more chops for Dan.

"Ah, Clarence," the bishop asked, "would it be possible for me to have one more of these superb chops?"

"I had anticipated that you might wish another, m'lord, and Dr. Randollph also. They will be done shortly."

When Clarence had gone, the bishop asked, "Is he clairvoyant?"

"No," Randollph answered. "He's a master craftsman, an artist. He understands how to estimate the wishes of— what are we, his clients?—before they know themselves what they want."

"That's a good description of what I hope to accomplish today," the bishop said. "We must anticipate the action of Good Shepherd's board before it knows how it is going to act."

"I see the proliferation of nuclear weapons as a moral issue—see it as plain, clear-cut, no two sides, just one possible attitude. It's bad, period."

"Dan," the bishop answered. "You have the soul, the mental makeup of a prophet."

"Well, I'd never thought of myself that way." Dan sliced into another chop. "But could be. I believe Jesus identified with the prophets. And my favorite book in the Old Testament is Amos."

"Ah, Amos," the bishop said. "The first of the great literary prophets. If I remember correctly, the mood of the people in Amos' time was not unlike the mood of the people in America today. It was a period of great prosperity for the fortunate."

"As a matter of fact, the last period of prosperity for Israel and Judah," Randollph said.

"And," the bishop continued, "the people were zealous in their worship because they believed God was on their side and that piety would pay off in continued prosperity. They wanted to hear only optimistic talk about the future. They didn't want attention called to the desperate plight of the poor, the corruption of justice in the courts. They said the day of the Lord was coming, was almost here. And Amos asked then why they desired the day of the Lord, for, he said, 'The day of the Lord is darkness, and not light.'"

"He was right, he called the turn just the way it hap-

95

pened," Dan said. "And I'm right about the threat of nuclear war being the great moral issue of our time."

"Oh, I agree. The prophet in me agrees," the bishop said, then added, "But Amos would have been a complete failure as an administrator."

"I don't see why," Dan insisted stubbornly.

"Because," the bishop explained patiently, "the prophet won't, indeed can't compromise. On the other hand, the essential element in the character of a successful administrator is his skill at compromise. My inclination is always to seek out a compromise that will give everyone some of what they want, but no one everything they're asking for. That way, no one can claim victory or be angry because they suffered defeat."

"You want me to compromise on this?" Dan sounded belligerent.

"I didn't say that, Dan. In fact, I would be disappointed in you if you did. You see, when genuine moral issues are concerned, I permit my prophetic role to dominate my administrative role. You may be confident that I will stand behind you."

"Then what do you want me to do, bishop?" Dan seemed puzzled.

"Nothing."

"Nothing?"

"That's right. This is a situation for C.P. to handle."

"And I'm sure you have some suggestions as to how I should go about it," Randollph said.

"Yes, C.P., I do."

"I'd be grateful if you'd outline them for me, Freddie. You know I'm in total agreement with Dan on this."

"I know that. Now here is what I expect will happen. Someone, maybe several members of the governing board, will raise the issue at the next board meeting. They will probably accuse Dan of meddling in politics, conduct unbecoming a clergyman . . ." The bishop stopped to smile. "I saw the punch you, what is the word, decked that chap

96

who attacked you with, Dan. It was on the television news clip, you know."

"I know," Dan said, sounding more cheerful. "I'm sorry I broke the bas—the bum's jaw. But not as sorry as a good Christian ought to be."

"You can ask God to forgive you for your failure to be sufficiently contrite," the bishop said. "And then, someone is bound to accuse you of damaging the public image of the church. Good Shepherd is very sensitive about its public image."

"You haven't mentioned what I'm supposed to do to stem this tide of accusations, Freddie."

"Patience, C.P., I'm getting to it. First, though, Dan, you will attend the board meeting, but don't say a word in your defense."

"What! Not defend myself?"

"That's right. As you know, I'm not given to being authoritarian—"

"Oh yes you are, Freddie," Randollph corrected him. "You're just not given to the use of the authoritarian manner. You're just as authoritarian as General Patton was. The difference is that you are polite about it."

"Let's not quibble over semantics, C.P. How would General Patton tell Dan to be silent under verbal attack?"

"He'd say, 'Keep your'—well, we can omit the adjective. He'd say, 'Keep your mouth shut. That's an order.'"

"Thank you, C.P. That sums up nicely my instructions for Dan. Now," the bishop continued, "if the issue arises —and I expect that it will—I want you, C.P., to point out that the proper procedure is to bring the complaint before the Pulpit and Personnel Committee, and for the committee to bring in a report before the Governing Board. Any discussion prior to the submission of the report is contrary to the stated procedure."

"Won't that just postpone dealing with the problem, Freddie?"

"That's the point, C.P. Some problems, if they can be

postponed, just quietly disappear, or at least are greatly minimized. I usually deplore administrative red tape. But there are times when it does have its uses."

"Freddie, Freddie," Randollph couldn't restrain his laughter, "and they used to call me Con."

"The Scriptures enjoin us to be wise as serpents and harmless as doves," the bishop said. Randollph thought he looked quite pleased with himself.

VIII

Lieutenant Michael Casey was in a foul mood as he walked the long, monotonous corridor looking for the office of Helga Jackson. The office doors, identical and equally spaced, reminded him of a minimum-security prison where white-collar lawbreakers were sent to pay their debt to society in comfort if not luxury.

His foul mood had been generated by a session with his immediate superior, Captain John Manahan. Captain Manahan did not like Lieutenant Casey. Manahan didn't like the new breed of college-educated cops who, while competent, were promoted too rapidly. Manahan thought of himself as having come up the hard way. Actually, he'd been promoted rather rapidly because he possessed the right ethnic qualification for success in the Chicago police, a mastery of police politics, and his powerful Chinaman in the police hierarchy. But he saw the Michael Caseys as a threat to the established system, which meant they were a threat to him. He resented them.

He was careful, though, to conceal this resentment when dealing with Casey. Casey was clearly going to move up, so it was better to have him as a friend than an enemy. And Casey was good. He knew how to handle important people, and this made Manahan look good.

But Manahan had come close to chewing him out this morning. As close as he ever came.

"Mike," Captain Manahan had said as he settled back and brushed cigar ash off his generous belly, "you ain't gettin anywhere with this Trent thing." It was an accusation.

"That's true," Casey had replied, because he knew the captain was right. He also knew that Manahan was getting heat from his superiors.

"How come?"

Casey tried to frame a conciliatory reply. "It isn't that I haven't been working on it. I have. Working hard. But there just aren't any promising leads."

Manahan relit his cigar. "What about the widow? Chance she did it?"

"She's got an alibi."

"Airtight?"

"Seems to be."

"Business enemies?"

"We haven't found any. We'll keep looking."

"Yeah, I know." Manahan puffed at his cigar and surveyed the haze of smoke as it floated lazily toward the ceiling. "Papers keep sayin' he was a model of the upright businessman." He thought a moment, then said, "That's why you've got to clear this thing up—and fast." Manahan's voice had hardened. "This Trent, he's just some nobody gets himself knocked off, the papers don't care. The politicians and the commissioner don't care. But this here's the Splendid Samaritan. That sells papers. You don't come up with something pretty quick, I might take it out of your hands. That wouldn't do your career any good."

Casey knew this was an attempt to build a fire under him. Manahan, though, wasn't worried about Casey's career. He was worried about Manahan's career.

Casey finally came to a door with a plaque on it that

100

read H. Jackson. He was also irritated with Helga Jackson, though he'd never met her. She'd at first refused to see him at all. She was an auditor for a large insurance company and traveled much of the time, so he'd had to put a little pressure on her. She'd finally set a time when he could talk to her, but indicated that there wasn't much she could tell him.

When he knocked on her door, he heard a voice say, "Come in, please." It sounded like an order. Helga Jackson's office was surprisingly large but crammed with filing cabinets, a word processor, computer, and other paraphernalia he supposed was necessary to the efficient performance of her job. The room was completely impersonal—no pictures on the wall, no gewgaws on the desk, nothing that said a human being inhabited this place.

Helga Jackson did not rise to greet him. What he could see of her above the desk was a woman in her early thirties with blonde hair clipped short, a nose a little too long and a small, almost petulant mouth. She was wearing, at least on what he could see of her, a plain, well-cut maroon jacket, which he assumed was the upper half of a suit. She wore glasses pushed up into her hair. She had startling blue eyes that looked at him as if issuing a challenge. Casey thought it probably wasn't a pleasant experience for whoever she audited if his books weren't in perfect order.

"I'm Lieutenant Michael Casey," he announced.

"I assumed that you were," she replied in a voice with no warmth in it. "Please take that chair." She indicated a straight-backed steel office chair with a seat thinly padded in brown vinyl. It looked uncomfortable and was.

"I'll get right to the point," Casey said.

"Please do."

"I am, as you know, investigating the murder of James Trent."

"I know. You've been hounding my mother."

Casey decided it would do no good to treat Helga Jackson gently. "That's not true, Miss Jackson. This is a murder investigation, and it would be a dereliction of duty if we didn't ask questions of the family of the deceased. I have not hounded your mother. She was most cooperative."

"I don't have to answer any of your questions."

"No. No you don't," Casey said. "It would be helpful if you did. We can, however, get the information about you we need by asking other people, running checks on your activities. We have our methods for gathering information, and they are most thorough."

He started to rise from his chair, but Helga Jackson said, "I'm sorry. I didn't mean to be rude. I have nothing to hide. Ask your questions."

"Some of them will be rather personal."

"I said I had nothing to hide."

"Can you tell me where you were the evening Mr. Trent was killed?"

"Yes. I was in New York City. A business trip." The answer came quickly.

"Would you describe for me your relationship with Mr. Trent?" He thought he detected a flash of fear or anger in those startling blue eyes, but it was gone before he could identify it.

"What does that have to do with your murder investigation?" Casey could tell that Helga Jackson was not quite so sure of herself as she had been a moment ago.

"Probably nothing," he answered her pleasantly. "It's just a part of painting a picture of the deceased. We have a clear picture of how the public saw him, but—"

"The Splendid Samaritan." She said it in a flat voice with just a hint of sarcasm at the edges.

"Exactly. But there's a private picture, too. We need to paint that also—and it takes a lot of work."

"Well," she said, "I'm afraid I can't help you much on that."

"Why not?"

"Because I had much less contact with him than you would imagine."

"Why was that?" Casey knew the answer he was going to get.

"Because when he, he came into our lives, well, you see, I, my brother and I, were away at school most of the time. And when we were home, he was often away. We didn't see all that much of him."

Casey remained silent. It seemed to unnerve her. She became fidgety, picking up a pen, then putting it down, shifting restlessly in her chair. She was not, Casey thought, a fidgety person. He let the silence hang.

Finally she spoke. "I suppose I should have felt affection for him. After all, he was my mother's husband." She thought about that for a minute, then added, "He could be charming. He had a, well, a personality, a strong personality. He could persuade people to see things his way. But he—" she searched for words "—he, it was like he rationed it. He didn't waste much of it at home. No, Lieutenant, I can't honestly say I had any affection for him. I feel like I hardly knew him."

"Did you ever hear him mention, or do you have any knowledge of, any enemies he might have made?" Casey knew this was probably a useless question only prolonging the interview. But it was a routine question in a homicide investigation.

"He never mentioned any in my hearing," Helga Jackson answered. "But then, he wouldn't. He never discussed his business at home. Nor do I know of any enemies he had, but—" she paused, as if uncertain about saying more.

"You were going to say?" Casey pressed her.

"I'm a businesswoman. Because of my job, I am acquainted with many businesspeople, some of them at top management levels. And the bigger you are, the more enemies you have. Business, at the top anyway, is a rough game. You don't get to the top without cutting a few throats along the way."

"You infer, then, that Trent had made enemies?"

"He was at the top of the top. If he hadn't pushed some

people out of the way . . . well, that's how the game is played."

"Even by the Splendid Samaritan?"

Helga Jackson puckered her small mouth as if she'd just tasted something nasty.

"Ha!" she said. "It's easy to play the Splendid Samaritan when you've got the power and the money."

Casey thanked her and left. He had the feeling she'd told him more than she'd intended to, but not as much as she knew.

Malcolm Jackson's law firm was located in a building not far from where his sister worked, but miles from it in elegance and prestige. It looked as if it had squatted there for long years and was saying, "Look, I'm built to last. I'll be here when all these fancy new steel-and-glass structures are worn out and gone." But Casey knew its days were numbered. As soon as some real estate developer assembled enough of the properties surrounding it, the wreckers would finish it off and yet another characterless high-rise would be born.

The directory in the lobby listed Jackson and Murphy, Attorneys at Law, as occupying offices on the third floor.

Jackson and Murphy's offices were not furnished to impress prospective clients. A middle-aged secretary with her hair done up in a bun sat primly behind a desk in a room with a dingy brown carpet and a collection of chairs that appeared to have been assembled at random. Two men and a woman, none of them very prosperous-looking, waited in dejected silence for the opportunity to talk with either Mr. Jackson or Mr. Murphy.

"Yes?" the secretary said in a voice that combined impatience and disinterest.

"I'm Michael Casey," he told her and flashed his police identification. "I have an appointment with Mr. Jackson."

"I'll tell him you're here," she said, dialing a number with a pencil. "Casey from the police is here," she said into the phone, listened, then hung up. "You may go right

104

in." She sounded as if Casey should be grateful for her permission. Casey went toward the door the secretary indicated, followed, he imagined, by the baleful stares of the waiting clients because his immediate access to Attorney Jackson would delay theirs. Or maybe they just didn't like policemen.

Casey's reception from Malcolm Jackson was not at all like that he had received from his sister. Jackson rose from his chair immediately as Casey entered, came from behind his desk with hand extended and a welcoming smile. "I'm Malcolm Jackson," he announced in a friendly voice. "Casey—it's Lieutenant Casey, isn't it? You're young to be a lieutenant in Homicide. Please sit down. Excuse the mess." He indicated the clutter of papers on his desk and several thick books piled on the floor, some of them open. "I'd like to tell you that I usually keep the office neat, but that would be a lie. It always looks like this—sometimes even worse."

Unlike his sister, Malcolm Jackson had many personal items in his office. There was his law school diploma on the wall, several pictures featuring Malcolm Jackson in the company of what Casey supposed were judges or politicians, and on his messy desk three expensively framed photos of his sister, his mother, and a man Casey didn't recognize. Jackson noticed Casey looking at the pictures. "The three people I love most," he said. "You no doubt recognize my mother, and my sister. The man is the late Martin Jackson, my father. A finer man God never made. I still miss him, miss him terribly."

Casey, who normally admired order, liked Malcolm Jackson's rat's nest of an office better than the sterile and impersonal quarters of his sister. For one thing, the chair Jackson had offered him was quite comfortable.

"I'm curious," Casey admitted. "Do you specialize in a particular branch of the law?"

Jackson laughed. "You can tell that we aren't corporate attorneys. No self-respecting corporation would want to be connected with a place that looks like this. Sean Murphy

105

and I were roommates at law school. We decided we'd be bored silly in some big firm drawing up wills for rich old ladies and finding tax loopholes for people that already had more money than they could ever possibly use. So we decided to form a partnership and specialize in criminal law."

"So you decided to help the other end of society?"

"I'd like to tell you, Lieutenant, that Sean and I were two young idealists dedicated to helping unfortunate people who couldn't help themselves. But we weren't. We just wanted to have some fun out of our practice."

"Have you?"

Jackson considered his answer. "Yes, we have. Criminal law these days is mostly plea bargaining. The courts are too full, the jails are overflowing. So we spend much time trying to get the best deal we can out of the state's attorney's office. Or if a case comes to trial, we know how to maneuver to see to it that our client is brought before a soft judge instead of some moron or hardnose. It's a game of wits."

"Do you keep pretty busy?"

Jackson smiled. "You mean how are we making out. We do quite well. We aren't getting rich, but it's a comfortable living."

"What did the late Mr. Trent think of your profession?"

Jackson's genial look disappeared. "He thought I was a fool. Not about being a lawyer, but for passing up the highly lucrative branches of the law. He wanted me to let him use his influence to get me a job in a big and important firm. I refused. I didn't want his help."

"You didn't get along well with him?"

Jackson thought about it, then said, "We didn't have enough to do with each other to say we didn't get along. He was a domineering man. Oh, I know he was the Splendid Samaritan and the very model of the generous Christian businessman. But he became very upset when anyone crossed him—at least, when I crossed him, which I did a few times."

"You didn't like him?"

"I suppose, to be honest, I didn't. But since, as I said, we didn't see much of each other—I expect my mother or my sister has explained to you why that was—"

"Yes."

"Well, he went his way, and I went mine. Let's say we weren't close, that I didn't seek opportunities to be with him."

"Where were you the night he was murdered?"

The genial look returned to Jackson's face. "Now you sound like a prosecuting attorney. I was attending a fund-raising bash for one of our deserving politicians. He's crooked as they come, but an amiable crook. And he does steer some business our way."

"Where was this bash held?"

"At the Bismarck. The favorite watering hole for our local politicians."

"And when did this bash break up?"

Malcolm Jackson grinned amiably, which, Casey noticed, made the ends of his luxuriant mustache wiggle up and down. "You mean do I have an alibi." He pondered his answer. "Speaking as a suspect—"

"I didn't say you were a suspect," Casey interrupted him. "I'm just collecting facts."

"I know." Jackson's grin set his mustache twitching again. "But I know the police always look first at the family of a murder victim. So, speaking as a suspect, I have a strong alibi. However, thinking as a prosecuting attorney would think, well, he could find ways to cast a little doubt on it."

Casey found himself liking this friendly young man. "You're being remarkably candid," he said.

"That's because my heart is pure," Jackson said, smiling again. "No, it's because you'd find out anyway. I know something of your reputation, Lieutenant. Word is, you don't miss much."

"That's nice to hear," Casey said.

"The kind of clients I have are pretty well informed about our police and judicial system. You are on a list—

107

which is not nearly as long as it ought to be—of police-men, state's attorneys, and judges who can't be bribed."

"I am pleased," Casey said.

Jackson abruptly switched to a let's-get-down-to-business voice. "You'll want to ask me if Trent had any enemies. No, I'm not omniscient. My sister called me just after you left her office. My answer is the same one she gave you. I am not aware of any enemies he may have had. But, given his wealth and success, it's a fair bet that he had some. Also, though he never let it show when he was playing the Splendid Samaritan, he was, as I've mentioned, a domineering personality. People like that nearly always make enemies."

"Did he dominate your mother?"

Jackson's friendly expression turned grim. "I'd rather not talk about it."

"But, Mr. Jackson, you must know it's a subject I have to pursue. If you won't talk about it, I'll just have to find people who will."

Jackson sighed. "I suppose you're right. Here's what I know about it." He took time to assemble his thoughts, then said, "I never saw him be anything but polite to her. But I never saw her cross him. What he wanted, she did. What went on between them when they were alone, I wouldn't know. She never talked to my sister or me about him, their relationship."

"Then why are you reluctant to talk about it?"

"Because she became progressively more unhappy after she married him."

"How do you know that?"

"It was like her spirit was slowly being drained out of her. Every time my sister and I were home from school on holiday, she'd be noticeably worse."

"Did you ask her about it?"

"Yes, many times."

"And?"

"She'd just pass it off. Say she hadn't been feeling well,

108

that she wasn't as young as she used to be, indefinite excuses like that."

"But you didn't believe her?"

"No. Neither did my sister. We talked about it. We both thought Trent was the cause of her unhappiness. But we didn't know why, and she wouldn't tell us. But then," he added, "we'd both loved our father very much. We may have—no, I'll rephrase that—we did resent Trent for taking his place. We really couldn't be very objective about him."

Casey prepared to leave. "I don't mind telling you that we aren't getting much of anywhere on solving this murder," he said.

"And the papers are screaming for a solution, which means your superiors are giving you a hard time."

"Yes."

"It could have been that Trent walked in on a burglary."

"Possible. But how do you explain the light, the bound hands, and the bloody hundred-dollar bill?"

"I can't," Jackson said. "But then, I don't have to explain it. You do."

When Casey entered the reception area of Acme Enterprises, he was confronted by a quite lovely antique desk, and a quite lovely young lady, if you liked the lacquered look favored by receptionists at the better grade businesses. The young lady appraised Casey in a fraction of a second. She saw a six-foot, well-built young man dressed in a camel-hair jacket, gray slacks, and a blue button-down shirt with a navy knit tie. This told her that he was too young and too casually, if fashionably, attired to be an important executive. On the other hand, there was an air of authority about him that suggested that he was somebody who carried weight. Maybe he was one of those young hot-shot businessmen who owned their companies and thus could dress as they damned pleased. She decided he was worthy of her grade-A welcoming smile. She flashed it at him and said, "Yes. What may I do to help you?"

Casey, aware of her appraisal, grinned at her when he displayed his credentials and said, "I'm Lieutenant Michael Casey, Chicago police."

"A policeman?" She could have saved her grade-A smile. A policeman rated a grade C at best. He was an attractive young guy, though. She wondered if he was married.

"We're still investigating Mr. Trent's murder," Casey informed her.

"What a terrible tragedy," the receptionist said, wiping off her smile and replacing it with a look of infinite sadness. Casey wondered if she'd practiced the sad look in front of a mirror. There was no sadness in her eyes.

"Is the late Mr. Trent's personal secretary still employed here?" Casey asked. Routine dictated that this was the place to start. Personal secretaries usually knew more about their bosses than anyone else.

"Mrs. McWilliams? Yes."

"Would it be convenient for her to spare me a few minutes?"

"I'll see." She dialed one number. "Amanda, Lieutenant Casey of the police is here to see you. OK. I'll send him back." She turned to Casey. "It's the last office at the end of the hall."

"I know," Casey said. "I've been there before."

Amanda McWilliams was just as beautiful as but more natural than the receptionist. Her greeting was friendly. Casey supposed that anyone who got as far as James Trent's office automatically rated a warm welcome. Her dress, the color of pale sunlight, was simply cut. It didn't shout "Hey, see how sexy I am," but subtly suggested that it covered interesting charms. The lacquered-looking receptionist could learn something about how to dress from Amanda McWilliams, Casey thought.

"Lieutenant Casey, this is my husband, Andrew," Mrs. McWilliams indicated a large man with thinning brown hair seated in a corner. He came out of his chair with the ease of movement characteristic of an athlete. Casey

110

thought he looked like a retired linebacker whose belly was beginning to bulge.

"Call me Andy," McWilliams said, stepping forward to crunch Casey's fingers in a friendly handshake. "You want to talk to Mandy about Trent's murder. I can disappear."

Casey had a sudden feeling that he'd like to have McWilliams present for this interview.

"No, Mr.—Andy, you're welcome to stay. Nothing very secret about the questions I need to ask."

"Andy came by to take me to lunch. Isn't that nice?" Mrs. McWilliams had a charming, natural smile.

"Andy and Mandy, sounds like a vaudeville act, doesn't it?" McWilliams said, looking fondly at his wife.

"How can I help you, Lieutenant?" she asked.

"I'm trying to discover if Mr. Trent had any enemies, anyone who had it in for him," Casey said. "Perhaps some employee who felt he'd been treated unjustly and was very angry about it. "

"Oh, Mr. Trent was liked and respected by the people here. Always polite, always thoughtful." Her answer came quickly and sounded like a public relations statement.

"I'm not an employee, but I didn't like the son-of-a-bitch," McWilliams said.

"Oh, Andy," she sounded distressed.

"I'd be interested to know why," Casey said to McWilliams.

"Because every time he looked at Amanda he undressed her with his eyes."

Amanda giggled. "I think it's sweet that Andy is jealous."

"Did Mr. Trent, ah, ever, that is—"

"Make a pass at me," Amanda supplied. "No, never. And I'll answer your next question. So far as I know, he never made passes at any of the other girls. And I think I'd know."

"Figures," McWilliams said. "He had to keep his Splendid Samaritan mask in place around here. I'll bet he was a chaser, though."

"Let me ask you again about angry employees."

"Tell him about Harry Walpole," McWilliams instructed his wife.

Amanda looked annoyed. "Mr. Walpole isn't a murderer," she said crisply.

"You told me he threatened to kill Trent."

"Oh, Andy, that was just big talk."

"I think you'd better tell me about it," Casey said.

"Well, Mr. Walpole displeased Mr. Trent, and Mr. Trent fired him," Amanda said reluctantly.

"What Walpole did was bungle a bribe, and lost Acme a multimillion-dollar contract," McWilliams said. "Trent fired him, and used his influence to keep Walpole from getting another job."

"You'd better tell me the whole story," Casey said.

Amanda wrinkled her brow as if trying to recall something she had forgotten. "You see, Lieutenant, Acme is a conglomerate. We have an electronics division that does, that bids on government contracts, mostly military. Mr. Walpole was our sales manager for that division. He offered money, quite a lot of money, to someone in the Pentagon to award us the contract. Mr. Trent found out about it, and well, that was the cause of the trouble."

"You're telling me, then, that Trent was angry about Walpole's dishonesty? Walpole, it seems to me, had no legitimate complaint."

"Come on, honey, tell the whole story," McWilliams said. "He'll find out anyway. Would you rather I tell him?"

"Go ahead, Andy." Amanda sounded resigned to the inevitable. Casey guessed she was so accustomed to protecting the reputation of the Splendid Samaritan that she couldn't break the habit.

"Trent wasn't mad because Walpole offered a bribe," McWilliams said. "He was mad because Walpole bungled it. He was an idiot. You don't offer a general or an admiral with a juicy contract-to-let cash money. That isn't how it's done."

"How is it done?" Casey asked.

112

"You cultivate these guys. You invite them to, oh, maybe a weekend at the company hunting lodge, fly them in the company plane. Or get them a special deal on a fancy car. Then you let them know that your company is looking for experienced administrators with a military background and when he retires, well, you're certain that there's a high-salaried slot for him in your company. It's a bribe, but a legal bribe. Then this guy looks after your interests. He sees to it that there are no problems when you come in with your cost overruns. Hell, it's just the taxpayers' money."

"Then why didn't Walpole do it that way?"

"He was too eager, way I get it." McWilliams looked at his wife, who was looking out the window. "This guy he'd lined up was in financial difficulty. Extravagant wife, or kids in college, something like that. Several companies were hot after this contract, and Walpole figured the way to beat them out was put cash on the barrelhead. Now nobody high enough in the military to control multimillion-dollar contracts is going to risk his career and pension by taking an outright bribe. He doesn't have to. So Trent—Acme, Inc.—lost the contract, and Trent found out why. And fired Walpole. Not because Walpole did something illegal and unethical, but because his bungling cost Trent several million dollars."

"And Walpole threatened to kill Trent?" Casey asked. "How do you know?"

"Mandy told me."

Casey turned to Mrs. McWilliams, who was looking miserable. "You'd better give me the details."

"It wasn't because Mr. Trent fired him," she said.

"The stupid bastard was at least smart enough to know he had it coming," McWilliams said.

"Then why?"

"When he found out Trent was keeping him from getting another job," she said.

"Trent had a mean streak," her husband said.

113

"How did Walpole make the threats?" Casey asked. "By phone, in person, letters?"

"Letters," Amanda answered.

"How did you know?"

"Because I opened and read all of Mr. Trent's mail unless it was marked personal. Much of it required only routine answers, which I could handle without bothering him."

Casey took out his notebook. "I think I'd better have Harry Walpole's address. "Did these letters bother Trent?"

"No. He just laughed and threw them in the wastebasket."

"Sensitive, compassionate guy," McWilliams said. "Dedicated to serving his fellow man. Isn't that what his publicity always said?"

"Oh, Andy," she reprimanded her husband. "Mr. Trent just never let things upset him."

Casey got up to leave. "I hope you enjoy your belated lunch. I'll leave you my card, Mrs. McWilliams, and if you think of anything else that might be helpful, please call me."

"Oh, I will," Amanda said.

"Nice to meet you, Andy." Casey decided not to shake hands with McWilliams a second time. His fingers still hurt from the first one. "What kind of work do you do?" It was a polite rhetorical question rather than a search for information.

McWilliams chuckled. "I'm a salesman, the top salesman, I might add, for a company that—well, you could call it a defense contractor."

IX

Randollph, like Casey, believed in the benefits and efficacy of routine. Casey, Randollph knew, believed in routine because he had been taught that following certain rules of procedure in his work was the surest way to achieve results. Casey actually had an affection for the routine of his craft.

Randollph, on the other hand, thought of routine as a defense against a world that blithely supposed he had nothing better to do than what it wanted him to do when it wanted him to do it. It was a method for reducing an unmanageable job to the barely manageable. Back at the seminary when he was teaching fledgling divines how Saint John Chrysostom got himself exiled for preaching against the styles in women's clothing favored by the Empress Eudoxia, or how John Knox reformed the Church of Scotland by abolishing the dictatorial office of bishop and substituting for it the dictatorial office of superintendent, he'd followed a routine, of course. Not that there hadn't been plenty to do. Lectures, conferences with students, keeping up with the literature in his field, grading papers.

But it had been a benign routine. He'd discovered, in the short time he'd been pastor at Good Shepherd, that the demands placed on the pastor by a large holy business were brutal. You established a routine or you'd be swamped in a week's time.

He'd come to think of his procedures as a pastor as analogous to the pattern of the professional football player he'd once been. You worked toward Sunday. You might play a splendid game on Sunday, have the crowds cheering you. But, come Monday, yesterday's game was history. You had to begin preparation for next Sunday. After a game with a mean team like the Raiders that delighted in creaming the quarterback, you hurt all over on Monday. But that didn't matter. You had to get up the next day and get ready to do it again.

For a preacher, this meant getting next Sunday's game plan established. You had a sermon to prepare. Usually this demanded doing some biblical research on your text and some reading in the areas of faith and practice you were explicating in this particular homily. Miss Windfall, he knew, thought when he was researching a text or reading a book of theology he was soldiering on the job. Dr. Arthur Hartshorne, his predecessor, never cracked a book and, according to Dan Gantry, didn't know much about the Bible. "Old Arty mostly told funny or weepy stories," Dan had said. "Told 'em real good, though."

Setting up Sunday's game plan also included a conference with Tony Agostino, Good Shepherd's organist and choirmaster. Hymns and anthems had to fit with the sermon theme, or at least not clash with it. Randollph could reject hymns with weak and sentimental texts, or hymns that expressed a dubious theology. But, to his regret, he couldn't read music. He'd often select a hymn with a strong and well-written text only to have Tony point out that the tune to which it was set was all but unsingable.

But getting ready for next Sunday was only part of the routine.

He had to set aside time to write the pastor's column for

116

The Spire, Good Shepherd's weekly newsletter, which must be mailed in time to arrive Friday or Saturday to remind members that divine worship was an option for them come Sunday.

Then there were the occasional responsibilities. Weddings, which required a rehearsal you knew about in advance and could fit into a schedule, however crowded. Funerals, though, could not be anticipated. He'd go weeks without one. Then there would be a period of a week or two when he'd have several last rites to conduct. Funerals took time, lovingly given, but time. And for Randollph they were emotionally draining. He hadn't yet learned to be professional about death.

Randollph set aside two afternoons per week to make calls on Good Shepherd's members so unfortunate as to be confined to a hospital. He averaged three evenings each week meeting various boards and committees deemed necessary to keeping the machinery of Good Shepherd lubricated with holy oil.

And then there were the people who needed "a minute of his time." These included church goods salesmen, professional fund-raisers looking for business, denominational executives seeking his support for their agency's newest program to move the world, or at least the church, a notch or two toward salvation, representatives of supposedly worthy community causes seeking the best-known speaker they could persuade to address their annual banquet sans honorarium.

Fortunately, Miss Windfall had an unerring eye and instinct for those worthy of admission to the temple, and those who didn't need to see the high priest and could be shunted off on Dan Gantry or Bertie Smelser. Or just turned out into the cold.

But Randollph had an unbreakable rule that he would see anyone who genuinely needed pastoral help or counseling. If it was an emergency, he'd see them at any time. But he'd set aside one afternoon each week for people who required or thought they'd be helped by a spiritual advisor.

This was the part of his multidimensional job for which he felt the least prepared and, in performance, the most inadequate. He hadn't expected ever to be a pastor, so he'd taken only the required course in counseling when earning his seminary degree. He'd talked to the bishop about his lack of training and experience as a counselor.

"Nowadays," Freddie had said, "the seminaries are doing a good job in preparing students for the role of counselor. In my days as a student, they didn't teach us anything about it."

"What did you do when you were a pastor, then?" Randollph had asked.

"The best I could."

"Are you saying that I've just got to muddle through?"

"Not entirely. There's quite a bit of good literature in this field nowadays. Get the professor, I can't think of his name, at our seminary in Evanston to recommend a reading list. You aren't too proud to ask for help, are you, C.P.?"

"Is a drowning man too proud to seize a life preserver? But what do I do in the meantime? Some weeks I'm swamped by the number of people with problems they expect me to solve, or at least help them to solve."

"I can give you a few general rules to follow, C.P. Rules I learned from experience, from my failures—and some successes, too."

"Please do."

"Rule number one," the bishop had said, "is to use common sense. I like to think I have been blessed with a goodly amount of common sense. And I know you have it."

"Could you be a little more specific, Freddie?"

"Many people will come to you with messes they've gotten themselves into. They are so close to their problem they can't see the options open to them. Don't tell them what to do. Point out the choices they have."

"I've already figured that one, Freddie."

"Thought you might have."

118

"I get many people coming to me with marital problems. Almost always the wife."

"I know," the bishop had sighed. "In our culture, men feel it is an admission of weakness to seek counseling. You have to remember, though, to be wary of one spouse spelling out the sins of the other spouse. We all want to present ourselves to others in the best possible light. These situations can occasionally be the total responsibility of one spouse, but not often."

"I haven't had much luck in patching up these marriages."

"You won't."

"Why not?"

"Because when a marital problem gets to you, it is usually too late. Once in a while you can help turn a sour marriage sweet again. Not often, though."

"That's almost like saying marital counseling is a waste of my time."

"I know. Early in my ministry I always felt a terrible sense of defeat when I failed to put a broken marriage back together. Then I learned that often I could help the party— usually, as I said, the wife—through the agony of separation, over the trauma of a life that had crumbled."

"I wouldn't have thought of it that way. That helps."

"Two more rules or bits of advice, C. P. You'll occasionally get a genuine psychotic. Learn to sort them out quickly."

"Give me an example."

"Well," the bishop had replied, "I'd get people who were convinced they'd committed the unpardonable sin. Or that God had chosen them to be His special messenger. Don't try to play psychiatrist. These people are beyond your competence. Do your best to get them the kind of help they need. And one more thing."

"Yes?"

"Never waste time on an alcoholic. There isn't a thing you can do for them. They'll convince you that you've cured them, that they'll never take a drink again. They

119

believe it. But they'll hit the first bar they come to after they leave your office."

"Do you just abandon them, Freddie? That doesn't sound like you."

"Oh, no. The best thing you can do is to persuade them to get in touch with Alcoholics Anonymous. You know about them?"

"Of course."

"Their method, I think, is psychologically sound. Much of it resembles Christian theology, though they are nonsectarian. And their success rate is astonishing."

The bishop's counsel had been helpful. Randollph, if not entirely confident of his skills as a counselor, was at least more comfortable with this part of his job.

Today was his afternoon for open counseling. When he returned to his study after lunch Miss Windfall, apparently restored to health after a one-day absence, handed him just one card with the name and meager personal data furnished by whoever it was that had requested a hearing.

"Just one appointment," Miss Windfall had remarked, unnecessarily, since Randollph could see that for himself. What Miss Windfall meant was that things had gone slack in her brief absence, and that with a light afternoon's schedule, Randollph could complete the tasks that he should have taken care of yesterday.

In his study Randollph glanced at the card Miss Windfall had handed him. It read: *Name*—Mrs. A. Everleigh. *Member of Good Shepherd*—no. *How was appointment made?*—by phone. *Was reason for appointment stated?*—Personal problem.

Personal problem. That nearly always was a euphemism for marital trouble. He wondered if Mrs. James Trent had sought any help for what it now seemed certain was an unhappy marriage. Not from her pastor. Perhaps from another pastor who did not know her? The bishop had told him he'd get members from other churches as counselees because they were too embarrassed to tell their troubles to their own pastor. Maybe Mrs. Everleigh was a member of Fourth Presbyterian or St. James Episcopal.

The intercom on his desk squawked and Miss Windfall's slightly distorted voice announced that Mrs. Everleigh had arrived.

Mrs. Everleigh, Randollph's quick appraisal told him, was probably a prosperous matron in her very-well-preserved fifties. He was sure Samantha would approve of her stylish but conservative brown tweed suit accented by an orange silk scarf. She moved gracefully toward him, hand extended, smiling.

"So nice of you to see me, Dr. Randollph." Randollph liked her smile.

"Let's sit over here at what I call my conversation center," Randollph steered her to the comfortable old leather sofa and sat facing her in one of the matching chairs.

"This is a delightful room, so masculine, yet not overpoweringly so. May I smoke?"

"Yes, of course." He located an ashtray while Mrs. Everleigh fitted a long black cigarette into a white holder. Randollph found matches and lit her cigarette because she seemed to expect him to.

"Dr. Randollph," she began pleasantly, "I am the owner and operator of the most expensive and luxurious bordello in Chicago."

Randollph hoped he didn't look as startled as he felt. All he could think of to say was "Oh?"

"Does that shock you?"

"No. Nothing much shocks me anymore. Surprises me, perhaps."

"Because I don't fit your stereotype of a whore or a madam?"

"One wouldn't guess your, er, profession by looking at you I admit."

Mrs. Everleigh laughed. "I'll take that as a compliment. Actually, I'm a businesswoman providing a service that is much in demand. My work is dealing with personnel, public relations, maintaining my property, my house, keeping accurate records. We've installed a computer system for our records." She seemed proud of this. "Incidentally, Everleigh is not my name."

"I thought it probably wasn't," Randollph replied. "Once you told me your line of business, I recalled that there was once a famous, er, house here in Chicago run by sisters named Everleigh. I suspected that you borrowed the name."

"I'd heard that you were pretty sharp. I heard right. You're wondering why I made an appointment to see you."

"I am intrigued."

"I have some information the police might like to have, and the best way to give it to them I thought would be through a priest or clergyman who can't be forced to reveal the source of his information. I chose you because I'm a football fan. I figured if you'd led the life of a professional athlete, well, you'd been around and wouldn't give me a bad time, or a lot of pious talk, or try to reform me."

"Do you feel the need to reform?"

"No." Mrs. Everleigh spat it out. "I run a high-class business, even if it is illegal. I have strict rules. I don't permit drunkenness or anything but normal sex on my premises."

"I'd be interested in your definition of normal sex."

"Anything that doesn't involve violence or physical abuse."

Randollph thought this left a rather wide latitude for sexual activity, but didn't say so.

"In spite of my business, I consider myself a good citizen," Mrs. Everleigh continued. "I pay my taxes. I give generously to several charities. My girls are well paid and treated with consideration. Can you understand what I'm saying?"

"I think so." You're saying, Randollph thought, that you want to think well of yourself even though you make a living through what society considers a disgusting and immoral business.

"What I'm asking you to do, Dr. Randollph, is to tell the police what I'm going to tell you without divulging the source of your information."

Mrs. Everleigh stubbed out her cigarette, replaced it with another one, which Randollph dutifully lit for her.

"Why can't you go directly to the police yourself?" he asked. "I would think that you have some contact with them."

"You mean do I bribe them? Of course I do. It's just part of my overhead expense." She laughed, a low, tinkling sound. "Some policemen, some pretty high up, are among my regular customers. Their visits are on the house." She laughed again. "That's a terrible pun, isn't it?" She quickly shifted to a serious attitude. "I can't go to the police, because I'd have to tell the story to Lieutenant Michael Casey. He has a reputation as an honest cop. He'd feel compelled to report me to his superiors, who'd then be forced to do something about my establishment even if they didn't want to. That kind of trouble I don't need. You see," she added, "I've thought this through very carefully. This is the best way to do it. I want to do my duty as a citizen, but I don't want to be persecuted for it."

"You have, I take it, some knowledge of a crime, which you wish to communicate to the police through me."

"That's it. And I want your promise not to reveal your source."

"So far as I'm concerned, anything told me by a counselee is a privileged communication."

"I'll accept that. All right, here it is. You are familiar with the murder of James Trent, the one they called the Splendid Samaritan?"

"Yes." Randollph didn't think it necessary to reveal how much he knew about Trent and the murder.

"I don't know if it has any bearing on the case, is a clue or whatever—but the Splendid Samaritan was one of my most frequent customers." Mrs. Everleigh leaned back, puffed on her cigarette, and smiled what Randollph could only interpret as a smile of triumph. She confirmed it by saying, "So Mr. Perfect, upright, pious citizen wasn't all that he pretended to be."

"Few of us are," Randollph said. "I'm surprised, though, that he risked his reputation by—"

"Oh, he always came disguised. A blonde wig and mustache. And used an assumed name. Many of my customers do that, of course. I've gotten pretty good at seeing through disguises. And his picture was in the paper all the time. I'm sure he knew I knew who he was, but we pretended I didn't. So he didn't risk much. I protect the identity of my customers, and I don't go in for blackmail."

"Is there any more information about Mr. Trent you wish me to pass along to the police?"

"No, that's the main thing. Trent, the girls told me, was insatiable. He wanted a different girl every time. Sometimes he'd request a black girl. Then an hour or so later, he'd send her away and ask for a Japanese girl. Or it might be a Scandinavian girl, then a Chinese."

"Is this kind of, ah, behavior rare in your establishment?"

"No. Fairly common. Some men want a new girl every time. Not many used two girls an evening, though, like Trent. They seem to need variety, Trent and his kind. Others get attached to one girl, and want her every time." Mrs. Everleigh tucked her cigarette holder into her purse, gathered her coat, and prepared to leave.

"I can count on you to tell the police, Lieutenant Casey, about this, then? I don't know if it will help, but if it helps catch a murderer, I'll be glad."

"I'll talk to Casey."

Mrs. Everleigh extended her hand and put on her friendly smile, which, Randollph suspected, was the one with which she greeted her customers. "Thank you for helping me, Dr. Randollph. If you were anyone but who you are, or what you are, I'd offer you the hospitality of my house."

"Let me offer you the hospitality of my house," Randollph replied. "Any Sunday morning at eleven o'clock."

"I just might take you up on that," she said, and left.

* * *

Casey settled himself comfortably on the sofa recently vacated by Mrs. Everleigh, propped his feet on the somewhat beat-up coffee table, and asked, "So what's the information I need to hear?"

"It may not mean much of anything," Randollph said, regretting his hasty call to the lieutenant after Mrs. Everleigh's departure. "I may just be wasting your time."

"That's a good description of what I've been doing with my time the last several days. Might as well waste it here as someplace else. This Trent thing is at a dead end, if you'll excuse the feeble pun. What have you got for me?"

Randollph told him about Mrs. Everleigh.

"Mrs. Everleigh would be Penelope Vanderbilt," Casey said. "I doubt if that is her real name either. Probably started life as Maude Jones or Daisy Smith or something like that. But she's got an obsession about being high-class. So she probably rechristened herself with a name that sounded classy."

Randollph was astonished. "You know her?"

"I know who she is," Casey answered, then added hastily, "I've never been in her establishment."

"I didn't think that you had," Randollph assured him.

"Every cop knows about her," Casey, relieved, continued.

"Then if you report what I've told you, your superiors will know the source of the information. I promised her anonymity."

"Don't worry. She won't be bothered. She pays too well for protection."

"Does her information have any value?"

Casey thought about it, then said: "It tells us that the Splendid Samaritan had a few holes in that holy robe in which he draped himself."

"So how does that help?"

"If he wasn't as upright and moral as he pretended to be, then maybe along the way he pulled a few crooked

125

deals, ruined business competitors, or even seduced the wife or daughter of someone who decided to take revenge." Casey did not look happy with his conclusions. "That would mean investigating his past life rather thoroughly, which takes a lot of work and manpower. And with no assurance whatever that you'll turn up anything."

Randollph was disappointed that his information wasn't much help.

"It could also indicate that he was set up by a woman," Casey continued. "Guys like Trent, who crave variety in sex partners, which you say Penny Vanderbilt, Mrs. Everleigh, claims he did, they're easy marks for a smart woman. Problem: Find a woman who hated him enough to kill him. I like that theory. He's at his office late at night, when no one else is around. Purpose—a romantic rendezvous. Or so he thinks. Instead, she puts a .22 bullet in his brain."

"That doesn't explain the bound hands, the light, the bloody bill, and the robbery."

Casey slumped farther into the leather sofa. "I know. It doesn't make sense."

"It made sense to whoever did it," Randollph reproved him. "You are the one who taught me that. No matter how senseless a murder appears to us, it was the sensible thing to do from the murderer's point of view."

"Yeah, I know," Casey said. "I guess I'm just so frustrated on this one that I'm forgetting things I ought to remember."

"We all do that at times," Randollph told him gently.

"Take that bloody hundred-dollar bill grasped in Trent's hands. That's a very theatrical touch, to say the least. Can you make anything out of that? Oh, I know I said the murderer did it to make some kind of statement. But what is it saying?" Casey was almost talking to himself now. "It's a symbol. The killer wants it to tell us something about Trent. But what?"

"What does money mean?" Randollph asked Casey.

"A million things—and nothing."

"It could be a symbol of greed," Randollph said. "After all, that's one of the seven deadly sins. To my mind, the ugliest of the seven."

"Uglier than lust? Trent, according to your information, was guilty of lust. I can't think of anything uglier than ordering up girls for his use like you'd select your dinner from a menu."

"I admit that grading sins as to their degree of repulsiveness is tricky theological business," Randollph said. "But lust is a perversion, a misuse, of something good, a gift of creation. In its highest expression, it makes us more human. Perverted into indiscriminate and unbridled sexual appetite, it dehumanizes the victim."

"So I think that's uglier than greed," Casey argued. "Why don't you?"

"Greed is not a gift of creation gone wrong," Randollph explained. "It is the desire to acquire more and more— there's never enough. The greedy man wants more than he can ever possibly need, more than he can ever possibly use. It is pure original sin. And what's worse," he went on, "society condemns the lustful person—as it should—but often praises and honors the greedy."

Casey abandoned the argument. "So you think the hundred-dollar bill is saying, 'James Trent, the Splendid Samaritan, was a greedy man'?"

"Perhaps. But don't forget that the killer went to some trouble to see that the bill was bloodstained. I'd guess that is a part of what the murderer was trying to say."

"Blood money. Trent's money was blood money. Is that the message?"

"Perhaps."

"But that doesn't get me anywhere," Casey complained. "Does it mean that he killed somebody in order to make his fortune? Does it mean he sucked the blood out of some other business for his own benefit? How am I going to find out what it means?"

"When you've collected enough facts. You always say that by collecting the facts you find the pattern."

127

"So I do," Casey admitted. "Now, good doctor, do you have any suggestions as to where I find more facts? That's all I've been doing, chasing after facts, and finding damn few that help much."

"Since you ask, Lieutenant, I think if I were you, I'd do a little digging into the personal history of James Trent. I've a feeling that bloody bill means something important. It's just too bizarre to be pointless."

"You're probably right," Casey said without enthusiasm, "but it's not a job I look forward to. Oh, it's easy enough to find out the basic facts about him. Where he was born, his business career, how he made his money. But what he might have done to make someone want to murder him, well, they don't publish facts like that."

"Sorry I got you over here for nothing," Randollph said, "though it's always nice to see you."

Casey looked happier as he got up to leave. "It wasn't for nothing. I'll thoroughly enjoy telling Captain Manahan about Penny Vanderbilt's information. It'll be fun to watch him squirm."

"Oh? Why will he squirm?"

"Because," Casey said, "he's a regular patron of Penny's bordello. And he knows I know it."

Randollph was surprised. "Isn't he endangering his career? He's breaking the law."

"Oh, that's not a problem. Penny extends the courtesy of her house to any police officer high enough in the hierarchy to carry some weight. Anyway, if Manahan got into a little trouble, his Chinaman would protect him."

"His Chinaman? I do not consider myself dense," Randollph said, "but it escapes me entirely how a Chinaman could protect a police officer."

Casey laughed. "Sorry. 'Chinaman' is a bit of Chicago police patois. Your Chinaman is someone powerful in the police hierarchy or a politician who is, well, sort of your sponsor. He helps you in your career. Drops the right word in the right place to get you a promotion. And, if you get into a little trouble, he helps get you out of it. The New

York police call their mentor their rabbi. Here, it's China-man." Casey was about to open the door when he stopped and asked Randollph, "By the way, when is Sam going to have one of her dinners she says are for people she likes? I hope she still likes Liz and me. Liz loves them, and I confess I get hungry for Clarence's cooking."

"Be assured that you're still on the list of people Samantha likes. I'll ask her and let you know."

After Casey had gone, Randollph pondered what Casey had told him about policemen who hoped to rise in their profession needing a Chinaman, or in New York a rabbi. On casual inspection, it seemed a corrupt, or potentially corrupting system. But, on reflection, he had to admit that he'd had his Chinamen, too.

There had been his high school coach, who had tried so hard to get him a football scholarship at a major university. He hadn't managed to do it, but did land him one at a small, obscure college.

Then there'd been his college coach, a rough and pro-fane man, who discerned in Randollph a potential for greatness as a quarterback. When none of the pro teams drafted Randollph, the coach used his friendship with the offensive coordinator of the Los Angeles Rams to get his protégé a tryout as a free agent. Two Chinamen whose help had made his career as a pro star possible.

And then there was Freddie.

Freddie had seen something—worth? value? talent?—in him at their first meeting. He'd carefully guided his graduate education and his career as a teacher. Then he'd brought him to the pastorate of the Church of the Good Shepherd. It was to Freddie he now turned for counsel and help. Freddie was his Chinaman. He decided that someday, at just the right moment, he'd say, "Freddie, did you know you're my Chinaman?" No, he thought, Freddie would probably prefer the New York term. It would be fun to go one up on the bishop by saying, "Freddie, you're my rabbi."

129

X

Everett Stagg carefully lit one of the long, fat Montecristos his tobacconist managed somehow to smuggle in from Cuba for a few select customers. He savored the rich smoke as it saturated his tongue and trickled through his nasal passages. This was supposed to be Castro's favorite brand. Well, the son-of-a-bitch was a no-good Communist, but he did know tobacco. Everett had to give him that.

Stagg was not a reflective man. He thought he enjoyed his Montecristo only because he appreciated a fine cigar. A psychologist, though, could have told him that this expensive tube of tobacco was for Stagg a symbol of his success, his power, and his money. He had the money to buy anything he wanted. And if he wanted something illegal and difficult to obtain, he had the influence to get it.

Stagg wouldn't have understood this. What he did understand was that he was immensely pleased with himself. He'd come to Atlanta and set himself up in the real estate business. At first he'd concentrated on selling houses. Atlanta was, still was, a boom town. He branched out, buying and selling business properties. Then land development. Then acquiring rental properties. He boasted that Stagg and Company could sell you a shopping mall in an Atlanta suburb or rent you an executive-grade vacation home in the Bahamas. Anything you wanted in the way of real estate, he could furnish.

Like most successful people, he attributed his success entirely to his own skill, brains, and superiority over the herd of humans he watched trudge to their dreary jobs every morning, then wearily drag themselves home every evening. Like most people who rose from humble origins to the top of whatever world they had chosen to sit on, he never considered luck a factor in his rise. He never thought about how he had sold his Acme Enterprises stock for a small fortune, which had furnished the capital for getting started in the real estate business. Nor did it ever cross his mind that it was because he had married a lady from Atlanta that he'd moved here just at the right moment when only a dolt could fail in the real estate business. Or that his wife knew the city, and had a nose that could smell out low-priced land that was sure to become valuable.

His feelings of well-being, nearly always with him, had been tempered considerably by those newspaper clippings he'd received a few days ago. Nothing else in the envelope. Postmarked Chicago. He'd been shaken more than he cared to admit. Was it a warning? A threat? Or had someone found out by chance that he'd once been associated with these two men and mailed him those newspaper stories just as a mean trick? With the optimism of a salesman, he selected the best alternative. It was just a mean trick. After all, he told himself, Big Al and Timmy were the main men. He was just a silent partner. Who'd bother with him? Stagg, incapable of living in the past very long, resolutely put the clippings out of his mind.

He was wondering if he enjoyed his business so much because it produced a constant flow of large profits, or because it was like roulette, with all the thrill of putting a pile of chips on a project and seeing if the ball dropped on your number, when his secretary buzzed him.

131

"There's a Robin Hartley calling about the Lemaster place. Insists on speaking to you personally. Do you wish to take the call?"

"Yes, I'll take it," he said eagerly. He'd told the Lemasters that it wouldn't be easy to lease their house, mansion that it was, for a year at five thousand per month. This was the first inquiry he'd had about it.

"My name is Robin Hartley," a husky voice said to him. "My company is considering establishing a branch in Atlanta. "I'll need to lease a furnished house for a year while we complete all the necessary surveys and lay the groundwork. It must be spacious enough to entertain, and elegant enough to reflect the best possible image of our company. Friends in Atlanta tell me you are advertising a house that might meet our requirements."

"Indeed I am," Stagg said heartily.

"Tell me about it."

Stagg went into his sales pitch enthusiastically. "It's in one of our fanciest suburbs. Five bedrooms, four baths—"

"I'm more interested in the facilities for entertaining," the husky voice interrupted him.

"Yes, of course," Stagg quickly switched directions. "The main room, the living room, is eighteen by forty feet, fireplace, a large fireplace, at one end. A smaller room, they call it the library, adequate for entertaining small groups."

"What style?"

"What style? Oh, you mean the architecture. Antebellum." He'd not known what antebellum meant, he reflected, until coming to Atlanta and entering the real estate business. He'd learned in a hurry, though, that nomenclature was vital to selling real estate. If you developed a subdivision, the property would sell twice as fast if you named it Twin Oaks or Lee Valley or anything that sounded like a desirable address.

"Antebellum," he repeated, "very impressive-looking. You'll like it."

"How much?"

"It's a mite expensive."

"How much?" the husky voice sounded impatient.

Stagg had a sudden inspiration. If a corporation was paying the bill, it was only tax money. "Sixty-five hundred a month." He was glad he hadn't mentioned the price in any of his ads.

"If the house is suitable, the price is satisfactory," the husky voice replied. Stagg silently congratulated himself on his business acumen.

"When would you like to inspect it?" he asked.

"Tonight. I'm calling from New York. I'll fly to Atlanta later today. Let me see. I'll rent a car at the airport. I should be able to meet you at the house by ten o'clock tonight. Please have all papers with you. If I like the place, I'll move in tonight."

"Good, good." Stagg was mentally rubbing his hands together. He always rubbed his hands together when he'd scored a victory. This one, he was sure, was all wrapped up. A difficult property moved with unexpected ease. "I'll have one of my top salesmen meet you at the house—"

"No." The husky voice was cold.

"Uh, I don't understand," Stagg sputtered.

"I do not do business with subordinates. I'll expect you to be there."

"I, I have an engagement," Stagg sputtered. He thought of the long, boring evening ahead. Dinner at the Cecil Applegarths. The Applegarths were old Atlanta, socially prominent. But, Stagg knew, despite their gracious and expensive lifestyle, they were on their uppers financially.

He'd helped Cecil Applegarth make some money by tipping him to a few good real estate deals. In return, the Applegarths included the Staggs in what was supposed to be Atlanta's social elite. Stagg's wife loved it. She'd give him forty kinds of hell if he backed out of tonight's dinner in favor of a business deal.

"Very well," the husky voice said. "I have the names of some other respected real estate people in Atlanta. No doubt one of them can find something for me."

133

That did it. The almost certain prospect of unloading the Lemasters' place, his commission on the deal—fattened by his bold decision in jacking up the price—plus the pain of losing out to a competitor, was more than he could bear.

"I'll cancel my engagement," he said hastily.

"About ten o'clock, then. What's the address?"

He gave it, then said, "The best route from the airport would be—"

"I'll find it," the husky voice said, and hung up. It was some time later that Stagg realized he didn't know if Robin Hartley was a man or a woman. Robin was one of those unisex names. And the husky voice could have been either a man's or a woman's. Oh, well, it didn't matter as long as he or she had the bucks.

Everett Stagg knew he ought to call his wife and tell her he couldn't make the Applegarths' dinner, but he didn't. He had his secretary prepare the lease papers. When he instructed her to type sixty-five hundred dollars in as the price per month, she raised her eyebrows. This pleased Stagg. "Client sounded prosperous, so I raised the price a little," he told her. "Didn't get any static." He wanted his secretary to know how clever he'd been. Not so much to impress her, though that didn't hurt. Mainly, it was a way of confirming his self-image as a clever businessman.

When the papers were prepared, he slipped them into a briefcase. It was nearly closing time.

"Now," he told his secretary, "the client's flying in from New York and we're meeting at the Lemaster place at ten o'clock. Client insisted it had to be tonight. I'm sure the deal will go through."

"Of course it will, with you handling it," she said. She knew he loved to be flattered.

"What I want you to do is to call my wife and tell her I've suddenly been called away on a very important business deal. Tell her I tried to get out of it, but just couldn't. Lay it on heavy."

"Oh, I will, I'm good at that." She should be, she

thought, she'd had plenty of practice. She didn't like Mrs. Stagg and her pretension to high social position. She enjoyed these little opportunities to upset the old girl's life.

"Know you are, dearie." Stagg absently patted her. "Just don't call till you're sure I'm out of the building. Tell her to go ahead to the dinner, make my apologies, and say that I hope I can get there in time for cigars and brandy with the gentlemen."

"Will do," she said.

As Stagg's elevator dropped him rapidly toward the lobby, his spirits rose. Oh, he knew he was in for a bad time at home. But he was a man who let the future take care of itself—except, of course, in the business of buying land that would vastly increase in value over the years.

He felt good, first, because he'd escaped a boring evening. Second, he'd have dinner at Santini's Little Italy. Stagg loved Italian food, especially pasta. But his wife considered pasta peasant fare and wouldn't let their cook serve it. There was no dignified way, his wife claimed, to eat spaghetti. And as for sopping up the sauce with bread, well, no civilized person would ever think of doing something so crude. So, whenever he had to stay downtown, or his wife was dining with members of the several charity committees she belonged to, Stagg had dinner at Santini's. He was a valued customer, and the attention he received from barmen, waiters, and Romeo Santini, the owner, was almost as welcome as the food.

Third, he was going to close a profitable business deal. Sign some papers, and money would automatically roll in for a year. He did not plan to tell the Lemasters about the extra fifteen hundred a month he'd be getting. After all, they hoped to get five thousand and would be pleased with that. What they didn't know wouldn't hurt them—or him.

Stagg double-parked his tan Cadillac sedan in front of the restaurant. One of the parking-lot boys was opening the car door for him almost as soon as the car came to a full stop. Stagg was known for the generosity of his tips.

135

"Evening, Jimmy," he said to the boy. "Be sure to park it where it won't get scratched or dented."

"Oh, I'll take good care of it, Mr. Stagg, sir."

"I know you will, Jimmy. You always do."

Santini's Little Italy was not an imposing place. It made no pretense of luxury or plush decor. It consisted of one large room, tables covered with red and white checkered cloths and decorated with candles stuck in Chianti bottles. Except for the lull between lunch and dinner, it was nearly always full.

Romeo Santini, a short, stout man with glossy black hair and heavy drooping mustache, saw Stagg and went to greet him.

"Ah, Everett," he said, shaking Stagg's hand vigorously, "you've no doubt had a hard day evicting widows who couldn't pay their rent. How many people have you cheated out of their life savings today?"

"None yet today, Romeo, but the day's not over yet. How many virgins have you seduced today?"

"Not a one since yesterday, I'm sad to report." Santini assumed a mournful look. "But my day's not over yet either." You were an important person in the city if Santini engaged in this light, insulting banter with you. It added to Stagg's sense of well-being that he was one of the favored few.

Santini led Stagg to a table. "I will personally take your order," he said. "Your usual vodka martini?"

"No. I'd like one, but I've got a, er, business conference later. Want my head to be clear. I'll settle for a half bottle of that dago red you tramp out with your own feet,"

"Is true. Well, sometimes I let my mamma help with the tramping. She complains her feet have turned purple.

"You old fraud," Stagg said. "Bring me a plate of antipasto. And don't cheat on the marinated eggplant."

"And then perhaps a plate of veal piccata? It is extraordinary tonight."

"Veal I can get at home. I want a plate of spaghetti with lots of meat sauce." He and Romeo always went through this routine. Romeo never failed to suggest what he considered something excellent, knowing that Stagg would call for some form of pasta. It was another familiar touch that made Stagg feel accepted.

Stagg thought how pretty the plate of antipasto looked as the waiter set it in front of him. The bright red sweet peppers, pale yellow eggplant, wrinkled black olives with their slightly bitter taste, mottled slivers of salami, small dark strips of anchovies, radishes with their red and white surrounded by large green olives—this was a sight that always stimulated Stagg's appetite. He buttered a chunk of crusty Italian bread and dug in. Without really articulating it in his mind, he realized that he was a most fortunate man.

Everett Stagg arrived at the Lemasters' mansion well before ten o'clock. He turned the switch that bathed the two-storied porch supported by thin pillars in light. This, he knew, would impress the client. Then he went through the house, turning on lamps, chandeliers, overhead lights, making sure that each room was illuminated so as to show off its best qualities. He almost neglected to light the swimming pool. He mentally kicked himself for such carelessness. The client wanted a place suitable for entertaining, and a swimming pool added something extra toward fulfilling that requirement. He blamed himself for having that extra glass of dago red when his half bottle didn't last to the the end of the spaghetti. He still felt slightly, just slightly, befuddled. The thin fog of alcohol numbing his brain would, he felt certain, dissipate any moment now.

He chose the library as the room in which to do business. There was an excellent and no doubt very expensive copy of an antique escritoire—maybe a Louis something or other—but it was against the wall. Stagg preferred to be on one side of a desk facing the client on the other side. There was a nice library table, also against the wall. He switched it so that the end abutted the picture window overlooking the swimming pool. Nice touch, he thought.

137

The sight of the pool would remind the client that this was true luxury housing and that its exorbitant cost wasn't really out of line. He wondered if he should have jacked up the price another five hundred a month.

He found two comfortable chairs and put one on each side of the table. Then he took two copies of the lease papers and placed them on the table in front of the chairs. He reviewed the scene and was pleased with it.

It was well past ten o'clock when Stagg heard the slam of a car door. He hurried into the main room, then counted to ten before answering the chimes announcing a visitor. Another trick of the profession. Never appear overeager.

When he opened the door, he did a swift appraisal of the client. Not large, but an authoritative bearing. Wearing perfectly fitting gray slacks and a tan jacket that hadn't come from any cut-rate store. This client had money, or represented money. Junior executives or flunkeys didn't dress this expensively or carry that commanding presence. He wished he'd added that extra five hundred to the lease price.

Stagg extended his hand, put on his professionally cordial smile, and said, "I'm Everett Stagg. You must be Robin Hartley."

"Were you expecting someone else?" the client said, ignoring Stagg's extended hand. One up for the client, Stagg thought. He hoped this didn't mean a lot of haggling. He'd figured this for a sure thing.

The tour of the house went much more rapidly than Stagg had expected. The client looked over the large room and the library and said, "Adequate." The kitchen, bedrooms, bathrooms, and servants' quarters received only a cursory examination.

"It'll do," the client pronounced. "You have the papers ready?"

"In the library." Apparently there would be no haggling. Stagg was disappointed that he hadn't had much chance to deliver his sales pitch. He excelled, he thought, in the sales pitch. He'd turned many a recalcitrant customer into a buyer with it. Oh well, he thought, at least I'm not going to haggle over the price.

"I have to get something out of the car," the client said. "I'll join you in the library in a minute."

Stagg went to the library and sat in the chair he had selected for himself. The other chair was placed to give the best possible view of the lighted pool. That, it seemed, was now unnecessary. When they had inspected the library, the client must have noticed the pool, but had not commented on it. He looked at his watch. This business had gone much more rapidly than he'd anticipated. He'd probably have plenty of time to get to the dinner party for after-dinner drinks, which might placate his wife a little.

The client came in lugging a couple of bulky black cases.

Stagg's curiosity was aroused. "What's that, those?" he asked.

"Just some equipment," the client replied, opening one of the cases. For some reason Stagg began to feel a little uneasy, but he didn't know why.

"Now," the client said, straightening up, "what I am pointing at you is a pistol. I'm doing this to assure that you will obey my orders."

"Wh-what is this?" Stagg managed to stutter. He only half grasped the situation, partly because of shock, and partly because all that wine was still robbing him of some of his wits.

"You'll find out soon enough. Now place your elbows on the table and put your palms together. And don't get any foolish ideas about lunging at me across the table. I'm very good with this gun. Practice all the time. I could shoot you through either eye I chose before you were half out of your chair. You were thinking about it, weren't you?"

"Y-y-yes."

"I could see that you were. Now I'm going to wind this wire around your wrists. There. It hurts some, I know. It's very thin wire. But nothing like it will hurt if you struggle to free your hands. It would cut you badly. It might even

139

cut deeply enough that you'd bleed to death and ruin this expensive but unattractive carpet. By the way, I don't care much for this house. Showy but dull, really."

Stagg, disoriented by a situation he couldn't comprehend, managed to say, "If it's money you're after, please take everything I have."

The client laughed contemptuously. "Would I go to all this trouble for a few dollars? You're a fool, Stagg, as well as a criminal. Now if you'll excuse me, I have some equipment to set up. Just remember that I have the gun, and I'll be watching."

Stagg watched in horrified fascination as the equipment was set up.

"What's this all about?" he asked.

"There," the client said, "I think we're ready now. What's this all about? Do you recall the name Palmquist?"

It hit him like a vicious punch to the jaw. Now he understood what was happening. "You."

"Do I need to introduce myself?"

"You, I can't believe it, you're—"

"That's right. That's who I am. It took a long time for your sins to catch up with you, but now they have."

"But I didn't do it," Stagg was pleading now. "It was Big Al and Timmy. Timmy's idea. I didn't do it."

"Were you a founding member of Acme Enterprises?"

"Uh, well—"

"Were you?"

"Yes, in a way." Maybe, Stagg thought, he could talk his way out of this. "I was just one of the original investors, I had nothing to do—"

"Did you do anything to stop the swindle?"

"Ah, oh, you see, I was in the minority. I couldn't have—"

"Did you get rich through your share of Acme stock?"

"It's, it isn't like you think."

"It's exactly like I think."

Stagg saw this wasn't getting him anywhere. He tried a new tack.

140

"I'll pay you a million dollars to let me go. In cash. Tax-free." Who could resist an easy million?

"You greatly overvalue your miserable life. As a person, you aren't worth a dime. And where would the million come from? It would be like the man you swindled reaching out from the grave and handing it to you. That's no way to balance the books. The law can't do it. So that leaves it up to me. I'll balance them."

"You mean—" Stagg choked on his terror and couldn't finish the sentence.

"That I'm going to kill you, is that what you're asking? Oh, yes, yes, of course. I just want you to suffer some before I shoot you."

Stagg began to beg. "Oh, please, please, I've got a wife and—"

"Quit blubbering. You can comfort yourself, as you die, that you are leaving a rich widow, thanks to Norbert Palmquist. He didn't leave a rich widow."

Those were the last words Everett Stagg ever heard.

The client took a small, sharp knife and made a deep cut in Stagg's dead arm, then dipped a hundred-dollar bill in the little pool of blood and forced it between Stagg's bound hands. Then, quickly dismantling part of the equipment and packing it, the client picked up the cases and left.

XI

Until he'd become a pastor, Randollph had rarely pondered an exact definition of "church." He'd grown up singing "Onward, Christian Soldiers," a hymn he heartily disliked. He'd heard all the descriptive clichés—the church is the body of Christ, the church is the visible Kingdom of God, and a multitude more of nice-sounding words and phrases with imprecise meanings.

Actually, he had come to think of the church as an automobile—at least when the Governing Board of Good Shepherd met. Good Shepherd, or any other church, was an assemblage of parts with a variety of functions put together and hooked up for the purpose of keeping the whole contraption working. The meeting of the Governing Board was a monthly check to see that the church was operating on all cylinders. The Governing Board, like a mechanic, had to inspect the carburetor, test the spark plugs, line and balance the wheels, do whatever was necessary to keep the church in good running order.

Randollph supposed that using a car, however elegant, as a metaphor for a church was vulgar and inappropriate.

He was certain that proper theologians would disdain it. He doubted that anyone would ever write a hymn with the line "Like a mighty Rolls-Royce moves the Church of God."

Randollph had begun to think of himself—at least when the date for a meeting of the Governing Board rolled around—as Mr. Goodwrench. He actually saw to it that necessary adjustments and repair work was done by others. But he was shop foreman.

Usually these monthly tune-ups were routine, predictable, and boring. Sometimes, though, they ran into potentially damaging problems. Tonight, Randollph was almost certain, was going to be such an occasion. For one thing, attendance was larger than usual. It was considered a mark of distinction to belong to the board. People liked to say, casually, of course, "I'm a member of the Church of the Good Shepherd's Governing Board." This, presumably, established their credentials as someone of merit and social standing. Some of them, though, while enjoying the prestige of being a board member of a church everyone knew included in its congregation many of the city's wealthy and socially prominent citizens, didn't show up as regularly as duty dictated at board meetings. Tonight, Randollph estimated, there were few absentees. And there was a palpable tension hanging like a threatening rain cloud over the boardroom as the members clotted in a dozen or more conversational groups awaited the chairman's gavel.

"Looks like the word's gotten around that there'll be a little hell raised tonight," Dan Gantry whispered to Randollph.

"You sit by me," Randollph said.

"Afraid I might need to be restrained, boss?" Dan's smile was thin and without humor.

"Christian patience isn't one of your virtues," Randollph replied.

"I promised the bishop I wouldn't say anything, and I'll keep my promise, even if I'm maligned and despitefully used by some of the old bastards on this board. If I forget

143

myself and try to speak, you have my permission to clout me one across the mouth."

"We'll hope that won't be necessary," Randollph said. "I think Tyler is about ready to get things going."

Tyler Morrison, chairman of the Governing Board, had made himself a millionaire with a chain of cut-rate drugstores. He'd come from a downstate town and a modest background, so had not inherited his membership in Good Shepherd. Miss Windfall had been shocked when the board elected him chairman. She believed that no one, no matter how rich, should occupy the chief seat in the synagogue if he had made his money in common commerce. It was not that she didn't respect money. She did. But for her to approve of it, it had to be old money. And had to be possessed by people whose roots in Good Shepherd went very deep. Either no one had ever told her that some of the early members of the church had earned their affluence by selling booze to the roughneck population during the city's infancy, or through the messy but profitable business of cutting up pigs for the market, or she considered these facts irrelevant. Time, in her view, sanitized wealth, no matter how crass or dubious its origins.

But Randollph thought Tyler Morrison just about the ideal chairman of the board. He possessed the unflappable good nature of the salesman combined with the executive's impatience with wasting time.

Morrison took his seat at the head of the board table and banged his gavel. "Time t' start, please take your places," he ordered. The table (actually three tables joined) was large enough to accommodate a banquet in a medieval castle. The clots of people began dissolving as members moved toward their seats.

"All stand," Morrison directed. "Dr. Randollph will open the meeting with prayer." The conversations quickly quieted and people dutifully bowed their heads. Randollph briefly invoked the blessing of the Almighty on this meeting, and petitioned that its end result would further the holy purposes that were the mission of this and all churches.

144

This, Randollph reflected as he said amen and the bustle of board members getting themselves seated again punctuated his prayer, was traditional piety. He wondered if God ever got bored with these perfunctory blessings.

"Y'v all been mailed a copy of the minutes of last month's meeting," Morrison said. "Any questions or corrections? Chair'll entertain motion to dispense with reading 'em." He received a quick "so move" and "second." "Favor say aye. Motion passed. First item on agenda, the financial report. Reverend Smelser."

The Reverend Mr. O. Bertram Smelser, duly ordained to preach the word and administer the sacraments, seldom performed any of the functions for which the laying on of hands had qualified him. He had been a member of Good Shepherd's pastoral staff for more than twenty years. He was a dull and bumbling preacher. And Randollph sometimes wondered if Bertie Smelser would know which end of a baby to baptize. But he was a whiz at managing the church's business interests. The Lord's money, which flowed into Good Shepherd's treasury from a multimillion-dollar endowment, rents from offices that occupied part of the building, income from the corporation leasing the hotel, and contributions from members and visitors that, if not a tithe, came to quite a tidy sum, was Bertie Smelser's responsibility. He was God's moneyman.

Smelser, small and gray, seemed to grow taller as he rose and adjusted his gold-rimmed eyeglasses.

"You have the current financial report before you," he announced. "I wish to call your attention to a few items."

Randollph noticed Tyler Morrison slumping in his chair, and other members of the board listlessly leafing through the long and intricate report. They all knew what was coming. Bertie would provide lengthy and brain-numbing facts, statistics, comparisons, projections, to which hardly anyone would pay much attention. But there was tacit, if reluctant, understanding that the little gray man deserved this monthly moment on stage. The Reverend O. Bertram Smelser failed to inspire affection but had earned respect for his careful and astute management of Good Shepherd's finances.

Randollph was unable to concentrate or even pay attention to Bertie Smelser's reports. He'd once mentioned this to the bishop, and Freddie had reprimanded him.

"You don't understand how fortunate you are to have Bert on your staff."

"Why, Freddie? Oh, it isn't that I don't appreciate what he does, but—"

"C.P., since you've never served as pastor prior to Good Shepherd, you wouldn't be aware of the fact that all too many churches get into unholy rows over money."

"Could you expand on that, Freddie? I fail to understand why."

"Because," the bishop answered, "most churches never have enough money to operate properly. So they spend far too much time arguing about how to get more and spend less. Time they should be using for the consideration of other concerns, such as improving Christian education or doing better at ordering and conducting the worship of Almighty God. Too many of our churches follow worship practices that are trendy, ill-constructed. They almost border on the irreverent. Who was it that said 'Getting and spending we lay waste our powers'?"

"Wordsworth."

"He was talking about churches, or many of them—though he probably didn't know it. Now Bertie Smelser makes all that unnecessary at Good Shepherd. He manages the money, and people trust him. Of course," the bishop added, "it helps that you don't have to worry about getting the money. Good Shepherd is assured of an overflowing treasury. I'm not certain whether this is a blessing or not."

"Now you're contradicting yourself, Freddie."

"I know I am. Even bishops are permitted mixed feelings now and then—though it's best we don't disclose them to the public."

"I do listen to enough of Bertie Smelser's reports to know that a handsome sum from Good Shepherd's income goes to pay our denominational assessments. Do you have mixed feelings about that?"

"Oh my no, C.P. I have no mixed feelings about the moneys that accrue to this office—except that there's never enough."

"It sounds to me, Freddie, that you are guilty of sophistry."

"Of course I am, C. P. All executives are. Though we prefer to refer to it as being pragmatic."

Randollph remembered that he'd laughed. "Freddie, Freddie, I can't ever win, can I?"

"Bishops aren't supposed to lose arguments with their clergy. It damages the episcopal image."

"OK, Freddie, I concede, leaving your episcopal image intact. I promise to value Bertie Smelser more highly than I have. But I don't promise to listen to his reports. That's more than even a bishop has a right to ask."

As Smelser droned on about return on investments, cash balances, and prospective changes in interest rates, Randollph let his mind wander. The board, in theory, was a select group of Christians charged with the oversight of Good Shepherd's spiritual as well as temporal affairs. It struck him that the agenda always began with the financial report. Did this suggest that temporal concerns occupied the position of first priority? Saint Paul, he recalled, spoke of finances in his letters to the churches under his supervision, usually mixed in with counsel concerning theological and spiritual problems.

At any rate, the church was supposed to improve people in the grace and knowledge of God. That's what his sermons were designed to do. He wondered gloomily if his homilies came anywhere near this mark. Sometimes, just after he'd delivered what he assessed as a first-rate sermon, the postpartum euphoria that accompanied these occasions convinced him that he'd hit the mark. But how could one ever be sure? He guessed that all pastors who took preaching seriously had to live with this uncertainty.

Dan nudged him. "Wake up, boss, Bertie's finally run out of gas."

Randollph pulled himself back to the present. "Was I that obvious?"

"No," Dan said, "you've got your act down pretty good. Now Tyler, he doesn't bother to look interested. But anyone looking at you would think you were listening with fascination."

"Then how do you know I wasn't?"

"Well, first, I know you. Stuff like this bores the hell out of you. Second, I've learned to detect that glazed look in your eyes when you're off in dreamland or wherever your mind goes when Bertie's got the floor."

Tyler Morrison quickly shepherded through the approval of several routine reports, then said, "Last item on agenda, special report from the committee on membership and evangelism. Mrs. Conway."

Peggy Conway was a not particularly beautiful woman in, Randollph guessed, her mid-forties. Randollph noted, though, that she seemed surrounded by a nimbus of energy and good nature that lent an attractiveness often absent in women who were just blessed with a strikingly beautiful face and figure. He was able to comb out of his memory the information that she was the wife of a successful surgeon. Everyone on this board, he reflected, was successful —either because they were fortunate in their ancestors or through personal achievements in their chosen field of endeavor. He wondered if it would be a better governing body for the church if it included a few people who hadn't done so well in life's battles. Those the world rejected, though, because of inadequate education, natural incompetence, or minority status, were not attracted to the Church of the Good Shepherd.

Peggy Conway bounced to her feet, swept the board members with a dazzling smile, and said, "This is a special report for two reasons. One, we received over two hundred new members last year. That's a record number, at least in recent years." She paused, giving the board members an opportunity to clap.

"Then," she continued, "our committee did a survey, requesting the new members to state why they chose to join Good Shepherd." She beamed at them again. "Would you like to guess the number-one reason these new members gave for joining us?"

No one spoke for a moment. Then a lady, ancient and regal, and who, Randollph remembered, represented the aristocracy of Good Shepherd by Miss Windfall's standards, and whose name was Pembroke, said, "Undoubtedly because of our church's standing and prestige in the city."

"Wrong," Mrs. Conway replied. "Oh, I'm sorry, I shouldn't have spoken so abruptly. Please accept my apology, Mrs. Pembroke." Mrs. Pembroke nodded a curt acceptance.

Tyler Morrison spoke up. "Just guessin' an' puttin' it in business language, I'd say it was the quality of our product. An' I'll bet—shouldn't talk about bettin' in church, should I?—that most of 'em chose us because of Dr. Randollph's sermons. Know that's the reason I get out of my warm bed and get myself here every Sunday."

"On the nose," Mrs. Conway said. "Nearly ninety percent listed Dr. Randollph's preaching as the main reason they were attracted to Good Shepherd, and every new member, every one, listed it among the reasons they came here."

Randollph was stunned. He took what Clarence Higbee called the legitimate pride of the craftsman in his sermons. But he'd had no idea that they'd had this kind of impact. Oh, people often said nice things about the sermon as they departed after the service. But he had ascribed most of the comments to conventional politeness.

Peggy Conway shuffled through her report. "Want to hear some of the comments? Here's one. 'The sermons have helped me understand what my Christian faith really means.' Here's another. 'I look forward to the sermon be-

149

cause I know it will help me to be a better Christian.' And here's a good one. 'It's hard for me to believe that someone who used to spend his Sundays getting beat up on the football field can preach such scholarly sermons and at the same time be so interesting. I hate football, but I love Dr. Randollph's sermons.'"

This brought a hearty laugh from the board members, and relaxed the tension of waiting for a bad scene that everyone knew was coming.

"Care t' make a comment, Doctor?" Tyler Morrison asked Randollph.

Randollph found that he was just short of being choked with amazement and emotion. He stood up and said, "Mr. Chairman, Mrs. Conway, I'm speechless." This brought another hearty laugh from the board members.

"Guess it's OK for you t' be speechless now, Doctor," Tyler Morrison said, "but not on Sunday morning."

"Needless to say, I'm gratified by Mrs. Conway's report," Randollph continued. "There is the danger, though, that all this will lead me to think more highly of myself than I ought to think. However, I'll hope it will prompt me to try all the harder to make the sermons meaningful, helpful, and interesting." He paused and turned to Mrs. Conway. "And incidentally, Mrs. Conway, will you tell the person, whoever it is, that hates football that I forgive him —or her?"

Another laugh from the board members. The atmosphere in the room was becoming downright pleasant. Maybe, Randollph thought, there won't be the nastiness everyone had been anticipating.

Peggy Conway smiled at Randollph. "If it will help preserve your modesty, Dr. Randollph, most of the new members listed the music—they usually mentioned both the organ and the choir—as reasons for choosing Good Shepherd. And the dignity and beauty of the worship. But," she continued, "there were many who also mentioned the programs for youth, young adults, and other endeavors, many of which were originated by and continue to be supervised by Reverend Gantry."

"Like I guessed, quality of product," Morrison said. "Motion to express board's gratitude to Mrs. Conway and her committee for this interestin' an' enlightenin' report? Second? Favor say aye. Motion passed. Now," Morrison peered at the paper in front of him, "seems that finishes th' agenda. Chair'll entertain motion t' adjourn."

There was a "harrumph" and a small man with slicked-down brown hair and carefully curved wispy mustaches that didn't quite meet at the middle of his thin upper lip stood up and said, "Mr. Chairman." Dan whispered to Randollph, "Here it comes. I figured it'd be Torgeson leading the lynch mob."

"Steady on," Randollph whispered back.

It was not good, Randollph thought, that Torgeson was leading the lynch mob, as Dan had put it. Torgeson, in addition to being wealthy and prominent, was president of Good Shepherd's Board of Trustees. He carried a lot of weight in this church. When Randollph first came to Good Shepherd, the bishop had cautioned him to be wary of Torgeson.

"They call him Little Bobby, perhaps from affection, though that is hard to imagine. He's astute enough, but one of those chaps—most churches have one—who is unable to imagine that he could possibly be wrong about anything. He thinks he's the boss, and does his best to exercise all the prerogatives of his self-appointed position. He enjoys power."

"You're a boss, Freddie," Randollph had replied. "You exercise the prerogatives of your office."

"So I am, and so I do," the bishop, unoffended, had said. "But I didn't appoint myself boss. I was elected and had the responsibility thrust on me. But I don't try to push people around the way Torgeson does. Though I admit that some of my more obstinate clergy need a little nudge now and then. Anyway, watch out for Torgeson."

"Y' got somethin' to bring before this body, Mr. Torgeson?" Tyler Morrison asked. Randollph was all but certain that Morrison knew what was coming.

Torgeson, who habitually began his speeches with a raspy harrumph, and usually scattered a few more along the way, said, "Harrumph, yes, Mr. Chairman. I have a serious matter that we must act on. This, harrumph, church—which means a, means very much to some of us, has been receiving too much bad publicity lately. It's damaging, very damaging."

"Could y' be more specific, Mr. Torgeson?" Morrison asked.

"Yes, yes. There was the shocking murder of Mr. Trent, one of our city's best citizens, known as the Splendid Samaritan, and with good reason. He was, harrumph, and everyone knew it, a prominent member of Good Shepherd. Dr. Randollph conducted his funeral, even though that chaplain fellow delivered the eulogy." It sounded as if Torgeson was accusing Randollph of complicity in the crime of sullying the good name of the church, though the transgression was somewhat mitigated because the Reverend Mr. Hamilton Haynes Reynolds actually took the lead role in consigning Trent to his ultimate destination.

"We're all sorry about th' unpleasant nature of Mr. Trent's passin'," Tyler Morrison said. "But I don' see how that reflects adversely on Good Shepherd."

"Harrumph, it raises questions, people wonder," Torgeson said. "But some of us are more concerned by the recent, er, unseemly behavior of one of our pastors."

"You know somethin' I don't, Mr. Torgeson?"

"Of course you know about it, Mr. Chairman," Torgeson replied irascibly. "I mean the brutal attack by the Reverend Gantry on a patriotic citizen who was standing up for his country, our, harrumph, country, against a mob of, of Com—of left-wing radicals who'd spit on the flag."

A noisy murmur of voices broke out around the board table. These people were on their feet yelling, "Mr. Chairman, Mr. Chairman!" Little Bobby had done a good job of orchestrating the protest, Randollph realized.

Tyler Morrison banged his gavel and ordered quiet. When things calmed down, he said, "Mr. Torgeson, I saw those clips on the TV news you're referrin' to. Now as I saw it, Mr. Gantry was jus' marchin' along peaceful when this big guy rushed out of th' crowd watchin' the parade, grabbed the sign Mr. Gantry was carryin' an' started beatin' Mr. Gantry with it. I have information, too, that this fellow was shoutin' some pretty ugly stuff at Mr. Gantry."

"He deserved it," Torgeson growled.

"That mean you approve of obscene language, Mr. Torgeson?

For once, Little Bobby was speechless.

"Now," Morrison continued, "the way I saw it on the TV news, it was the big fellow who attacked Mr. Gantry, not the other way 'round."

"Gantry broke his jaw and put him in the hospital."

"Yeah, that was a nifty punch the reverend threw," Morrison said. Then, hastily, "He was jus' defendin' himself, way I saw it."

"That fellow might sue the church," Torgeson retorted. "How would that look in the papers?"

Randollph decided it was time to intervene.

"Let me assure Mr. Torgeson and this board that neither Mr. Gantry nor the church will be sued."

"How do you know?" Torgeson asked truculently.

"I will state that I have it on good, on impeccable, authority that the man has no plans to sue either the church or Mr. Gantry." Randollph paused for this to sink in, then turned to Torgeson. "Does that satisfy you, Mr. Torgeson?"

"No it doesn't. Gantry had no business being in that parade in the first place. And he was leading it."

Randollph wasn't sure the bishop would have wanted him to continue this verbal sword-crossing, but he felt he had to get the issue clarified.

"You disapprove of legal, peaceful demonstrations by people who feel strongly about a moral issue, Mr. Torgeson?"

"This isn't a moral issue!" Torgeson was almost shouting now. "It's a patriotic issue. Gantry and his radical pack are trying to undermine the defense efforts of our country and help the Russians take over."

There was a sparse but noisy clapping of hands for Torgeson's statement. This was, to Randollph, an optimistic sign. Torgeson's supporters were no doubt angry and prepared to raise all the hell they could. But there weren't many of them.

"Y' got somethin' more to say, Mr. Torgeson?" Tyler Morrison asked mildly. Randollph wished Morrison hadn't encouraged Torgeson. On second thought, Morrison perhaps had made a calculated move to let Little Bobby, his judgment obtunded by rage, overstep himself and swing the board's sympathies toward Dan. It was the kind of tactic the bishop would approve.

"I certainly do!" Torgeson shot back. "I move that the Governing Board of the Church of the Good Shepherd censure Mr. Gantry for participating publicly in the un-American activity, and dismiss him from his position as a minister of this church!" There was a quick shout of "second," followed by "question." Then several people were on their feet yelling, "Mr. Chairman, Mr. Chairman." Randollph was pleased to see that some of the shouters were people he'd bet had risen to defend Dan.

Morrison thumped his gavel, and said in a voice whose calmness did not disguise its authority, "Everyone sit down and be quiet." With order restored, Morrison turned to Randollph and asked, "Doctor, I'm a little rusty on the proper procedures in a situation like this. Ought to study up on 'em, I guess. Could you refresh m' memory?"

Randollph would have wagered a packet that Morrison could recite the rules applying here by heart. He was giving a little time for things to calm down. His main purpose, though, Randollph guessed, was to give Randollph an opportunity to defuse Little Bobby's bomb.

This, Randollph judged, was the time to be conciliatory. He felt little of the Christian charity he ought to have felt toward Torgeson. What he would have liked to do was to give Little Bobby a good dressing-down for his rudeness and his narrow definition of patriotism, and to defend the right of a pastor to take a stand on a moral issue, no matter how unpopular that issue might be with some or all of the congregation.

But he didn't.

He stood up and said, "Mr. Torgeson, or any member of this board or church, has the right and privilege of questioning or objecting to the performance of a pastor or other employee." Out of the corner of his eye he could detect a twitch of Little Bobby's mustache which could have been a smile of approval or even victory.

"However," he continued, "there are procedures—clearly defined by our denomination and also incorporated in the charter and bylaws of this congregation—that must be followed when complaints arise."

"Could y' sum 'em up for us, Doctor?" Morrison asked.

"Certainly, Mr. Chairman. The complainant—in this case, Mr. Torgeson, a long-time and valued member of this congregation—" he paused long enough to let Little Bobby lap up the cream of reconciliation just placed before him, then went on, "and any others who care to join him, must petition the Committee on Pulpit and Personnel for a hearing. The committee will then take the complaint, investigate it, and—if it finds the complaint to be of substance—report its findings and recommendations to the Governing Board, this board."

"That all?" Morrison asked.

"Not quite."

"You mean this board can't fire Gantry if the committee says to?" Torgeson was on his feet again.

"Let Dr. Randollph finish, he's got the floor," Morrison said. It was said quietly, but it was a reprimand.

"The Governing Board may take the Committee on Pulpit and Personnel's recommendation and debate it if it so chooses. Then it may make a recommendation to the bishop as to how it wishes the matter disposed of. The final decision rests with the bishop."

Torgeson looked to be gathering his thoughts for another speech, but Tyler Morrison clearly thought it was time to go home.

"Thank you for clearin' this up for us, Doctor. Motion t' adjourn? Favor say aye. Meetin's adjourned."

The bishop and his wife, Violet—who insisted that anyone on a Christian name basis with her address her as Vi because "No one names a girl Violet anymore, thank God"— lived in the hotel attached to and owned by Good Shepherd. Freddie had asked Randollph and Dan to stop by and report after the meeting of the Governing Board.

The episcopal apartment was surprisingly spacious for a hotel suite. The living room was large with windows affording a glimpse of the lake, though it was largely obscured by a thicket of high-rise buildings. It was furnished with antiques, authentic and good, Randollph supposed, although he knew little about such things.

When the bishop admitted them, Dan immediately made for the sturdiest and most comfortable chair in the room and sagged into it as if he'd spent a hard day loading cargo on the docks. Randollph sat with the bishop on a somewhat fragile-looking sofa upholstered in a multicolored fabric that he thought of as needlepoint, though it probably wasn't.

"Would you care for coffee or tea?" the bishop asked.

"You wouldn't have a slug of Scotch, would you?" Dan responded.

"I'm afraid not, Dan. I don't keep spirits in the house. I'm not sure whether this is because I don't care for hard liquor, or because I think it inappropriate for a bishop to serve it—though I'm not censorious of those who use it moderately. I do, however, have wine." He chuckled. "Jesus used wine, so it should be in keeping with episcopal protocol to serve it. Also, I'm fond of good wine. May I offer you a glass of sherry?"

"Yes, if it's large enough and on the rocks."

"Put ice in good sherry?" The bishop seemed horrified.

"I'll pretend it's Scotch," Dan said.

"Perhaps, after this evening, you're entitled to this, ah, eccentricity."

"I'll settle for coffee," Randollph said.

"Let me pass the order on to Vi, then you can tell me about the board meeting."

Once they were supplied with their choices of liquids, the bishop said, "Tell me what happened, C. P., not omitting any relevant details."

Randollph told him.

The bishop sipped his tea for several moments, then said, "Just about what I expected. And Dan didn't say a word?"

"I'd promised you, Bishop," Dan answered. "It wasn't easy, sitting there listening to that mean little bas—to Torgeson lying about me."

"We're supposed to love our enemies, Dan, if we follow the teachings of Jesus."

"I know," Dan said morosely. "I have a lot of trouble following that one."

"So do we all. It is an ethical mandate well-nigh impossible of achievement." The bishop gave Dan time to absorb this, then said, "There is something to be said in Mr. Torgeson's favor."

Dan was immediately belligerent. "You mean that he was right?"

"Some of the things he said were true."

"Name one."

"I intend to name two," the bishop replied. "First, though the Church of the Good Shepherd is in no way culpable in the murder of James Trent, the continuing publicity the murder is receiving and the weird and utterly mysterious nature of the crime, would—in the eyes of someone like Mr. Torgeson and no doubt many others—reflect adversely on the Church of the Good Shepherd."

Randollph set his cup on the coffee table in front of the sofa. "I don't see that, Freddie. It doesn't make sense."

"Bad publicity doesn't have to make sense, C.P. The

157

circumstances of Trent's murder are bound to cause some people, many people, to wonder if the man was as saintly as the press has painted him. The world loves it when an idol is perceived to have feet of clay. It makes people who see that the supposedly good person wasn't as good as he pretended to be feel better about their own moral shortcomings. A truly good person often makes other people quite uncomfortable."

"But how does that hurt the Church of the Good Shepherd?"

"In two ways."

"Which are?"

"First, the Church of the Good Shepherd is anything but an obscure institution in this city. That's what's bothering Torgeson. To have one of your prominent members murdered with apparent malice and forethought is most disturbing to your members, especially members of Torgeson's type. They want only good news about the church exposed in the media. I'm sure you have some of the same feelings as Torgeson on this, C.P."

Randollph reflected a moment, then answered, "Yes, I suppose I do. What's the second way it hurts us?"

"I believe you reported that Torgeson said the murder raises questions."

"That's as I remember his words."

"He's right. People who don't know much about Good Shepherd, some people, will wonder what kind of institution it is that has members who get themselves slain in such a strange way."

"That's irrational."

"I know, C.P. I said bad publicity doesn't have to make sense. Torgeson is no doubt exaggerating the adverse effect Trent's murder is having or will have on the church, but he's got a point."

"Could I have some more of this sherry?" Dan asked. "It isn't bad.

"Certainly, Dan." The bishop took Dan's glass, disappeared briefly, and was back with the refill. "Don't forget that sherry is a fortified wine," he admonished Dan as he handed him the glass. "It isn't as innocent as it tastes."

"I don't drink to get drunk, Bishop," Dan replied. "Oh, I've been drunk. Back in college. I didn't like it. Haven't been since." Switching the subject, Dan asked, "You said Little Bobby was right about two things. What's the second one?"

"He said, if C.P.'s report is accurate, something to the effect that the Church of the Good Shepherd means a lot to him."

"So he did," Randollph said.

"Wouldn't you say that's laudable, Dan?"

"Sure. I care about the church, too. I care a lot."

"Isn't it ironic, then, that Torgeson's motive for attacking you is his concern for his church?"

"I don't get it, Bishop."

"He sees you as a threat to the institution he loves and serves."

"And I see him as pig-headed, trying to block the church from what it is supposed to do in the world."

The bishop sighed as if the weight of his responsibilities were sometimes too heavy a burden to be borne by a mere mortal. "Do you know the most vexing single problem a bishop has to deal with—apart from finding enough money to do all the things the denomination says he must do?"

"Enlighten us, Freddie," Randollph said.

"Handling the relationship between pastors and their churches. Of course," he added, "the problem crops up in many forms."

"You're planning to enumerate them for us, I take it," Randollph prodded.

"First," the bishop mused, more to himself than to Dan and Randollph, "there is the incompetent pastor."

"I know a few of them," Dan said.

"I wondered about the competency of some of my students when I was teaching in the seminary," Randollph said.

"They can't preach, they muck up the administration of even the smallest parish, they lack the personality to deal with people. I don't know how they manage to get accepted for ordination, but they do. I take un-Christian comfort in the fact that we also have incompetent doctors, lawyers, and business executives."

"How do you deal with them, Freddie?"

"Keep them moving from one small parish to another. It isn't fair to inflict them on one congregation for more than a year or two. Oh, I feel sorry for them. Some of them are very dedicated to their calling. Sincere, decent people. Just incompetent."

"I can't weep for you if that's the worst of your problems, Freddie."

"Oh, it isn't, C.P. The bright, capable, even gifted pastor who has an abrasive personality is much worse."

"You mean someone like me?" Dan asked.

"No, no, Dan. You're bright, and you're gifted. You're not very strong on seeking compromise with those who disagree with you. But you're blessed with a pleasant personality. Most people like you and respect you. Not all, but most. However, this dust-up over your espousal of the antinuclear cause is an example of what I deal with all the time."

"You don't mean there are all that many pastors marching for nuclear disarmament," Dan said.

"No. It isn't the particular issue I'm talking about, Dan. It's the way pastors and their churches get crosswise of one another because they have different concepts of what a pastor's job should be."

Again Randollph asked, "Could you be a bit more specific, Freddie?"

"Yes. Many pastors, like Dan, believe Jesus identified with, was indeed a successor to the Old Testament prophets. They have a self-image as a prophetic preacher. They pronounce on current social issues, the ills of society as they see them."

"As they should," Randollph interjected.

"Yes, as they should, C.P., though my task would be easier if they didn't. You see, most—I've never taken a survey, but experience has taught me—most laymen think the obligation of a pastor is to perform the traditional tasks of his office. They see him as one who marries, buries, baptizes, and calls on members, especially the ill. They want him, or her, now that we have so many women pastors, to preach sermons that comfort them, inspire them, and show them how to use their faith to get ahead in the world."

"That's what Trent preached, how you can use Christianity to be a big winner in business," Randollph said.

"I know, C. P. And look how popular his Business Executives for Christ had become. Positive thinking, by whatever name you call it, is the ticket today."

"Much of what Jesus said was harsh and unpopular," Randollph observed.

"And they hung him, C.P. Don't forget that." My point, though, is that I frequently, too frequently, have to step in and try to reconcile a pastor who disturbs people with his preaching and a congregation that wants to hear only pleasantries from the pulpit."

"I'm glad I have no ambition to be a bishop," Randollph said. "To coin a phrase, if nominated, I will not run, and if elected, I will not serve."

"Oh, we never lack for candidates," the bishop commented. "But one more example. The most troubling of pastor-versus-parish problems arises when a good, capable, even outstanding pastor finds that he has been appointed to a church that is split down the middle. That could happen at Good Shepherd."

Dan had been quietly nursing his glass of sherry, but suddenly sat up straight. "You mean Good Shepherd could split over me?"

"Yes," the bishop said.

"Then, Freddie, I think you'd better tell us how you handle a split congregation."

"That's what I've been getting around to with all this

161

talk," the bishop said. "The dissident part of a split congregation nearly always uses the pastor as the whipping boy for their anger, whether the pastor had anything to do with it or not. They keep the pressure on. They devise strategies to undermine him. Angry and hostile church members can wear a pastor down. He's always looking back over his shoulder."

"So what do you do, Freddie?"

"It depends on the pastor. If he can, what is the phrase, keep his cool and not answer hostility with hostility, and continue to treat those members who are after his hide with respect and kindness, why then I let him stay on if that is his choice. If he tells me he can't take it anymore, then I arrange to transfer him to another parish."

"This is meant for me, I take it, Bishop."

"Yes, Dan. Insofar as it applies. You have done nothing wrong. You're caught in a situation not all that uncommon. I wanted you to know that I'll stand by you."

"I appreciate that," an uncharacteristically humble Dan replied. "I'm hoping that it won't come to a split. This evening's action at the board will defer the problem." The bishop watched Dan swigging at his sherry. "The question is, Dan, can you treat Torgeson and whatever cronies he has in this with Christian courtesy."

"I can sure as he—I can try, try hard."

"You do that, Dan. It will not only be good for your soul, but will also act as a maturing agent."

"You mean it will help me grow up?"

"I wouldn't put it quite that way, Dan. Shall we say that the experience will build your inner resources."

"I guess they could stand some building."

The bishop turned to Randollph. "I suppose you are in touch with Lieutenant Casey?"

"We talk frequently."

"Is he making any progress at all on this Trent murder?"

"No, he's baffled."

"I do wish he'd get it cleared up. Partly because I agree with Torgeson. I want people to forget his connection with

Good Shepherd. And partly, I confess, I've a vulgar curiosity about the who and the why of the murder of the Splendid Samaritan."

"The lieutenant is glum about it. Says he can't find a handle on it anywhere. We may never know the answer."

When Randollph finally got to the penthouse, he found Sammy sitting on the sofa, feet tucked under, reading a book with a lurid dust jacket. She turned up her face and said, "Kiss me."

"The most pleasant duty I've performed this evening," Randollph said, bending over and kissing her.

"Call that a kiss?" Sammy said. "And don't call kissing me a duty. That isn't how Rolfe kisses Monica."

"Whatever are you talking about, Samantha?"

"Listen to this." She turned a page in her book. "'Rolfe suddenly clasped Monica to him, his lips crushing hers. With one hand he ripped her blouse from her and cupped a ripe breast. She felt the flames of a desire that could not be denied rise in—'"

"Enough," Randollph laughed. "I get the idea."

"No, I've got the idea. I've been reading this trashy novel for an hour. Mostly sex scenes. Now I'm horny as hell. Take me to the bedroom and treat me like Rolfe treats Monica. You can skip ripping off my blouse, though, it cost too much. Just light the flame of a desire I can't deny. No, it's already lit. You can fan it a little, though."

Randollph collapsed on the sofa laughing helplessly. "Samantha," he managed to say, "I do love you so very much."

"Why?"

"Because, well, because I never know what to expect. Because you're so entertaining."

"Those are good reasons," she said. "That is, so long as they aren't the only ones."

"You know they're not."

She put her arms around him. "I thought a little levity

163

would be in order. I hear you had a rough night at the board meeting."

Randollph was startled. "How could you know that so soon? You have spies?"

"I have a friend who has spies. Has them everywhere."

"Let me guess—Thea Mason."

"Give the man a cigar."

Randollph suddenly felt uneasy. "Is she planning on publishing something about what went on tonight?"

"She is a newspaperwoman—I should say a newsperson."

"She's a gossip columnist."

"It's her job. Just like preaching is your job. This whole thing with Dan isn't just a, well, it's in the public domain. People are interested. Yes, she'll publish something about it. Incidentally, she told me about the survey of why people are joining Good Shepherd. She's going to get in all the nice stuff about you. Agnostic that I am, I'm still awfully proud of you, C.P." She kissed him.

"I confess that it didn't hurt my ego. I hope she'll also report the nice things the survey said about Dan."

"She will."

"How do you know?"

"Because I made a point of telling her to do it. Anyway, she likes Dan. Enough of this, though. You hungry? You usually are after these meetings."

Randollph confessed that he was ravenous.

"Clarence left a cold roast beef sandwich with his own horseradish sauce in the fridge."

"Let me at it," Randollph said with enthusiasm.

They moved to the breakfast booth in the hotel-size kitchen, though they never ate breakfast there unless Clarence was away.

"You want a beer?" Sammy asked.

"No, milk. I want to be fully alert when it's time for dessert."

XII

Warren Helperin was worried. The world saw him as a successful attorney, which he was. It also saw him as a possible future governor of the state, which he hoped to be.

What the world couldn't see was in his heart. For this he was profoundly grateful, but he was also nagged constantly by the fear that some happenstance, some malign quirk of fate might do him in. Oh, he'd been careful. It had taken infinite patience to conceal his miserable childhood and substitute for it a legend of a happy life growing up in the bosom of an aristocratic southern family. He'd even had his name changed legally to fit the legend. He'd done it in an obscure hick town a long way from Chicago, and it was a million-to-one shot that anyone would ever dig that up.

Even as a boy he knew he was bright. He determined to get an education no matter what it cost him. But how does a young man entirely on his own and without resources get a college education and a law degree? He works hard, of course. That's the American way. But it isn't enough. He'd engaged in a number of activities as nasty and illegal as they were profitable. Fortunately he'd never been caught or he'd be languishing in some prison today. He'd hated being a crook. From the moment he could afford to be honest he'd been scrupulous about it. Now, for all practical purposes, he'd realized one ambition he'd nursed and nurtured since his youth. And another was within his grasp.

But something, some inner voice or fear, was telling him it could all blow apart unless he intervened somehow.

But how?

He tapped his teeth absently with a pencil he'd picked up from his desk. Then, decisively, he picked up the phone and asked his secretary, "Betsy, would you see if you can get the mayor for me?" He always couched his instructions in the form of a request. Maybe that was one reason his employees liked him. Especially women. Women, employees or not, were attracted to him. He knew that. He liked to think he had sex appeal. Courtesy and gentle manners were part of it. Courtesy and kindness paid off, he believed.

"Of course, Mr. Helperin. Right away."

Betsy, he was aware, adored him. She was a homely girl with slightly crooked teeth and no sense of how to dress attractively or style her hair. He wondered if she had sexual fantasies about him. No matter. She was the most efficient secretary he'd ever had.

When the mayor was on the line, he said, "Good morning, Madam Mayor, how goes the day?" They were good friends and he called her "Georgia" in private. But never by her nickname "Gorgeous George," adopted from the name of a former professional wrestler who always came into the ring beautifully groomed but played rough. No one called her that to her face, but he'd heard that she liked the nickname.

"Well, Warren, it keeps me busy filling the trough with swill for all our good political pals."

"Business as usual, then?"

"Business as usual. What's on your mind?"

"I need to see you as soon as possible."

166

"Hmm, let's see." Helperin could picture her looking at her calendar. "You're a priority with me, you know that. Only time today is lunch, which I'm having at my desk. Why don't you join me?"

"Splendid."

"What'll you have? I'm ordering a ham and cheese."

"I'll take a pastrami on rye, coleslaw, and a kosher dill."

"Goodness, a gourmet. See you at noon."

Helperin arrived at the mayor's office with the delivery boy from the delicatessen.

"Hello, Mr. Helperin." The mayor's secretary spoke with friendly respect. Warren Helperin was a political heavyweight. "You want coffee with lunch? I just made a fresh pot. You take it black, don't you?"

"You have an excellent memory, Maria."

"I'm a politician's daughter," she answered, as if that explained her memory. "Go right in. I'll bring the coffee."

The mayor was standing by her desk arranging the food as the delivery boy unloaded it. She'd spread two cloth napkins on the desk, one in front of her chair and one on the opposite side. She was a slim woman of average height. Probably in her fifties, Helperin guessed, though she tried to keep her age a secret. She was wearing a green suit, its quality discernible to an eye knowledgeable about ladies' apparel. Green was her favorite color, and she wore it often. The joke among the politicians was that she was fond of green because it was the color of money. Her light brown hair, whether that was its natural color or not, always looked as if she'd just returned from a trip to the beauty parlor.

The delivery boy, generously tipped, departed. Maria brought in a silver pot of steaming coffee and closed the door behind her as she left.

"Well, Warren, pull up a chair and dig in. I ordered two sandwiches, two for you, too. I'm starved." The mayor was famous for her voracious appetite. She'd swill beer with kraut and knockwurst at German parties, pasta and rich pastries at Italian gatherings—almost any kind of ethnic cuisine, even haggis—and usually ask for seconds. Yet she never added an ounce to her weight. Helperin's theory was that she burned the calories with the nervous energy with which she fairly crackled.

Helperin bit off a chunk of kosher dill pickle, enjoying the crisp texture and the sour spicy flavor.

"Hear you might run for the Senate, Georgia," he said, chewing on the thick pile of pastrami loaded between slices of rye bread fragrant with caraway seeds.

"Where did you hear that?"

"Around. Pour you some coffee?"

"I'll do it. I'm the hostess. Nah. Think I'll stick to my own turf. This is a better job than senator. More real power." But Helperin hadn't missed the little flash of pleasure in her eyes.

"Better think about it, Georgia. Not many women in the Senate. You'd be a national figure."

"I'll think about it. But you didn't come over to talk about me running for the Senate. I know you, Warren. You're sweet-talking me. That means you want a favor."

"Well, as a matter of fact, I do." No point in dissembling. She was too smart for that.

"I don't know whether I owe you one or not, I lose count. But with you, who's counting? What do you need?"

"This may take a little explaining."

"No hurry. I've got another sandwich to eat."

"It has to do with my running for governor—and Jim Trent's murder."

"Oh? Since you and I both know you've got the nomination sewed up, it must be Trent—the late Mr. James T. Trent—that's the problem."

"That's right."

"Well, go on."

"It's like this, Georgia. I've been very active in Trent's Business Executives for Christ organization."

"I know. You're president of the Chicago chapter."

The mayor, Helperin reflected, didn't miss much. Probably one reason she was so successful in the rough and corrupt arena of Chicago politics.

"I got involved with it for the political advantages it had to offer. It gives me a good image in the business community. And it can make the difference in the downstate vote, the Bible Belt areas."

"I can understand that," said the mayor, munching her way through her ham and cheese. "I'm a good Catholic, go to mass every Sunday, hobnob with the cardinal. I don't mind the voters knowing that at election time." She chewed thoughtfully, then said, "Let me guess. You plan to use Business Executives for Christ to rally the faithful to your run for governor."

"That's right. I plan to use our chaplain, name's Reynolds—Hamilton Haynes Reynolds III, sounds impressive, doesn't it?"

"It does."

"I plan to have him work hard at organizing new chapters downstate. He's good at it, and he's sold on the organization. Then, during the campaign, I'll work those chapters. Speak at all of them. Should get favorable coverage from the hick press. Polls show I can carry Chicago easy. But I need the downstate Bible vote to carry the state."

The mayor wiped her mouth with a napkin. "I understand the politics of what you're doing, Warren. But I don't see how the murder of Trent is a problem."

"It's like this, Georgia," Helperin explained patiently. "There's just too much continuing publicity about Jim Trent's murder. Papers screaming for a solution. People wondering about why a good man like Trent was murdered. It might, if this goes on, begin to reflect badly on Business Executives for Christ, and that would be very bad for me politically."

"What you mean is, the investigation could turn up

169

some evidence that Trent wasn't as pure as he pretended to be. You think he might have a skeleton or two in his nice clean closet, Warren?" She was looking at Helperin intently. "Level with me, Warren."

Helperin poured himself another cup of coffee before he answered. "I honestly don't know, Georgia."

"You suspect?"

"I'm more afraid. He, well, let me put it this way. It's my experience that businessmen who are as successful as Jim Trent, they don't get that way unless they cut a few corners, you know what I mean?"

"All right, Warren, between us I know Trent cut plenty of corners. I could give you the amounts of bribes he paid to quite a few politicians, and the names of the bribees. I could also give you a list of state legislators he had in his pocket. Of course, state legislators in Illinois come pretty cheap. But is this the way the leader of Business Executives for Christ should behave? Jim Trent was a phony. I always thought so. I still think so."

Helperin felt his chances of getting the favor he needed were very good indeed.

"So what do you want me to do, Warren?"

No point in stalling around about it, he thought. "Get the police to close out the case."

"Well, well, that's a big order."

"They could say their investigation had concluded that Trent was killed by a burglar, and they were following up leads. That would take the attention from Trent, and would protect the Business Executives for Christ. If a burglar did it, then it doesn't endanger the organization's image."

"I can see that."

"I want it out of Homicide. There's a Lieutenant Michael Casey in charge of the investigation. He's supposed to be Homicide's hotshot. If there's any dirt to be dug up on Jim Trent, he'll dig it. Get it out of his hands."

"I know Lieutenant Casey," the mayor said. "Nice-looking young man. Fine manners, dresses well. You'd

170

hardly know he's a cop. They say he's smart, and that he's a comer."

"That's the one."

"OK, Warren. You need this, and I can do it. I might have to knock a few heads together, but I can do it. You'll owe me one—a big one. But who's counting?"

XIII

Lieutenant Michael Casey was sifting through the file on the James Trent murder and silently cursing the day that the Splendid Samaritan had gotten himself knocked off. Every possible lead had been checked out. He'd had some hopes that Harry Walpole, the chap who'd bungled the bribe, been fired by Trent, and written letters threatening to kill the Splendid Samaritan, might have actually carried out his threat. He'd interviewed Walpole personally.

But Walpole was just another dead end.

Walpole was a bachelor who lived in a small but what Casey thought of as a deluxe apartment, not too many blocks in from the Gold Coast. Walpole, he saw when the ex-Acme employee invited him in with a salesman's calculated effusiveness, was somewhere in his mid-thirties. His sandy hair was thinning, but not enough for the hairpiece he'd probably be buying in a few years. Casey bet that Walpole jogged and played handball to keep his stocky figure from bulging. Noticing Walpole's expensive stereo equipment and bar stocked with prominently displayed bottles of the best gins and whiskies along with several exotic liqueurs, he also bet Walpole drove a Porsche or Jaguar. Harry Walpole was a Yuppie writ large. No wonder he'd pushed hard for that contract. He was probably up to his belly button in consumer debt.

"You've come to ask me about Jim Trent," Walpole stated pleasantly.

"That's right." Casey wondered if Trent's secretary had warned Walpole, then decided this was unlikely.

"You've probably heard that he fired me."

"I'd heard that, yes."

"So I'm a suspect?" He seemed quite casual about it, Casey thought. "Did you hear why?"

"I'm told you bungled a bribe to a military procurement officer."

"I sure did. Every time I'd get three drinks in him, he'd start whining about how much it cost to live in Washington on his salary, the exorbitant tuition he had to pay to send his kids to private schools. I thought he was telling me he wanted cash. So I offered him cash. Stupid of me. He was just a drunk crying into his beer, or rather whiskey. Not even a good brand, either. Speaking of whiskey, care for a drink, Lieutenant?"

"Can't. I'm on duty."

"You don't mind if I have one?" He moved to the bar and selected a bottle. "This is the best Highland single-malt Scotch you can get." He poured the whiskey into a brandy snifter. "Everyone's drinking single malt these days, without ice." Casey took this to mean that single malt was the "in" drink this year, or one of them. He wondered what it must be like to have your tastes, your lifestyle dictated not by what you preferred, but by what current fashion proclaimed as proper for those who wished to be included in the circle of the acceptable.

"You didn't resent Trent firing you?"

"I didn't like it, but I had done a stupid thing."

"You wrote him letters threatening to kill him."

This jolted Walpole. "You find them in his files? I thought he'd just throw them away."

"Why did you do it?"

"Because he's blackballed me all over town. Now that the hypocritical son-of-a-bitch is dead, maybe I can find something worthy of my abilities."

"You aren't sorry he's dead?"

"I didn't shed a tear."

"You know it's a crime to send threatening letters through the mail."

Walpole was surprised. "No, I didn't. If I'd known, I wouldn't have done it."

Casey was irritated. "Mr. Walpole, you had a motive to kill Trent, and you expressed an intention to do so in letters. Yet you seem unconcerned about it. Why?"

Walpole swirled the liquor in his snifter, tasted it, then said, "Because I have what you cops call an airtight alibi for the night he was killed."

"And it is?"

"A friend, a very lovely lady, and I drove up to a small exclusive hotel in Wisconsin, had dinner in its excellent restaurant, and spent the night there."

"And she'll be willing to testify to that?"

"Oh, yes. But it's hardly necessary. I've been there before. They all know me. And the parking attendant had the keys to my car. They have security twenty-four hours a day. They know when a car enters or leaves. You'll want to check?"

"We certainly will. I'll need the name of the hotel, its location, the name and address of the girl."

"Sure. Here, I'll jot it all down for you. Try the hotel before you talk to the girl, though, will you? Maybe you won't even need to see her."

Casey accepted the paper without committing himself. He glanced at the information Walpole had written. He saw that Walpole's car was a Porsche.

And, Casey noted as he looked over the sheet on Walpole, his alibi had held up. The girl, who had confirmed Walpole's story without embarrassment, could be lying. And he could think of ways that Walpole might have left the hotel unseen, driven to Chicago, murdered Trent, and then gotten back into the hotel undetected. But it would have taken very careful planning and perfect execution. Walpole loved himself too much to risk a killing. And Casey didn't think he was bright enough to lay out a complex plan for murder. Scratch Harry Walpole.

Casey didn't have a secretary. He did have an office, small and furnished with an institutional-gray metal desk, filing cabinets, and in addition to his fairly comfortable desk chair, three not-so-comfortable straight-back chairs for use when Casey needed to have a conference with other detectives. The city was not lavish in its expenditures on the comfort and convenience of its police officers below the rank of captain. But just having an office was a status symbol.

The desk sergeant stuck his head in the open door to Casey's office and announced, "There's a Mrs. James Trent, I guess *the* Mrs. James Trent, here to see you, Loot. Shall I bring her in?"

Casey was surprised, but his expression said he'd been expecting her. "Sure. Bring her in."

When the sergeant ushered her in, Mrs. Trent said, in a crisp voice quite unlike her spiritless tones that day he'd first met her, "Lieutenant Casey, I hope I'm not interrupting your routine."

"Not at all, Mrs. Trent. Let me get you a chair. I'm afraid it won't be too comfortable."

"That doesn't matter, Lieutenant. Would you please close the door?"

Casey closed the door, settled himself behind his desk, and asked, "To what do I owe the honor of this visit?"

Mrs. Trent smiled slightly. "I came to confess that I murdered my husband."

It took all of Casey's experience to prevent his face registering shock. He managed to react as if high society ladies confessing to murdering their husbands was a frequent experience in his office.

"But you've already established an alibi. Are you saying that your maid lied?"

"Oh, no. You see, I didn't do it personally. I—" she paused, searching for the right phrase "—I employed a professional criminal to do the actual killing."

For a moment Casey was confused as to how he should proceed. "Mrs. Trent, in a matter as serious as this, don't you think it would be best to have your lawyer present? I presume that you have one."

A brief smile flickered across her face. "Oh, yes, I have one. No, I don't want him here. This would just upset him. He's a fine man and a good lawyer, but something of an old fuddy-duddy." Again the brief smile.

"All right, Mrs. Trent, we'll go ahead without him if that is your wish. Tell me, please, why you murdered— had your husband murdered."

The answer came back promptly. "Because he abused me, had abused me for years."

"And that's why you had him killed?"

"Yes." No smile now.

"Could you be more specific as to the nature of the abuse? Was it physical? Mental or emotional?"

"I prefer not to talk about it."

Casey looked at her mouth. It was rigid. He wasn't going to get any more out of her on this subject. He switched directions.

"Who was the killer you employed?"

"I don't know."

"Why not?" Casey spoke a bit more brusquely.

Again the answer came back as if she were reciting a set piece. "He was hired through a third party. I have a—an acquaintance who knows how these things are done."

"What is his name?"

"You don't expect me to tell you that," she snapped.

"Sooner or later you'll have to."

"Never!"

Casey was becoming exasperated, though he tried not to show it. "Mrs. Trent, how do you explain the fact that the murderer knew exactly where to find your husband's safe? This was a burglary as well as a murder, you know."

She didn't hesitate. "I told the—the person who employed the actual killer about the safe."

"Why?"

"I wanted it to look like a burglary. To mislead the police."

"Yet now you're confessing. You went to a lot of trouble to mislead the police, then come in and confess."

"I hadn't planned to confess when I hired the—the murderer."

"What changed your mind?"

"I found I couldn't live with it. I've always been a Christian, perhaps not a very good one. I was brought up in Sunday school and church. I learned that 'Thou shalt not kill' was one of God's laws."

"Then it was your Christian conscience that finally drove you in here today?"

"That would be a good way to put it."

"And how do you explain your husband's, your late husband's, bound hands, a bright light shining on him, and a bloody hundred-dollar bill in his hands?"

Again the answer came right back as if memorized, this time with the flickering smile. "I can't explain it, Lieutenant. I've thought about it. My thoughts are that it was some quirk of the killer's. Aren't people like that usually a little, well, crazy?"

Casey didn't reply. She'd thought the whole thing through. She had plausible reasons for her actions. And how he would like to believe her, book her, and get himself off the hook on this frustrating crime. He ran her story through his mind like a recording. Yes, from what he'd already discovered about Trent's character, he could believe that, Splendid Samaritan though he was supposed to be, he could have abused his wife. Yes, it was possible that she'd paid someone to do the actual killing. She had a wide circle of acquaintances, and there were plenty of guns for hire in Chicago. Yes, she could have been moved to confess by a stricken conscience.

But Casey didn't believe a word of what she had told him—with the possible exception of Trent's abusing her.

Then why? Why was she confessing to a crime she hadn't committed?

Oh, people did that all the time. They'd already had half a dozen confessions from people claiming to have murdered Trent. They were the regulars. They were the crazies who confessed to every highly publicized crime.

But Mrs. Trent wasn't a crazy. She had a reason for doing what she'd done. But what?

She interrupted his reflections.

"Lieutenant, shouldn't you arrest me and take me to jail?"

Casey decided not to tell her that he had the authority to do just that.

"No, Mrs. Trent. Our procedure goes like this: I report what you've told me to the state's attorney. His office then determines if there is sufficient evidence against you to present to the grand jury. The grand jury then decides, on the basis of the evidence presented, whether to indict you for murder or not."

"But I've confessed. Isn't that enough?"

"We have our procedures," Casey answered, dodging her question. He very much wished he could go ahead and book her. But he knew it would be a mistake.

"You mean I can just go on home?" She sounded distressed.

"We'll keep you informed. The state's attorney will no doubt be wanting to question you in the next few days. I assume you'll be available?"

"Oh, I'm not going anywhere. I don't see why, though, you have to go through all this red tape. What good does it do to try and help—oh, never mind."

"Look at it this way, Mrs. Trent. You confessed, so you told me, to clear your conscience. Well, you've gotten this,

178

ah, crime off your conscience. That ought to make you feel relieved."

As she left, Elva Trent did not look like a woman who had just unloaded a burden of guilt.

After Mrs. Trent had left, reluctantly it appeared, Casey scribbled notes covering her confession and the story she had told. He thought about his next move. He decided he'd better tell Captain Manahan about it. He would have liked to skip Manahan, but that was procedure. The captain was very strict about procedure.

He took his notes and told the desk sergeant he'd be in the captain's office, then went on down the hall. Manahan's door was open. He was chewing a dead cigar and scowling at a paper on his desk. He looked up as he heard Casey's light tap on the door.

"Busy, Captain?" Casey asked politely. He wanted Manahan in as pleasant a mood as possible.

"Always busy, Mike. But come on in. Wanted to see you anyway. Heard you had an interestin' visitor." Casey wondered momentarily whom the captain had deputized to keep him informed, then decided it didn't matter since there was nothing he could do about it anyway.

"Mrs. Trent, you mean?"

Manahan took a kitchen match from a box on his desk, flicked it with his thumbnail, and applied it to his dead cigar. It was a habit or affectation that the boys in the squadroom joked about. "Thinks it makes him look like a sheriff in the Old West," they said. "Probably saw John Wayne do it in a movie."

Casey waited until the captain was sucking on the cigar, then said, "Yes. Mrs. Trent came in to confess that she murdered her husband."

Manahan choked on a lungful of smoke and went into a fit of violent coughing. "Oh, dammit," he finally managed to gasp. Then, recovering his breath, he said, "Tell me about it."

Casey didn't need to consult his notes, but he did. It

might impress Manahan that he'd been meticulous with his interrogation. He recited Mrs. Trent's story.

"Well, well," Manahan said genially, glad to wrap this one up. "Been a lot of pressure on me, you know."

"And on me," Casey reminded him.

"Yeah, you booked her?"

"No."

Manahan's grin changed to a scowl. "And why not?"

"Because she's lying."

Manahan became belligerent. "Now look here, Mike, you're not gettin' anywhere solvin' this murder, right?"

"Right."

"Then the widow comes in and hands you the solution on a silver platter. And you turn it down because you say she's lying. You crazy or somethin'? How do you know she's lyin'?"

"I can't prove it—not right now, anyway—but I know. Her story's too slick. And it's got holes in it big enough to drive a squad car through."

Manahan's mean little eyes narrowed. "You psychic or something? Get a warrant for her arrest, haul her in, and we'll give her a good goin' over."

Casey thought, or at least hoped, his face didn't show the contempt he felt for this stupid man who was his superior. "I'll do that if you order me to, Captain, but I strongly advise against it. "

"And just why? You questionin' my judgment?"

Casey was doing that, he knew, but wasn't going to admit it.

"Captain," he said in as placatory a voice as he could summon up, "I've been closer to this case than you have. I know Mrs. Trent, know her fairly well."

"What's that got to do with it?" Manahan angrily jabbed the stub of his cigar in a large ashtray.

"In the first place," Casey explained patiently, "you don't get rough with people like Mrs. Trent. She's no skid row bum. I know we're supposed to treat everyone alike. But you and I know we don't."

Manahan grunted.

"In the second place, she wants to be booked. She was disappointed, no, I'll make that stronger, she was a little miffed when I didn't put her in jail."

"So let's accommodate her."

"Suppose we do. It will be page-one stuff, lead story on radio and television news shows. Then, when the grand jury refuses to indict for lack of evidence—which, believe me, it will—then who looks foolish? Who'll the media land on for being inept? Then we'll be right back where we started with an unsolved case, but this time with everyone laughing at us."

The captain pondered what Casey had said. Casey knew that his boss's pride was his vulnerable point. The idea of being the butt of jokes in the press, having the media call him incompetent, was enough to chill the captain's blood. This, Casey felt certain, was the train of thought making its slow way through Manahan's brain. This, if anything, would make him cautious.

The phone on the captain's desk buzzed. He picked it up, still mentally wrestling with the problem of Mrs. Trent, and muttered, "Manahan." He listened, then said, "I'll send him right down." Replacing the phone, he said: "A Malcolm Jackson is waiting for you. Says it's urgent. That's Mrs. Trent's boy by her first husband, I seem to recollect."

"Adopted by her and her first husband."

"Well, go see what's so urgent about him seein' you, then come and tell me."

"Right," Casey said, and left.

The desk sergeant, a grizzled veteran waiting out the years until pension time in a nice, safe job, nodded toward Casey's office. "I put him in there." It crossed Casey's mind that the sergeant was probably the one who kept Manahan informed of what went on in the squadroom.

"Thanks, Dave," Casey said. Casey made it a practice to be polite to the old-timers who shared Manahan's resentment of the new breed, the college-educated cop.

Malcolm Jackson was sitting in the chair so recently vacated by his mother. He stood up when Casey came in and shook hands perfunctorily. There was none of the genial, easygoing manner about him that he'd displayed the day Casey questioned him.

"Nice to see you again, Mr. Jackson," Casey said. "Please sit down." Casey moved around him and sat behind his desk. "What can I do for you?"

Jackson sat down. "I am here to confess that I murdered James Trent," he said.

Casey was able to suppress his surprise. He realized that there had been an unarticulated suspicion in his mind that this was exactly what Malcolm Jackson was going to say.

"You want to tell me this without legal counsel present, Mr. Jackson? You, of course, know your rights."

"I'll be my own legal counsel, Lieutenant."

"Then do you want to tell me why you killed Trent?"

"Because he abused my mother, had been abusing her for years."

"Then why did you wait so long to, er, take action?"

Jackson was beginning to relax.

"Because I only learned of it recently, learned of it for sure, that is. I'd suspected it, but Mother would never talk about it."

"How did you learn for sure, as you put it, that Trent was abusing her?"

"I finally forced it out of her. She'd been losing ground emotionally for some time. It appeared to be getting worse. So—oh, it must have been a couple of months ago—I sat her down and made her tell me."

"And you decided to kill him?"

"I was furious. My first thought was to give him a thorough beating and threaten him with a worse one if he ever abused her again."

"And why did you change your mind?" Jackson, Casey noticed, was looking less grim, even bordered on enthusiasm as he poured out his confession.

"When I'd cooled off, I realized beating him up wasn't

182

going to solve anything. He was a mean bastard. He had power and he had money. Mother's life would still be miserable. And there's no telling what he'd have done to me."

"So—"

Jackson held up a hand as a stop sign. "Let me finish, Lieutenant, while I still have the courage."

"Go on."

"I finally realized that killing him was the only solution. I know you're wondering why Mother didn't just divorce him—"

"It did cross my mind as the logical solution."

"He would have made her, well, he was the Splendid Samaritan, and he wasn't going to tolerate anything that damaged his image. He'd have found a way to make her out to be a slut, see that her reputation was ruined. You can do almost anything in our society if you have power and money."

Casey agreed, but didn't say so. He wondered if he was becoming cynical.

"So you decided killing him was the only possible way to solve your problem."

"Yes. I couldn't think of any other way to rid Mother of Trent, any way that would protect her. Anyway," Jackson continued with a faint smile, "the idea appealed to me."

"Tell me how you went about it," Casey said.

"Oh, I didn't do it myself."

"You're going to say you hired it done."

"That's right."

"And you're going to tell me that you don't know who actually killed Trent because you hired a professional hit man through a third party."

Jackson was obviously surprised. "How did you know that?"

Casey was tempted to tell him he'd already heard that story from Jackson's mother, but decided not to.

"Figures," he said. "You wanted him dead, but cold-blooded killing isn't in your line. You probably were afraid you'd screw it up somehow. You, being a criminal lawyer, would have no difficulty finding a professional gunslinger. The third party was probably one of your clients."

"I'm amazed," Jackson said. "How did you guess all that?"

"I've heard stories like that before. By the way, I suppose you'll refuse to tell me who the third party was, the one who hired the hit man for you?"

"No, I don't mind telling you that. His name was Johnny DeVito. Small-time hood. I've represented him several times. Nothing important. Breaking and entering, heisting cars for chop shops. But he had the connections."

Casey hadn't missed Jackson's use of the past tense when naming DeVito. "We'll need to haul DeVito in and question him, you know," Casey told Jackson.

"Haul away—that is, if you can find him. He seems to have disappeared."

"Oh? Any idea where or why?"

"Not for certain. Word is he got a little too ambitious and tried to rip off some small-time Mafia operation. It's rumored he's wearing cement slippers at the bottom of the lake somewhere."

Very neat, Casey thought. Naming the go-between who'd hired the killer lent Jackson's story credibility. He supposed someone would have to check out DeVito. He'd bet, though, that Jackson knew no one would ever hear from the small-time punk again.

"Mr. Jackson, did you instruct your gunman—through the third party, of course—to burglarize Trent's office so that the police would be misled?"

"I think you're psychic, Lieutenant."

"No, just experienced. I suppose Trent was tortured to force the combination of the safe out of him."

"That's my guess. I can't think of any other reason."

"And how do you explain the light focused on Trent, and the bloody hundred-dollar bill in his hands?"

Jackson played nervously with the ends of his mustache. "I've thought about that, Lieutenant. I can't explain it. Of course, I don't know who actually did the killing. You get some pretty strange characters in that profession. Best I can do is guess it was some kind of idiosyncracy. People like that are usually a little nuts."

Jackson, Casey realized, had anticipated this question and devised as good an answer as was possible under the circumstances.

"One more question, Mr. Jackson. You tried to make the murder look like part of a burglary. Now, having gone to all that trouble, you come in and confess. Why? Your Christian conscience weighing heavily on you?"

Jackson actually laughed, which Casey thought tasteless of him. "You can drop the Christian part, Lieutenant. I'm not that religious. Otherwise, yes. It's been bothering me more and more. I don't want to go through life having nightmares about it." He stopped and seemed to be debating with himself, then said, "Maybe I shouldn't be telling you this, but I kind of want the world to know what a thoroughgoing bastard the Splendid Samaritan really was. Not very nice of me, is it?"

"Nicer than murder," Casey said coldly. Jackson had put on quite a performance. He'd anticipated every question. The only other thing Casey wanted to ask him was why he was confessing, the real reason. He knew that Jackson wouldn't answer that one.

"If that's all your questions," Jackson said, "might as well go ahead and book me."

Casey looked at Jackson intently before responding. "I could do that, as you know, Mr. Jackson. But I think we'll go another route on this."

"You mean—"

"As an attorney, you, of course, know what that is."

"You mean go directly to the state's attorney, and let him present evidence to the grand jury and seek an indictment?"

"If he thinks he has a case."

"But I've confessed."

"Several other people have also confessed to murdering James Trent."

Jackson seemed momentarily puzzled, then laughed. "Oh, you mean the nuts who confess to everything."

Casey didn't reply.

"You aren't going to book me?"

"Not at this time. We'll be in touch."

Jackson looked at Casey angrily. "Hell of a way to run a railroad," he said and left.

Casey went immediately to Captain Manahan's office.

"Come in, come in, Mike," Manahan said. "What did Junior want?"

"He wanted to confess to the murder of James Trent." Casey enjoyed seeing Manahan's mouth drop open in amazement.

"Well I'll be goddamned!" Manahan said.

"I'm sure he's lying, too," Casey said. "But if you disagree you'll have to decide which one you want arrested."

After Casey returned to his office, he sat and stared out of the one small begrimed window that, when clean, afforded a view of the precinct parking lot. He kept turning the two confessions over, then over again as if they were rocks with something slimy but important hidden under them. He just couldn't make sense of them. He needed, he realized, to talk about it with someone who could help him sort it out.

But who?

Not Manahan. Manahan was a moron. Not one of the other detectives in Homicide. Some of them were smart, but they were still policemen, thought like policemen, reacted like policemen. They wouldn't be able to unravel it any better than he could.

Then he thought of Randollph, and wondered why. He reflected on his relationship with Randollph. In a way, Randollph was the nearest thing Casey had to a best friend. Oh, he had plenty of friends on the force. People he liked and trusted. But the foundation of these friendships was professional. He, a Roman Catholic cop, had been best man at Randollph's marriage to Sam Stack—an honor of which he was enormously proud. After all, how often did the most prominent Protestant pastor in the city select an RC cop to serve him on such an important occasion?

And Casey enjoyed Randollph's company. He liked arguing theology with Randollph. He and his wife, Liz, were frequent guests for social occasions at the Randollphs'. Yet there was a curious kind of barrier that neither ever breached. They never called each other by their Christian names. Casey called Dan Gantry Dan. He called Samantha Sam or Samantha. And Randollph, he knew, wasn't averse to using given names. He'd even heard Randollph call the bishop Freddie. To Casey, it was impossible to imagine a priest calling a bishop by his first name. Unless, of course, the priest was also a bishop or had been a close seminary classmate of the bishop's.

He gave up trying to figure it out. What he did know was that he respected Randollph's mind. Randollph was smart. Randollph's education had taught him much about what motivates human beings to do what they do. And maybe Randollph's experience as quarterback of a pro team had conditioned him to look for things that weren't obvious.

He needed to talk with Randollph. He dialed the church's number from memory, hoping that this wasn't Randollph's afternoon at the hospitals, and that he didn't have a string of appointments.

Miss Windfall told him that Randollph would be free in an hour. Miss Windfall knew that Casey was to be granted access to Randollph whenever he requested it. Randollph had never instructed her to do this. She just knew. Anyway, she liked Casey.

Shortly before Casey was due to arrive at Randollph's office, the bishop appeared unannounced. No one knew whether Miss Windfall's capricious personal feelings included a friendly regard for the bishop or not. It didn't matter. The office of bishop mattered. At the Church of the

Good Shepherd, the bishop came first. She sent him right in.

"Ah, my rabbi," Randollph greeted him. "Do have a seat." Randollph wondered if the bishop owned a suit that wasn't black or oxford gray. It must be tiresome, he thought, to dress in a manner that never varied. Then he reprimanded himself for being too concerned with clothes. After all, he doubted that Saint Anthony of the Desert ever varied his costume.

"I've decided that being known as rabbi is something of a compliment." The bishop seated himself and crossed one plump leg over the other, exposing a length of black silk hose. "Did you know that a rabbi was originally a sort of resident scholar hired by a community to adjudicate any fusses and squabbles according to the Hebrew law?"

"Yes, I knew that."

"You would, of course. I lay no claim to being a scholar, but I seem to have been hired by the community —the particular religious community that is our denomination—to settle any internecine differences that arise."

"Are you thinking of Dan's problem?"

"I'm being reminded of it constantly. Mr. Torgeson appears to have organized a kind of mini-vendetta against Dan. Phone calls, letters—oh, not many, but they make up in bias, no, vitriol would be a better description, what they lack in numbers. And I've just come from being grilled by two, I suppose I should say newspersons since one was a woman, about Dan's case and what I'm going to do about it. Your friend Thea Mason's story about the meeting of your Governing Board has made it a hotly debated issue."

"What did you tell them, Freddie—the reporters, I mean?"

"Why, I smiled pleasantly and said that couldn't be decided until the matter had gone through specified channels."

"Did you tell them you'd base your decision on the recommendations of the Governing Board?"

The bishop steepled his hands as if in prayer, but his

188

cherubic grin indicated that he was not, at the moment, supplicating divine inspiration.

"No, C.P. Well, not exactly. The way I phrased it, though, might possibly have given them that impression."

"Freddie, Freddie," Randollph laughed, "you told them a lie. You'd better make an act of contrition, then say three Hail Marys and a Paternoster."

"Oh, I'm not guilty of lying."

"Dissembling, then."

"Not even that. I expect your board to bring in a recommendation strongly backing Dan. Then I can, in good conscience, act on it."

"But if it doesn't, you're not going to remove Dan."

"Not unless Dan requests it. But the reporters didn't ask me that. One thing I've learned in this office of bishop. No, two things. First, there is a difference between, ah, prevarication and honest but careful phrasing. The trick is to skirt close to ambiguity when a precise statement might be damaging. The second is never to volunteer the answer to questions you haven't been asked. Those reporters probably didn't know that I am the final authority in Dan's case and I have the power to dispose of it as I please—or, to put it in ecclesiastical jargon, as the Lord leads me. I saw nothing to be gained by enlightening them."

Randollph was still laughing when the intercom squawked and Miss Windfall announced the arrival of Lieutenant Casey.

The bishop rose to leave. "I'll just say hello to the lieutenant, then leave you alone. Perhaps he has some information about the Trent murder. If so, and if it isn't confidential, I'd like to have you inform me."

Casey was in the door before the bishop could open it. "Why, hello, Bishop," he said. "How nice to see you again. I hope I'm not interrupting an important conference on church business."

"No, I was just leaving."

"If you're not in a rush," Casey said, "why don't you stay. You'll be interested in what I have to report."

"Is it about James Trent, the late James Trent?"

"Yes."

The bishop turned around and headed back to the comfortable chair he'd so recently vacated. "Then I'll stay. That is, if C.P. has no objections."

"A wise pastor never objects to his bishop's wishes," Randollph said.

"Spoken like a good RC priest. Always obey the hierarchy. My pastor, dull and grumpy old bird that he is, would approve." Casey pulled up a chair. "I'll get right into my story. I'm baffled. I need to bat it around with someone, someone who might see something I don't. I thought of Dr. Randollph. You, Bishop, are a bonus." He quickly recited the tale of the two confessions.

No one spoke when Casey had finished. He finally said, "Well?"

"My experience, Lieutenant, has indicated that in dealing with a knotty problem, it is best to begin by considering every possible alternative."

"I've tried to do that, Bishop," Casey replied, "but it hasn't gotten me anywhere."

"You begin with the assumption that they're both lying?" Randollph asked.

"Yes."

"Their motive?"

"All I can think of is that each one is trying to protect someone they think actually did the murder."

"Yes, that's fairly obvious," the bishop interjected. "Now, who is the mother protecting? Whom does she suspect?"

"The boy, man, her adopted son, I suppose," Casey answered. "I think it is possible that there was more bad blood between Malcolm and Trent than we've been told."

"And who is the son trying to protect?"

"His mother, I suppose," Casey said.

"If he discovered recently that Trent had abused his mother, as he claims to have, then it would, well, he'd be likely to suspect or at least worry that she'd done it."

"If, Lieutenant, you thought one or the other had done it, that one of them was telling the truth, which one would you bet on?" the bishop asked.

Casey answered promptly. "The boy—Malcolm."

"Why?"

"Because it would have been simple for him to hire a killer. He is a criminal lawyer. He knows intimately the dirty underside of Chicago. He could have managed it with little danger that anyone could ever prove anything against him."

"Is there any significance to the fact that they both confessed the same day, only hours apart?" Randollph asked. "And they told essentially the same story as to motive and method."

"I don't much believe in coincidence," Casey said. "But for the life of me, I can't figure out why they turned up hours apart."

"As to motive, they might be telling the truth." The bishop wiggled around in his large chair trying to find a more comfortable position. "From what we've discovered about Trent, he was hardly the Splendid Samaritan. We don't know what sordid acts he was capable of. But you can't rule out abuse of his wife."

"The similarity of their stories, confessions, suggests the possibility that they might have conspired to do in Trent, then each confess to the crime," Randollph speculated.

"How would the double confession be to their advantage?" the bishop asked.

"Because there isn't enough evidence against either one to get an indictment, let alone a conviction," Casey said. "A good criminal lawyer could be almost certain of getting either or both acquitted."

"Sounds like something Malcolm might have thought of," Randollph said.

"If each of them is lying, it says something good about them," the bishop said.

"Oh, how is that?" Casey asked.

191

"It means that they are willing to risk everything to save someone they love. She'd be risking ruining a spotless reputation, receiving a long prison term, at best, and the loss of her inheritance from Trent's estate—which, I gather, she needs rather badly. Her son would face disbarment, prison, or even the death penalty. It takes a lot of love to give up everything you have, even your life, for someone else's sake."

"I hadn't thought about that, Bishop," Casey said. "Or at least I hadn't pondered it. It isn't easy for a Homicide detective to associate love with murder. Of course, the motive for their false confessions would have to be love."

"You still think they were both lying?" Randollph asked.

"Yes, Doctor, I'm going to proceed on that assumption until I can turn up evidence that genuinely implicates one or both in Trent's murder."

"If you are right in your assumption, Lieutenant, there is another possible, even plausible explanation for their confessions."

"Oh? I can't think of what it might be."

"You're a detective. Work on it. You'll figure it out," Randollph said.

XIV

Casey began the next day by reviewing his options.

He concluded that he was right, that Mrs. Trent and her son probably, almost certainly, were innocent. He didn't doubt, though, that each had a reason to suspect—or at least fear—that the other one was guilty. The similarities of their confessions weren't too hard to explain. They'd both established excellent, if not airtight, accounts of their whereabouts elsewhere at the time of Trent's murder. About the only alternative explanation for their guilt was the one they had offered. Malcolm Jackson would think of this immediately. Mrs. Trent was bright enough to figure it out. He would find it much easier to credit their confessions, one of them anyway, if it weren't for the light focused on Trent's wire-bound hands. And the bloody hundred-dollar bill. Why would a professional killer lug a high-intensity lamp with him? The wire-bound hands might have been the gunman's way of immobilizing Trent while he tried the safe. But the bloody bill was a bit of theatrics meant, Casey was sure, to send a message. No hired hit man would have any reason to do such a thing. He would have been there for only one reason—to make money, not give it away. Casey decided he wasn't going to invest any more effort on Mrs. Trent and her son unless and until he could fit the lamp and the bloody bill into the puzzle.

But what did he do next?

He realized he hadn't taken a very thorough look at Trent. He'd learned that the Splendid Samaritan as a person didn't match his reputation. He was a patron of whores, a businessman who apparently saw nothing unethical about bribery if it made money for him. Perhaps he was a wife-abuser. And there was evidence that he had a mean streak in him.

Yet Trent had made immense amounts of money. How had he made it? Was he a rich kid with the kind of shove up the ladder of success a packet of money can give? Or did he do it on his own? The odds were that if he'd been crooked and ruthless while playing the part of the Splendid Samaritan, he'd been ruthless and crooked all along the way. Maybe Trent's path upward was strewn with people he'd crushed and climbed over. Maybe one of them had hated Trent enough to murder him.

Conclusion—dig into Trent's past. It was a long shot. But, as far as he could see, it was the only shot he had. And, as he thought about it, he felt that peculiar tingling in his spine. It was a rare sensation for him. He'd felt it a few times before when he'd fought through a nearly impenetrable jungle of facts and theories to find nothing at the center except an unpromising small path. The tingle had always been a sign, a signal to try the path because it might lead somewhere. And it usually had.

Casey didn't like the tingle. It violated everything he believed about the proper procedure for a homicide investigation. He believed in careful, logical analysis of available facts. He believed that homicides could be classified into types, that murderers did what they did for a limited number of motives. Find the motive and match it to the suspects. He believed this as doggedly as his pastor believed in the infallibility of the pope when he spoke ex cathedra. This peculiar tingle smacked of black magic, extrasensory perception, or at best an irrational hunch—all of which Casey scorned as valid instruments of careful police work. He'd never told anyone about it except his wife, Liz.

But he couldn't ignore it. It prodded him. It whispered, "This is the way to go."

He slid his chair, which was on rollers, to one of the gray metal cabinets along the wall of his office. It wasn't much of a trip. He pulled the file on James Trent, then rolled the few inches back to his desk. The file was medium thick, but consisted mostly of laudatory news and feature stories about the generosity and goodness of the Splendid Samaritan.

Casey found a yellow legal-size pad in the pile on his desk and began jotting what facts he could find in the stories about Trent.

Born, he wrote, in Hollyhock Hills, Texas, a small county seat town not far from Houston. Worked as a salesman for various oil-drilling equipment firms. Invented an oil-drilling tool that was, as it turned out, a revolutionary improvement on anything in its field. Founded Acme Enterprises to manufacture and market it. Acme went public, and Trent became a multimillionaire.

There wasn't much more about Trent to be gleaned from the stories. Acme Enterprises had become a conglomerate. Not unusual. It acquired all sorts of companies, everything from nationally marketed bakery products to an empire in real estate. One story included a pious statement Trent had made in answer to a question from a reporter as to how much he was worth. "I don't count my worth in what I have," Trent had answered. "I count it in what I give, in the good I am able to do."

Casey leaned back and thought about the skimpy facts he had learned about Trent. There was some kind of inconsistency in what he had read. It took him a while to isolate it. Wasn't it unusual for a salesman with no training in engineering to have invented a highly sophisticated tool

195

whose principle had eluded the best-educated and most experienced minds in the business?

Again the tingle along the spine.

Casey knew he'd have no peace of mind until he did a research job on Trent's past.

But how to go about it? He began to lay out a logical procedure. The best way would be for him to visit Hollyhock Hills. He'd need to know more about the founding of Acme Enterprises. He'd want to find out what kind of person Trent had been before he became the Splendid Samaritan. He'd want a list of Trent's early business associates; he'd want to talk to them. There would be records to check. Who had furnished the start-up money for Acme Enterprises? Why had he moved his headquarters from Houston to Chicago?

Would the department authorize the expenses for a trip to Texas? Almost certainly it wouldn't. It would want to know why he thought the answer to Trent's murder was hidden somewhere in Trent's past. And all he could say would be, "Because I have that peculiar tingling in my spine." He shuddered to think of the guffaws that would greet such a statement. Word would get around that Casey had gone a little strange. It would cut off a promising career.

He could call the chief of police in Hollyhock Hills. He'd probably cooperate. Policemen everywhere felt they belonged to the same fraternity. It was a poor substitute for an on-the-scene investigation, but at least he didn't have to ask anybody for permission to make a long-distance call. He had begun to write out the questions he'd want to ask the Hollyhock Hills police when the desk sergeant stuck his head in the door and said, "Chief wants to see you, Loot."

Casey was annoyed. Manahan probably wanted to browbeat him about the Trent case because someone higher up was browbeating Manahan about it. He sighed and headed for Manahan's office.

Casey was surprised to find Manahan lighting a fresh cigar with a good half length of the previous one reposing

196

in the ashtray. Manahan customarily smoked and chewed his cigars down to stubs. He only lit a fresh one with half its predecessor unconsumed when he was in a jovial mood.

"Come in, Mike, and sit down. I have some good news."

Casey sat in the chair across the desk from Manahan. "Good news is always welcome, Captain. What is it?"

"You'll be glad to hear that we're closin' down the Trent case. Been a bitch for you, I know."

Casey was stunned. His first thought was that Manahan had arrested either Mrs. Trent or Malcolm. It was the kind of damnfool thing Manahan would do.

"You mean it's solved? You've arrested someone?"

"No, I didn't say it was solved. I said we're closin' it down, the investigation."

"With no solution? The media will tear us to shreds."

"No, they won't. We're makin' an official statement that our investigation has determined Trent was killed by a burglar."

"But that's ridiculous!"

Manahan bit down savagely on his cigar. "Don't you go sayin' anything like that to the press, or I'll charge you with insubordination."

Casey was speechless.

"Now, Mike," the captain said in a more conciliatory voice, "killed by a burglar is the official line. You might not agree. I even might have my doubts. But someone upstairs says that's how it's gonna be."

"You have orders?"

"You got it."

"From who? Why?"

"Now, Mike, even if I knew, I wouldn't tell you. But I don't. It just came to me from upstairs. They don't explain. Just call off the investigation, they said. They'll put out the press release."

"Then it had to come from the commissioner."

"If I was you, I wouldn't be speculatin' about that. My orders, they were handed down to me by someone who had

197

'em handed down to him, so I pass 'em along to you. Not ours to question why. You know that."

Casey was seething. His mind was a jumble of ideas, speculation, fury, disgust, and puzzlement. He didn't trust himself to speak.

"Look at it this way, Mike," Manahan said. "You weren't gettin' anywhere with this Trent thing. Now you got it off your back."

This, Casey suspected, was Manahan's way of gloating. He guessed that the captain was thinking, well, you young hotshot that's supposed to be so superior to us ordinary cops because you've been to college, this is one big important case you ain't goin' to solve and get your name all over the papers an' the tube callin' you brilliant. He took a deep breath to calm himself and avoid saying something he'd regret later.

"Well, Captain, if that's the way it is, that's the way it is." He got up to go.

Manahan contentedly blew smoke at the ceiling. "Glad you see it that way, Mike."

Casey crossed his ankles and stared unhappily at his pebble-grain loafers, carefully avoiding Randollph's gaze. "So that's it. We have a case we're getting nowhere with and the powers-that-be don't want the heat anymore. Murder by burglar or burglars unknown—case closed."

Randollph laid his arms on his desk top, interlaced his fingers and began twiddling his thumbs idly. He wondered why Casey had chosen him as confidant to hear what surely was one of the least pleasant professional experiences of his young career.

"Except," he said as idly as he twiddled his thumbs, "Captain Manahan notwithstanding—it isn't."

"No."

"It will peck around in the back of your brain, whatever other cases you are assigned to, and won't give up until it's solved."

Casey smiled sourly. "That's it. Pride, I suppose."

Randollph stared at his thumbs, and deciding twiddling them was inappropriate for the pastor of a large metropolitan church, stopped. Unconsciously, his hands sought a paper clip and began toying with it. *He wants me to help him,* he thought, and was so surprised that he said it aloud.

"You want me to help you."

Casey stared at him, surprised.

Looked away.

Nodded. "Yes, I suppose that's why I came. Not consciously, but . . ."

"What do you want me to do?"

Casey shrugged. "I don't know. I came on instinct so I hadn't thought of how you could help."

Randollph dropped the thoroughly bent paper clip and leaned back in his chair. "Let's see—Captain Manahan has made it clear that to pursue the case would cost you your career."

"Yes."

"So you can't go down to Hollyhock Hills or even call the police chief to inquire about the Splendid Samaritan's background."

"No."

"I can't call the police chief."

Casey smiled. "No, he'd think you were some kind of nut and hang up."

"Theoretically, I could go to Texas and poke around."

Casey shook his head. "I couldn't ask you to do that."

Randollph laughed. "But you certainly wish I would. Lieutenant—if you're going to start not-asking me for favors of this dimension and I'm going to start doing the unasked—I think I'd better begin calling you Mike and you'd better begin calling me C.P."

Casey's face showed openly just how stunned he was. "You mean . . ."

Randollph nodded. "The bishop would like this cleared up and I have some time off coming. Sam and I had been think about getting away for a few days, although," Randollph's expression became rueful, "I will admit—Hollyhock Hills, Texas, was not on any of the itineraries we discussed."

Casey shook his head. "Dr. Ran—er, I mean, uh, C.P., I can't believe..."

Randollph chuckled, enjoying the for once totally non-plussed state of his usually poised young friend. "Mike, I do believe I've startled you into speechlessness. It won't be exactly a new experience. Ever since I came to Good Shepherd I have been around violent death, murder." His face turned pensive and he stared away from Casey at the El Greco copy on the far wall as if answers resided in ancient Toledo. "It is almost as if the Lord called me not only to be a pastor, but to be an amteur detective as well."

The tan rental sedan crested a superficial rise in the Texas gulf country and exposed a small sandy town that was tired and unprosperous-looking, and might just as well have remained hidden from view.

"Hollyhock Hills," said Samantha.

"So Rand McNally would lead us to believe," replied Randollph.

She punched him playfully on the arm. "Some romantic you are—our first getaway in months and you bring me to this dump. Where are the hills?"

Randollph eased the rental sedan down the road leading into the center of town. "In the fanciful mind of some long-forgotten developer. Along, no doubt, with the holly-hocks."

Halfway down the main street was a sagging gray frame building with HOLLYHOCK HILLS HERALD in gilt lettering across a bay window too dusty for such golden splendor. Randollph pulled to the curb and asked, "Where shall we meet?"

They gazed around. Across the street a dirty diner advertised HOLLYHOCK HILLS HOME-BAKED BISCUIT HEAVEN. Sam and Randollph shared a grinning glance; their eyes met.

"How," she laughed, "could a minister of the Gospel

200

possibly pass up that self-confident preview of the world to come?"

"That," replied Randollph, "is merely the proprietor's prophetic vision. Nonetheless, when scouring rural America for palatable food—your best bet is breakfast. Even if you eat it for lunch or dinner."

Sammy opened the door and stepped out. "See you in heaven, Chess."

George Grafton, the editor and publisher of the *Hollyhock Hills Herald*, stared first at Samantha's buff business card and then at her long trim body in a caramel-colored skirtsuit. He was a tall leathery-lean man with silver hair, gray eyes above a hawk-nose, and the weathered red face of an outdoor drinker. A "good ol' boy" Texas style, thought Sammy.

Grafton reached a long leg from behind his battered desk and kicked a hardwood chair forward. "Setcherself, Mizuz Stack."

Samantha sat and tugged her skirt to cover two inches more of the lovely legs that drew the editor's eyes.

"Whut's a big-tahme tellyvision personality from Chicago doin' in a Godforsaken hole lahke Hollyhock Hills?" Sam's eyes widened; Grafton waved aside the modesty. "No account to be surprised, Mizuz Stack—and by the way, the name sure do fit—I've traveled a bit. Even been to Chicago. Caught your show one tahme."

"My station is thinking of doing a feature on the late James Timothy Trent—also known as the Splendid Samaritan."

Grafton snorted, "Splendid Samaritan." He scratched his chin and tugged at an excessively large earlobe. "Could tell you a thing or two 'bout Timmy Trent—folks around here always called him Timmy." He paused and grinned. "Well, sometahmes they called him other things. I could tell you a thing or two, but I don't *think* it is news that's fit to print—as *The New York Times* would say."

Sammy grinned. "What's the fun of investigating some-

201

body's past if you don't discover where the bodies are buried?"

Grafton laughed. "That's the pure truth. I'm a nosy fella myself. Ever hear of Norbert Palmquist?"

Sammy shook her head. "No, but I have a hunch I came to Texas just so you could tell me about him."

The Reverend Harry Emerson Jacobs was a fat man in a small study. The blistering heat of Texas late-morning sun seemed to reverse the law of physics, contracting the room even farther. The lack of air-conditioning, the smell of Jacobs' sweat, and the heat and humidity made Randollph dizzy and gave him the feeling the walls were moving slowly in on him like a horror room in Edgar Allan Poe's head.

"So you see, Reverend Randollph, I fear you have had a long journey for nothing. Considering the events surrounding the death of Norbert Palmquist—nothing was ever proved, of course—but with that in mind I don't see how the bishop of Chicago could possibly designate Mr. Trent as Illinois Layman of the Year. Even posthumously."

"No," said Randollph, feeling more than a little uncomfortable with the shabbiness of his cover story, "the bishop certainly could not nominate Mr. Trent, but I haven't had the journey for nothing. This could save the bishop and our denomination a considerable public embarrassment."

Harry Emerson Jacobs nodded and his jowls jiggled with the motion of his head. "Yes, that's true. I am glad I have been of service. Of course, one likes to speak well of the dead, but . . ."

"Quite," soothed Randollph. "What happened to the Palmquist family?"

"Tragedy," intoned Jacobs sepulchrally, "nothing but tragedy. Mrs. Palmquist struggled, but she was a frail woman. Died less than a year later. Three children, a girl and two boys. They were sent to live with relatives out of state. The eldest boy went to an aunt in Kissiminee, Florida. The younger two went to someplace up north."

"I wonder if church records might show where they were placed exactly?"

For the first time in the half hour they had chatted, Jacobs looked suspicious. "Why would you want to know that, Dr. Randollph?"

Feeling distinctly like a hypocrite, Randollph covered, "I know Mrs. Trent. She is a fine woman and, of course, knew nothing of the Palmquist affair. It occurred to me that she might be willing to make some sort of charitable amends to the children."

Jacobs brightened. "Ah! I see. That indeed would be a worthy work. I'll be glad to check with our secretary, Gladys. If we have the information, you're welcome to it, Dr. Randollph."

Randollph swallowed the last bit of biscuit-and-gravy, sipped his coffee and sighed, "Not a meal that Clarence would esteem, but I confess there are times when rude-and-hearty fare suits perfectly."

"Amen," said Samantha and grinned. "Sorry, Chess—I shouldn't steal your lines."

"Such mild theft and such a delicious thief. I don't mind at all. What prompted you to resurrect the nickname Chess? If memory serves, you haven't used it much since the first year of our courtship."

Sammy shrugged. "I don't know. It just popped into my head again. Why? Don't you like it?"

He smiled. "No, I rather enjoy it. It did, however, jog something in me. There are days, even weeks that pass that I am not conscious of my first name. I don't suppose my mother was thinking of Cesare Borgia and his equally murderous sister Lucrezia when she named me. Probably had just read a romance novel with a dark handsome hero named Cesare—but still—it got me thinking. What's in a name?"

"What has that got to do with the murder of the Splendid Samaritan and the information we've uncovered about the way Trent cheated for his original fortune?"

Randollph smiled smugly. "Everything . . . or nothing."

"Are you going potty on me or merely mysterious?"

"My beloved Samantha, I so seldom get one up on you that I can't help wallowing in it a trifle."

"Chess," she said warningly, "you *know* I can't *stand* it when you go all secretive and smug."

Randollph smiled again. "If we catch the afternoon flight home from Houston, we can be in bed in plenty of time tonight for you to *attempt* to worm it out of me."

Sammy snorted. "Your mother didn't name you after an Italian murderer—she named you after a Cheshire cat."

The next morning was sunny-blue-sky-white-cloud-summer's-coming as Randollph entered the lobby of the John Hancock Building, located the office name he needed, and entered an express elevator. One of those mental quirks that dog human brains came to him as he waited for his floor. He found it virtually impossible to enter the Hancock without remembering a vulgar joke. Like the Prudential Building, the Hancock had a revolving restaurant atop it with spectacular views of the city. Since, at the Prudential, it was known as the Top of the Rock, local humor dubbed the Hancock's restaurant the Top of the——. Randollph sighed inwardly as he emerged from the elevator and walked down a plushly carpeted hall. One ought, he thought, to be able to hear something like that once, decide it was unamusing, and discard it, forget it. That it always came to mind when he saw or passed or entered the Hancock was a sign either of original sin or far too many years spent in locker rooms, but he couldn't decide which.

The law firm of Stout, Wodehouse, and Simenon was either prospering or pretentious. Their reception area not only sported the customary contemporary and expensive carpet, wallpaper, and furniture, but also displayed an abstract sculpture and an abstract painting that even Randollph's untutored eye identified as a Henry Moore and a Jackson Pollock.

He was almost immediately ushered into a paneled conference room with a fine lake view and a sufficiency of occupants. As he slipped into an empty chair, he nodded to or smiled at or met the eyes of Mrs. Trent, her two children, Malcolm and Helga Jackson, Warren Helperin, and Hamilton Haynes Reynolds III.

The graying bankerish lawyer, previously introduced as Pelham Stout and who had escorted Randollph to the room, sat at the head of the table and spoke over steepled fingers in a cultivated baritone.

"We may now proceed, since all the legatees or representatives of legatee institutions are present. The last will and testament of James Timothy Trent is a rather lengthy and technical document owing to the size of his personal fortune and the diversity of his holdings. If there are no objections, I will merely read the relevant portions and answer questions afterward. Copies will, of course, be available to legatees and representatives of legatee institutions. I take it there are no objections?"

Stout paused to stare over his tortoise-shell bifocals. No one objected. He opened a folder and began flipping through a bound legal document. He cleared his throat.

"'To my dear wife, Mrs. Elva Cooper Jackson Trent, I leave the income from a previously established trust as well as our home in Lake Forest, all household furniture and possessions, the family automobiles, all other chattel goods and property, and the contents of our personal and joint bank accounts.'"

Pelham Stout paused to look at the window.

"The previously established trust mentioned, Mrs. Trent, was set up some years ago with initial capital of two million dollars. That has grown somewhat and the current annual yield is in the neighborhood of a quarter of a million dollars, tax-free."

He returned his gaze to the document.

"'To my stepson, Malcolm Jackson, and my stepdaughter, Helga Jackson, I leave the incomes from previously established trusts.'"

205

Again the lawyer paused to look at the concerned legatees.

"The trusts mentioned were set up at the same time as that for Mrs. Trent. With, however, slightly less initial capital. They currently return about a hundred thousand dollars per year, also tax-free."

The mother and children were pale and rigid as Stout flipped a page, then another, finally settled on the clause he sought.

"'The remainder of my estate is to be divided evenly between the Church of the Good Shepherd and Business Executives for Christ and shall be administered, respectively, by Dr. C. P. Randollph of Good Shepherd and jointly by Warren Helperin and Hamilton Haynes Reynolds III for BEFC.'"

Pelham Stout returned the document to the manila folder and closed it. He removed his bifocals and pocketed them. He looked very ill at ease to Randollph. He met no one's eyes and stared at a far wall. He cleared his throat in thunderous silence.

"The remainder of the estate, as the document so quaintly puts it, includes all of Mr. Trent's business holdings. Absolute accuracy prior to liquidation or transfer is impossible, but, exclusive of future revenues, a reasonable estimate would be—one hundred million dollars."

Malcolm Jackson's face was beet-red and he slapped the table with a palm producing a sound like a rifle shot in the room.

"IT WON'T STAND! WE'LL SUE!"

Pelham Stout stretched his neck against the constraints of the collar of his fifty-dollar custom shirt.

The lawyer's voice was soft, soothing. "You may, of course, contest the will and there are certainly precedents for such an action. I would, however, be remiss if I did not state that Mr. Trent was medically and legally of sound mind and body when the will was drawn. I must also state, on behalf of Stout, Wodehouse, and Simenon, that the document is correctly, precisely, and legally drawn."

Randollph was uncomfortable and the tension in the room was palpable. The thought crossed his mind that greed might well be the root-sin and all others mere manifestations in various disguises. He tried to pull his attention back to the situation. The lawyer seemed to find his hands fascinating and stared at them with fixed attention. Warren Helperin stared at his lap, as Helga Jackson did at hers. Chaplain Reynolds seemed stunned into a dreamy reflectiveness while Mrs. Trent stared out the window as if contemplating flying away. Malcolm Jackson's facial color was less red, but his anger was still visible.

"We'll sue," he repeated. "When I think of what Mother put up with . . ."

Stout said very softly, tentatively, "Our firm, as executors of the estate, would be obliged to defend such an action vigorously. It would be a long, tedious, costly, and sensational process. If I may suggest—there are also precedents for negotiations amongst legatees . . ."

Pelham Stout had shifted his gaze from his hands; he stared directly at Randollph.

Randollph also spoke quietly. "I cannot speak for Business Executives for Christ. Nor can I speak, unilaterally, for Good Shepherd. I will need to consult the bishop and my board, but I—personally—would not object to an attempt at negotiation."

Stout beamed at Randollph. There, he thought, is a rare breed—a lawyer without an appetite for litigation.

Warren Helperin looked up and cleared his throat. "Like Dr. Randollph, I cannot speak unilaterally, but I would also have no personal objection to negotiation."

Stout beamed at Helperin.

Malcolm Jackson nodded, still tight-lipped. "Fine. You consult who you have to consult. We'll be in touch. For myself, I don't care, but if my mother isn't dealt with equitably—we will sue and we will win."

Dan Gantry did a little jig in front of the penthouse window. The skyline was shadowed by the late-afternoon descent of the sun; the features of the tall buildings were flattened by the shadows, which made them appear as huge stones and obelisks; Dan looked, to Randollph, like an imagined Druid capering among the massive slabs of Stonehenge. He paused to sip from his Scotch on the rocks and smacked his lips.

"Boss," he addressed Randollph, "I just can't get over it. Fifty million smackers for Good Shepherd from that pious old fraud, Trent. With that kind of dough—we can really start to make a difference in this town. I can think of a dozen programs off the top of my head!"

Randollph set aside his unfinished martini on the rocks and smiled indulgently. "We haven't got it yet, Dan. And, if the bishop agrees with me, it won't be fifty million dollars."

Gantry stared pensively at Randollph. "You don't mean you *really* want to give a hunk to Mrs. Trent? A quarter million a year and a house in Lake Forest ought to be enough for anybody."

Bishop Freddie drained his cordial glass of its last drops of sherry and shook his head. "Dan, your grasp of proper personal proportion is impeccable, but your economics leave a bit to be desired. With taxes, upkeep, insurance, and obligatory lifestyle—the mere possession of a mansion in Lake Forest makes a quarter million a year insufficient."

Dan shrugged. "Then let her sell the house and move someplace cheaper."

Samantha frowned and crossed her legs. "You're pretty cavalier with other people's lives, Danny boy. I see your point, but I see Mrs. Trent's side too. He wanted her name and social prestige; she needed his money. His will welched on the bargain. Not the sort of bargain I admire or would make, but she has a right to expect that the bargain they made will be kept."

Again Gantry shrugged. "Pardon me if I don't bleed for the pampered rich."

"They are God's children also, Dan," replied the bishop. "Now, C. P., what sort of compromise did you have in mind?"

"Twenty percent," said Randollph. "I expect that Helperin would go along with that figure. Twenty million should pacify Mrs. Trent and her children. I also think we should put it to the Governing Board at the same meeting where the recommendation concerning Dan is made."

The bishop smiled and nodded, but asked, "Why? I'm interested in your reasoning."

"Fifty million dollars is an extremely large sum of money and more interesting to many people than the pros and cons of Dan's activism. If we submit that issue for discussion first, I suspect most of the energy and fractiousness will be drained off. By the time we get around to Dan—Little Bobby and his friends should be too tired to cause much more trouble."

The bishop's grin was wide, his face beatific. "My dear C. P., I couldn't have conceived or explicated it better. You're beginning to think like an administrator."

Randollph pursed his lips. "No offense, Freddie, but is that an entirely unmixed accolade?"

Near midnight, Sammy lay on her back beside Randollph and purred, "Darling Chess, you may think like an administrator, but you don't make love like one."

Randollph grinned. "Is that the voice of vast experience?"

Samantha slapped his side. "Is that any way to repay a heartfelt compliment?"

"No. I am properly chastened."

"Uh-huh. That'll be the day and I want to be here to see it. You seem to have had a problem-solving field day, but what about the murder?"

"As a matter of fact—the will situation presented itself to me as a trinitarian solution. I believe the negotiations not only can satisfy Mrs. Trent and get Dan off the hook, but may also resolve Mike Casey's troubles as well."

"How?"

"That will develop with the events . . . or not."

She pinched his shoulder. "Chess, dear," she said warningly, "if I didn't love you—I would kill you."

"Then I am doubly glad you love me."

As Randollph and Samantha bantered it was only ten-thirty on the West Coast. In Beverly Hills, California, the sun had slipped into the Pacific Ocean not long before and the postdusk light was in the playful state of not-full-dark, chimeric and illusory illumination, softened shadow, and mind-malleable shapes.

Crickets chirped contentedly on the vast, luxuriant, and pampered lawn of Daphne Dee's twenty-four-room mansion. A light breeze stirred the grass and caressed the trees, set up a faint sigh through the multitude of window screens. The only other sound in the house or throughout the estate was the discreet music from a portable cassette player that rested beside the outsize swimming pool in the shape of an arrow-pierced heart.

The lawn lights had not yet come on; the automatic timer was set for precisely 11:15 P.M.

Daphne Dee lay in the center of the swimming pool on an inflated plastic raft, which was tethered by plastic ropes so that it remained stationary in the line of the pool's arrow. In the semi-dark, Daphne's meticulously tanned body glowed, accented by the skimpy bands of her hot-pink bikini. She had had a few drinks, enough for a mild buzz, and her body felt warm and tingling from the soft air and her anticipation of the evening's agenda.

Life seemed pretty fine, at the moment, to Daphne Dee. It had been a long road from Hollyhock Hills to Beverly Hills, but she had come every mile of it and now she had it all. When she had realized that the money from Norbert Palmquist's invention was going to be terrific, but that her share of it wouldn't get her all she wanted, she had decided to use it to strike out on her own. Bobbie Belle Parker had been shed like last year's "in" disco. Daphne Dee had been born and Daphne Dee had created a near-religious fervor for success through selling cosmetics. Bobbie-Daphne had parlayed an initially small line of makeup, her syrupy southwestern charm, the arrow-pierced-heart logo, a revival-tent-meeting approach to sales motivation, and the color hot pink (pink clothes, pink lipstick, pink jewelry, pink limousines, pink everything) into a conglomerate that was not so large as Timmy Trent's, but not that far from the Fortune 500 either.

She really had it all.

The mansion in Beverly Hills; apartments and condos in New York, London, Paris, and the Bahamas; complete wardrobes in each of those locations; all the consumer goods money could buy and every credit card ever issued; personal managers, accountants, lawyers, doctors, and servants to cater to her every material or health need or whim; she even had her own personal, salaried astrologer to give her the latest developments in her chart at any time of day or night. She had a modest fame, having graced the covers of *People, Time,* and *Newsweek* in recent years as well as appearing on the *Tonight* and *Today* television shows.

She had it all.

For now.

The one discomfort in her life was the less-and-less-deniable knowledge that Bobbie Belle Parker had been born in Spavinaw, Oklahoma, before World War II. Her dressing-table mirror was less a shrine to worship at now, had slowly, subtly shifted to an unrelenting prophet with a disquieting message. From "What a gorgeous creature!" to "You're no longer young," to "You're getting old!" the unavoidable mirror spoke its truth without fear or favor. Getting old meant more collagen injections and another lift in the not-too-distant future, more ministrations by hair stylists, masseurs, dieticians, exercise gurus, cosmetologists,

211

and surgeons. Getting old meant there would come a time when their limits would have been reached. Worse—getting old meant death sometime or other. No more sun, fun, sex, money, fame, and things, no more . . .

Morbid, thought Daphne, and wished she'd had just one more taste to quiet that nasty little corner of her mind.

She drew her thoughts back to the evening's agenda and almost immediately a warmth spread through her body that was sweeter, stronger, and livelier than the mere climate could provoke.

Johnny Di Volte was going to "drop by" a little after midnight. *The* Johnny Di Volte, the Latin screen star lover known to his fans as The Hunk.

She knew what he wanted, of course. The grosses from his last three pictures had been poor. He was having trouble getting backing for his new script, his surefire "comeback" vehicle. Daphne Dee had plenty of money and had dabbled in pictures from time to time. (What was the point of living in Beverly Hills if you didn't?) She also had good connections with the studio Johnny was negotiating with.

That was all okay with her.

She liked sex with hunky studs and she was not interested in the confusion called love. And Johnny Di was a worthy notch to carve on her bedpost, proof to the world and herself that the mirror did, in fact, lie. And she'd heard things from a few friends who'd graced his bed. He was an indefatigable ram with a creative mind and delicious ideas, lovely kinks.

Anticipation calmed and excited her together.

Fantasy fogged her brain.

She heard no footsteps on the grass, only turned her head when she sensed another presence. The figure by the pool was dark, indistinct.

"What the hell . . ." she started, but then she froze.

One arm of the figure was extended toward her. Even in the dark, the oily shine of gunmetal was unmistakable.

The figure's voice was soft, but with a sardonic edge, "Howdy, Bobbie Belle. How y'all doin'."

"My name is Daphne Dee."

The figure's voice shed its cornpone affectation. "Cut the crap, Bobbie Belle. We both know who you are and I suspect we both know why I'm here."

Bobbie Belle Parker's heart began a hysterical hammering in her breast that felt as if it would rip her apart.

XV

Randollph glanced once more at the screaming headline:

COSMETICS QUEEN RUBBED OUT

Beverly Hills Murder   *Daphne Dee Dead*

Early this morning, Beverly Hills police discovered the body of Daphne Dee, the internationally known and wealthy cosmetics manufacturer and saleswoman, in the swimming pool of her Beverly Hills estate. Ms. Dee was lying prone on an inflated raft in the pool with her hands wired together in attitude not unlike prayer and clasping a bloody one-hundred-dollar bill. Apparent cause of death was a single .22-caliber bullet through the brain. A high-intensity portable light had been mounted at poolside and focused on the body as if, even in death, the celebrity businesswoman demanded the spotlight.

Initial reaction by the police was to note the apparent similarity between Ms. Dee's murder and recent homicides in Houston, Chicago, and Atlanta.

Little is known of Daphne Dee's background before she burst onto the celebrity circuit with the huge success of her makeup line some fifteen years ago . . .

He shoved the newspaper aside and took another sip of coffee before turning back to Lieutenant Casey.

"What does Captain Manahan say about this, Mike? Theorize that the mysterious and bizarre 'burglar' is a traveling man?"

Casey shrugged. "He says it doesn't change a thing. Says it could be 'coincidence.'" Casey made a grimace of distaste.

Randollph raised one eyebrow. "Perhaps we've misjudged the captain. He seems possessed of a more flexible imagination than I can manage. Sure you won't have one of Clarence's plum tarts?"

"No thanks, C.P. I'm trying to keep my lunches light. So you think this Daphne Dee was really Bobbie Belle Parker, one of the original group that swindled Palmquist out of his invention?"

"I'd bet on it, and they're all murdered now—Trent, Bobbie Belle, Big Al, and Everett Stagg. That makes it hard to see how the murderer could be anyone other than the Palmquist children."

"According to you, that's not much help, C.P."

Randollph smiled and shook his head. "I didn't say that, Mike. I merely said that the documentary trail runs out on them. The phone calls I made revealed that Orville, the oldest, lived with his aunt in Florida until he was eighteen. Then he joined the Navy and dropped out of sight. Rebecca and Norman, the younger children, were sent to a denominational home in Danbury, Connecticut. They were adopted a year or so later, but the records are legally privileged and sealed. It would take quite a court fight to open them."

215

Casey shrugged. "Like I said—not much help. Thank you for trying, C.P."

"Mike, that sounds like you're giving up. Where's your Irish?" Randollph stared out the window at the skyline and the lakefront. "And I don't think this problem is that tough to untangle. How tight a rein does Captain Manahan have you on?"

"What do you mean?"

"Would it be possible for you to check some alibis without his knowing?"

"Sure, I can do that."

"Good, then here is a list of five names that I think you should check out for the murder nights."

Casey accepted the scrap of notepaper, read the list quickly, and looked back at Randollph. "Okay but what have you got up your sleeve?"

"I think I can bring a little light to bear—literally and figuratively. Now here's what I have in mind . . ."

Casey leaned forward and listened intently.

Miss Windfall sniffed.

It was a habit the massive woman had acquired, and Randollph had learned that it indicated impatience with frivolity. It was, Randollph decided, a certain sign that she was feeling better. She had returned from her brief illness in a somewhat flustered, almost girlish mood. Felt guilty over her absence from her post, thought Randollph, and she was touched by the flowers I sent.

"The bulletin is waiting on your column, Dr. Randollph, and there are *several* days' mail piled up."

Definitely feeling better and ready to take control again, Randollph noted. Aloud, he said, "Happily, my column is ready and I have some time to devote to correspondence." He traded the few pages of his column for the stack of mail, hoping, for once, he had successfully spiked Miss Windfall's guns.

But no.

Her expression softened not at all and her next words

came in the tone of voice that Randollph had come to recognize as his secretary's condescending-to-mention-the-rabble diction.

"There is a couple waiting to see you; a Reverend and Mrs. Hamilton Haynes Reynolds III. No appointment."

The last two words, given Adelaide Windfall's sense of etiquette, damned the couple as not only rabble, but upstarts as well.

Randollph felt ridiculous. Here I am, he thought, a putatively mature man, not unfamiliar to the world and holder of a responsible station in life—and my middle-aged and somewhat intolerant secretary manages to make me feel like a mud-puddle-spattered truant.

"Show them in, Miss Windfall."

Her lips creased tightly, but Randollph met her gaze until she nodded irritably, turned, and left.

Randollph met the Reynoldses near the door to his spacious office and led them to the conversation grouping away from his desk. They sat together on the dark leather sofa and he took the matching easy chair placed obliquely to the couch.

"What can I do for you!"

They glanced at each other, and Randollph noted they were holding hands, decided they made a very attractive couple with their fair skin, blonde youth, and scrubbed aura.

Chaplain Reynolds answered, "We want you to take us into membership at Good Shepherd."

"I see. Do you have current membership in another parish?"

Tess responded, "No—it's a little embarrassing, what with Hamilton's position. We've only been in Chicago since he landed the job with BEFC, a little less than a year, and, well . . . after Mr. Trent's death . . ."

"What Tess is trying to say, delicately, is that I was on a year's probation so we weren't sure if the job would last, if we would stay in Chicago."

Randollph nodded. "So you delayed making a commitment. Quite understandable. And now?"

"The Splendid Samaritan's bequest has assured BEFC of financial stability and Mr. Helperin has told me that the organization is pleased with my work. They are going to offer me a long-term contract."

Tess cooed. "We've attended Good Shepherd several times and we really enjoy your preaching and the services. I was so disappointed that I couldn't attend the parsonage open house. Everyone says the penthouse is just fabulous.

Randollph nodded. "It is lovely. We'll arrange for you to see it sometime soon. I assume you've both been baptized—was it in this denomination?"

They smiled and nodded, said in unison, "Yes."

"Then there's no particular red tape to deal with and no classes required. We ordinarily receive new members quarterly. I believe the next service will be in about six weeks. Will that suit?"

Hamilton Reynolds smiled again. "Perfectly, Dr. Randollph."

"Then we'll process the paperwork and notify you of the exact date for the service."

"Thank you."

"Not at all. Thank you for the kind words about my homiletical efforts and your decision to honor Good Shepherd."

Randollph was less than a third of the way through the accumulated mail when Miss Windfall buzzed him and informed him that Warren Helperin was on the telephone line.

Interesting, thought Randollph, as he reached for the receiver.

"C. P. Randollph. How can I help you, Mr. Helperin?"

"Just checking to see what Good Shepherd's position on the bequest is going to be. Are you going to negotiate?"

"That is not certain. We are having a special meeting of the Governing Board tonight to discuss that issue. I can say that the bishop is amenable to some arrangement and I anticipate that his position will be decisive. How does Business Executives for Christ stand?"

"I think we'll go along. I am chairman of the Directors Committee for the national organization as well as Chicago chapter president. I've queried the other directors, informally, and I see no problem with negotiations. Have you considered a figure?"

"The bishop and I have discussed twenty percent as a reasonable compromise."

"That's in the ballpark with our thinking. I'm very glad to hear this, Dr. Randollph. If we can settle this without undue wrangling, I think it would be to everyone's benefit."

Especially to that of a certain embryonic political campaigner, thought Randollph, and chided himself for cynicism.

"Mr. Helperin, I've been thinking we might get all interested parties to sit down together. Perhaps we could all meet at my apartment, the penthouse here, for post-dinner refreshments and amicable discussion."

There was a long pause.

Randollph waited.

"I suppose ... I can't see any ... real objection. You would issue the invitations?"

"Yes. I can call you in the morning to confirm."

Another pause.

Helperin finally said, "All right. Why don't you do that, Dr. Randollph."

An hour and a half later, Randollph was nearly through the stack of letters and resolving never to let it pile up again when Miss Windfall interrupted him to announce that Malcolm and Helga Jackson waited outside desiring to see him.

Randollph suppressed a bemused grin. Curiouser and curiouser, as Alice said to the White Rabbit, he thought.

"Show them in, Miss Windfall."

Malcolm and Helga Jackson were neither smiling nor holding hands as he led them to the conversation area. They did sit on the sofa and he, again, took the easy chair.

Malcolm Jackson began aggressively, "We want to know what you're going to do about this unacceptable situation, Dr. Randollph."

"We don't care for ourselves," Helga chimed in, "but after all Mother has suffered—we won't allow her to be cheated by that . . . man!"

"What did she suffer?" asked Randollph.

Malcolm turned as red as he had the day before in the lawyer's office. "That's impertinent! My mother's private life is none of your business!"

"But Mr. Jackson, on the one hand you enter a demand for millions of dollars as reparations to your mother for her suffering. On the other, you refuse to reveal what sort of suffering justifies such large compensation."

Helga stared at her shoes, said tightly, "Dr. Randollph, do you have any faintest conception of the sort of man James Timothy Trent really was? I don't mean that Splendid Samaritan hogwash the press reported and people believed. I mean the real man?"

Randollph nodded. "As a matter of fact, I do. I know he was a swindler, a briber, and a ruthless employer in business. I know he was a womanizer and a slick-speaking hypocrite personally. I'm sure there is additional sordidness in his life that I am grateful not to be privy to."

The brother and sister stared at him.

She finally asked, "How . . . how do . . . how did you find out . . . all that?"

Randollph shrugged. "As the media are fond of saying, I'm not at liberty to reveal my sources." His voice dropped, but it held a power, perhaps a threat, for all its quietness. "Suffice it to say—I know."

There was a silence as they stared at him.

He shifted eyes from one to the other, met their gazes calmly.

Malcolm's aggressiveness had wilted and his voice

turned plaintive. "You still haven't answered the question. What are you going to do?"

"There will be a meeting of all interested parties at my penthouse apartment tomorrow evening. I would be pleased if you would attend. And, of course, your mother."

Malcolm and Helga looked at one another.

Slowly brought their eyes back to Randollph.

"We'll be there," said Helga.

Malcolm nodded.

The large conference room in the basement of Good Shepherd was alive with the electricity of human, animal energy and raw emotions stirred into a living anticipatory stew. Whispers, muted conversation, and furtive glances were the audiovisual manifestations of clearly perceived and undeniable tension.

Like armies of the night jockeying for the high ground, thought Randollph, and he surveyed his troops. At the head of the table, Tyler Morrison was upright and more attentive than he was for routine meetings. On Randollph's left, Dan Gantry was quite still and slightly pale save for his hands, with which he alternately and subconsciously squeezed then rubbed his thighs. To Randollph's right, the bishop sat placidly with his hands clasped over his small paunch and displayed a serene and smiling face. Freddie, Freddie, thought Randollph, however do you manage to stay so calm?

As if reading Randollph's mind, the bishop leaned close to whisper, "After you've been through enough of these dustups, you'll discover the unpleasantness is mostly of mild consequence and, in any case, has little to do with you personally."

Randollph shook his head. "I don't know if I'll ever achieve such splendid detachment."

Tyler Morrison glanced at his watch, then at Randollph, who nodded. Morrison banged the gavel three times rapidly and loudly. A charged silence ensued.

"Call the meetin' t' order. This is a special session of

221

the Governing Board of the Church of the Good Shepherd and our pastor has something t' say t' start off."

Randollph cleared his throat. "As most of you know, this session was scheduled to hear a report from the Committee on Pulpit and Personnel concerning some allegations brought against Reverend Gantry by Mr. Torgeson, a member of the church. However, before we get to that, there is another issue that demands our immediate attention. As many of you know from following the news yesterday and today, Mr. James T. Trent left a substantial bequest to the church in his will."

"How substantial, Dr. Randollph?" queried Tyler Morrison, as had been arranged.

"The exact value is only estimated at this time, but it would appear to be in the neighborhood of fifty million dollars."

The silence was broken by several gasps and then returned, seemed to deepen. Randollph noted a number of stunned faces, felt some of the premeeting tension dissipate, and grinned inwardly. Nothing, he thought, like truly big bucks to get people's attention or divert it.

He continued, "There is, however, one immediate problem. The widow and stepchildren were left what for most of us would seem large amounts, but they only amounted to a very small fraction of the estate. The balance was split evenly between our church and Mr. Trent's organization— Business Executives for Christ. The widow and stepchildren appear inclined to sue BEFC and Good Shepherd for a larger share of the estate."

"Can they do that?" someone asked, and a babble of voices posed other questions, seconded the original, and erupted into a stream of thoughts, emotions, answers, and general misinformation.

Randollph was pleased to see Morrison letting it run for some few seconds. More steam being let off. Again, he and the chairman exchanged glances, and after a few more seconds, Morrison banged the gavel once more.

"Come t' order, come t' order." Silence returned and

Morrison asked Randollph, "What about that question? Can they do that?"

Randollph nodded.

"They can, and there apparently are legal precedents for the success of such a suit. Courts apparently hold that a husband and father may not substantively disinherit his heirs."

Robert (Little Bobby) Torgeson, mustache twitching and eyes popping, pounded the table. "We won't let her get away with it! We'll fight! She's no right to try to take money from the church!"

Tyler Morrison drawled quietly, "We can fight, but then the court'll decide who gets what. Is there another option, Dr. Randollph?"

"Yes. A negotiated settlement."

"NEVER!" shouted Torgeson, and a fresh babble of argument, emotion, and opinion broke out.

Again Morrison let it run.

Randollph marveled to himself. *Five minutes ago, Torgeson and his friends didn't know fifty million was coming to the church, and now they were defending it with a death grip more befitting the disenfranchised heirs. I wonder if any of them have stopped to consider if Good Shepherd really needs that much more money?*

Morrison banged the gavel again. "Order! I say order!" Silence slowly returned. "What would you recommend, Dr. Randollph?"

"If we fight—the consequences will be a long court battle with Good Shepherd receiving *no* money until it is settled, which might take three or four years. In addition, the church would incur out-of-pocket expenses for trial costs, which would run into six figures annually, and how much the church would eventually receive, if anything, would be in doubt. If we negotiate, we would retain some control over how much the church receives; we would save the costs of legal fees, we would receive the money sooner, and we would avoid further public sensation—an issue

223

that Mr. Torgeson has recently indicated concerns him deeply."

The discussion became more orderly and continued for another fifteen minutes before the chairman judged it was time for a vote and asked, "Somebody want t' make a motion?"

Peggy Conway said, "Move that the Governing Board empower Dr. Randollph to negotiate with Mrs. Trent and her children on behalf of Good Shepherd concerning the distribution of Mr. Trent's estate."

Tyler grinned. "Nicely phrased, Mrs. Conway. Second?"

The motion was seconded.

"Motion's been made and seconded—further discussion?—chair calls the question. All in favor raise your right hand."

Randollph counted fifteen hands. The board had twenty members plus the chairman, who only voted to break ties.

"Opposed same sign."

Torgeson and three others raised their hands.

"We have fifteen for, four against and one abstention; motion carries. Chair calls on Mrs. Conway for the next order o' business—report o' the Committee on Pulpit and Personnel."

Peggy Conway opened a folder and began reading.

The report summarized Torgeson's charges and interviews with Dan Gantry, Randollph, the bishop, Lieutenant Casey, and eyewitnesses at the demonstration as well as a poll of a cross-section of the church membership. Finally, she read the committee's findings and recommendations.

"The evidence seems conclusive that Reverend Gantry was involved in a legal and peaceful demonstration when he was set upon and attacked without provocation. While the vigor of his defense of his person appears inconsistent with the pacifist view he was espousing, it also appears not only understandable, but justifiable in the circumstances.

"As to Reverend Gantry's participation in public causes —while the committee neither endorses nor disclaims his

224

views, it affirms the right and duty of a minister to exercise his prophetic voice.

"Further, the committee has found Reverend Gantry to be an energetic and able pastor who executes his duties at Good Shepherd with spirit and creativity.

"The committee, unanimously, rejects the motion to dismiss Reverend Gantry. Further, it rejects the motion to censure him, but does recommend that the Governing Board commend him for his excellent performance to date."

Dan Gantry's face was aglow.

Randollph kicked his associate's ankle under the table and whispered, "Humility would be more becoming at present."

Torgeson said, "That's outrageous!" He spluttered and fumed and was joined by some of his colleagues, but the fire was dissipated. They soon ran down.

The board voted to commend Gantry for his pastoral performance by a margin of sixteen to four.

Afterward, the bishop instructed Dan, "No gloating, Dan. You escaped a sticky situation for the moment, but, given your propensity for controversy, it won't be the last run-in you have with laymen. C.P. and I will protect you to the best of our abilities, but you must make our lives more tolerable by securing a firmer rein on your personal abrasiveness."

Gantry deflated. "What's the fun of beating the bastards if you can't gloat?"

"Harsh judgment of your fellows—even as unsatisfactory a specimen as Mr. Torgeson—is not your business, Dan. By all means, be a prophet, but exercise a gentler and more forgiving voice."

The bishop turned to Randollph and smiled ecstatically.

"C.P., that was as bravura a performance as I have ever witnessed. I came fully prepared to exercise episcopal authority and was not required to speak a single word."

225

"Freddie, are you going to call me an administrator again?"

The bishop chuckled. "Not the worst thing to be, but let us merely say—you are growing in grace in your work."

Sharing late-night coffee and the day's events with Samantha, Randollph recanted. "I like to twit Freddie about administrative compromise, but... I must admit I'm coming to take some pride of craft in defusing and solving organizational problems."

Sammy grinned. "It's like the bishop said—you're growing into your job. You're becoming a pastor."

"I suppose I am. What odd turns our paths take."

"Yup. You never guessed you would be a preacher-detective."

"What spurs the latter noun?"

"Dear Chess, don't kid a kidder. The guest list for tomorrow night's soiree tells me murder will be discussed as much as money."

"Mmm—isn't it interesting that I homed in on five people and they all contacted me this afternoon."

"Did you learn anything?"

"They all left their cards face-up, yes."

"Suppose you tell me about it. Better yet, I have a frilly new peignoir—let me have one more shot at screwing it out of you—so to speak."

Randollph grinned. "Ah, the tortures of the third degree."

XVI

Mike Casey's telephone voice was glum. "It's no go, C.P."

"You mean you couldn't check the alibis?"

"No, that was easy enough, but they're all eliminated. Warren Helperin was downstate, in Bloomington, when Trent was murdered. He's open for Houston and Atlanta, but he was in a late-hour meeting when Daphne Dee bought it. Reynolds was also out of town when Trent was murdered. His wife was here, but she was also here when it went down in Houston and Beverly Hills. Malcolm Jackson was definitely in Chicago on all the murder nights. Helga Jackson comes closest. She was in Chicago when Trent was killed and out of town during the Atlanta and California murders, but she seems to have been here when the Houston killing took place."

"Don't be depressed, my friend. You did well and—that's about what I expected."

"Huh...I mean, you want to run that by me again, C. P."

"You're too young or you don't watch enough old movies."

"That's too cryptic, you'll have to translate."

"The idea came to mind while watching an old Hope-Crosby road picture."

Casey sighed. "I still don't get it."

"Mike, if you come to the gathering at the penthouse tonight—I guarantee to be a lamp unto the world."

Casey snorted. "Wonderful. I wouldn't miss it. In fact I'll come early so you can fill me in on the substance behind this chaff you've been handing me."

Randollph was as nervous as on the day of his ordination.

Not a bad analogy, he thought, to calm himself. I'm unsure of what I think I know and I'm apprehensive lest I've taken on more than I can fulfill.

Samantha was entertaining the guests while Clarence was providing a table of refreshments including coffee, tea, brandy and cordials, cakes, biscuits, and pastries.

He looked at Casey, asked, "Think we've let them sweat enough, Mike?"

Casey nodded. "If anyone has murder on their conscience, they should be plenty jumpy. Sure wish we had some evidence to support your theory."

"I know," Randollph nodded, "you'd rather go by the book. Sometimes we can't, though. Sometimes we just have to trust and go ahead."

Casey grinned nervously. "A theology of criminal investigation, C. P.?"

Randollph chuckled. "Not an impossible subject, Mike."

They stood up and left the kitchen, made their way to the living room where seven people waited with money and murder making them tense.

Casey stood in the doorway while Randollph crossed to the love seat, stood next to Samantha. He nodded in turn to Mrs. Trent, the Jacksons, the Reynoldses, and Warren Helperin.

"I apologize for keeping you waiting. I believe you all know Lieutenant Michael Casey of CPD Homicide Central. I asked him to join us because I believe our discussion may well range farther afield than Mr. Trent's estate. May, in fact, speak to his murder."

"What the hell, Randollph?" exclaimed Malcolm Jackson. "The police have closed the case. Murdered by a burglar. Where do you get off bringing it up?"

"Because James Timothy Trent was not murdered by a burglar any more than Albert Evans, Everett Stagg, or Daphne Dee—also known as Bobbie Belle Parker—were."

Randollph sat and Casey leaned against the door frame.

Warren Helperin said, "You got us here fraudulently."

"Not at all. I believe we should discuss the distribution of Mr. Trent's estate. Mrs. Trent, Good Shepherd, and BEFC are prepared to negotiate. Can you give us an idea of what settlement would satisfy you?"

Mrs. Elva Cooper Jackson Trent raised a pale face to Randollph and met his eyes. A third incarnation, thought Randollph, not the spiritless victim or the merry widow, but a frightened woman holding tight to her courage.

Her voice was soft and her eyes said to Randollph that she no longer cared about the money. "Malcolm says I ought to have half, but Malcolm is . . . emotional."

"Mother! We ought not discuss this in this . . . hostile atmosphere."

She glanced at her son. "Malcolm, the time has come to . . . face things."

"Mother!"

She ignored him. "What do you think I ought to have, Dr. Randollph?"

"I think you ought to have relief from your fear."

Their eyes locked.

"If you could do that . . . you could name your price."

Randollph shook his head. "It isn't a condition of agreement. Mr. Helperin and I had discussed twenty percent as a rational figure. The other thing is unconditional."

Helperin spoke angrily. "Count me out. All bets are off, Randollph!"

Randollph did not move his eyes from Mrs. Trent's. "I think not, Mr. Helperin. Mrs. Trent?"

"Mother, don't!"

Elva Trent nodded. "Done," she whispered.

Randollph sighed. "You and your son both confessed to your husband's murder. The confessions were patently specious. Lieutenant Casey wasn't fooled for a moment. Obviously, you were frightened for someone. Protecting a loved one. Each other? I didn't think so, but you might both have been trying to protect Helga."

Mrs. Trent put a hand on her daughter's arm. Helga trembled and Elva asked Randollph, "Is this how you relieve my fear?"

"Yes. With the truth. I assume you had your reasons for thinking your daughter sufficiently motivated to murder your husband. But your mental processes are jammed by your fear. It often does that. What motive could Helga have had for murdering the others?"

She turned to look at her son.

Malcolm Jackson muttered in surprise, "He's right, Mother . . . we lost sight of the whole picture . . ."

"Through some background information discovered in the unwholesome and unlovely locale of Hollyhock Hills, Texas, it became clear that the murders were the consequence of a long-ago swindle of a man named Norbert Palmquist. And were likely done by one of his orphaned children." Randollph's voice had been soft, now became harsh. "Warren Helperin—are you Orville Palmquist?!"

The businessman sat upright. "What the—"

Randollph's head snapped to his right and he shot out, "He's not, is he, Becky?"

Mrs. Reynolds dropped her brandy snifter and it rolled on the carpet.

"He's not, is he, Norman?"

Reynolds flushed and reached into his jacket.

Casey saw the motion and reacted, jerking his .38 out with swift deftness, but too late as the Colt Woodsman .22 in Hamilton Reynolds' hand jerked, made a light cracking sound, and the bullet ripped Casey's arm, sent his pistol flying across the room.

Teresa Reynolds reached into her handbag and produced an identical .22 automatic. They stood. He looked at Randollph.

"What tipped you off, Randollph?"

"A number of things. The high-intensity light for one. Initially, it was thought to be part of the grilling and torture process, but they weren't all tortured. Perhaps it could have been part of the symbolism, like the wired hands and the bloody bill—a spotlight on the victim's hidden villainy. But it also occurred to me that the lights were the same kind used to light videotaping. And you popped into mind. A video nut, self-proclaimed."

"But I had an alibi. I was in California when Trent was murdered."

"Yes. That made me think of teamwork, what Hope and Crosby used to sing about in their road movies. But a husband-and-wife murder team seemed unlikely when only one spouse had a powerful motive, especially with such bizarre, ritual, and gruesome murders. But when we found out about the Palmquist children—you two—Samantha reminded me of my namesake, Cesare Borgia, and his sister, Lucrezia. They are reputed to have murdered many. I'm curious—did you really videotape the killings?"

She nodded. "We did. How else could both of us have enjoyed the revenge? But that can't be all that made you suspect Ham—no need for that any longer—made you suspect Norman."

"No, but I remembered our brief talk on matters theological and scriptural right after the Trent murder. He seemed woefully ignorant even for a graduate of Harvard Divinity. I called them this morning. They never heard of a Hamilton Haynes Reynolds III."

"Very clever."

Randollph worked at keeping his eyes on the murderer's faces and not on their black, shiny, and deadly automatics.

"Was the vengeance worth its price?"

231

Rebecca Palmquist's eyes gleamed and her voice was intense. "Yes," she hissed. "Yes! It was wonderful after all those years of poverty and institutions and all the smug cretins looking down their noses at us! All that time and always knowing *we* should have been the rich ones, *we* should have been respectable, *we* should have had the good life!"

Her voice was rising and the room was centered on the mousy woman revealed as predator. Her gun barrel drifted with the uncontrollable nervous energy of her arm, her limbs. It wandered about the room, stopping at Warren Helperin's face, moving on, hesitating at Helga Jackson's head, continuing, drifting . . .

"Knowing those scum had stolen what was rightfully ours! Knowing they'd stolen it because . . . because our father was a *weakling,* a *fool* and a COWARD!"

"BECKY!"

Norman Palmquist's face was drained of color, shocked.

"It's true! If he hadn't been a coward—he'd have killed them. Right then, right there. Instead he killed himself and left the job to us. We said we'd kill them for him, but it was for us. I killed because they robbed *me!*"

"Becky. . ."

"And yes, Dr. Randollph—I loved it. I loved their fear, loved to see them grovel and beg, loved when their masks of arrogance and self-satisfaction dropped off, loved to see the creepy little gobs of slime show themselves." Her voice rose again, "LOVED THEIR PAIN, LOVED THEIR SCREAMS!"

She was shaking and panting and her face was a mask of hatred and evil visible.

"Becky, oh Becky!" wailed Norman. "It wasn't supposed to be like this. Come on, let's get out of here. We've got our money and passports. We'll run like we agreed."

His sister seemed to come back from her reverie of bile.

Turned her head and looked at her brother.

With disgust.

"Don't be a fool, Norman. We're finished."

232

"NO!"

Casey, woozy on his feet, holding his bloody arm, said softly, "I'm afraid that's true, Norman. We took the precaution of having the building surrounded and the lobby infiltrated with plainclothesmen. You'd better surrender."

"You see, Norman? Finished. But," she smiled and whispered intensely again, "we can at least have the pleasure of taking them with us."

She turned her head back to her literally captive audience.

Laughed.

Norman stared at her in horror.

"Becky, we agreed! We said we'd stop with those four."

"So what? Why should the Jacksons live to enjoy *our* money, the money stolen from us? Why should Helperin live? He always treated you like a flunky and me like dirt."

As she spoke in a silky whisper that caressed emotional cruelty and savagery, she swung the barrel of her Colt Woodsman from face to face—Malcolm Jackson . . . his mother . . . Helga Jackson . . . Warren Helperin . . .

"Why should Casey live? Or Randollph? They trapped us."

Randollph stared down the tight black hole of death.

He realized he was holding his breath and wondered if everyone else was.

When he noticed he was wondering how long he could hold it—he knew his mind was trying to leave the situation, deny it, escape.

—O Lord, spread your protection and love to all thy children here.

He was pleased he had fallen back on prayer in crisis and remembered the old observation about the paucity of atheists in foxholes.

"Or why not Randollph's pretty bitch?"

She swung her pistol to Samantha.

The nose was less than five feet from Sammy's head; Becky could hardly miss; Randollph had a nightmare vision of Samantha's exploded skull, blood drenching her

233

long beautiful red hair. He arched his feet and tensed his legs, hoping he could create enough struggle and confusion as he was killed that the murderers could be overcome. He knew he could never sit by and watch Samantha murdered, so he prepared to die.

"I think she should go first, Norman. I want to see suffering on la-de-da Randollph's face."

"BECKY! NO!"

"YES!"

She raised the pistol and grasped it with both hands in a shooter's stance.

Sighted on Samantha.

Randollph leaped.

The corner of his eye caught Clarence Higbee shoving Casey down and sprawling, out of the way, while he flung a huge frying pan at Rebecca Palmquist like a lethal discus with a handle.

Two shots cracked loud in the confined space.

A bullet hit the frying pan and another whistled past Randollph's moving ear.

Bodies were diving, flying, hurtling everywhere.

Randollph was almost to her.

The gun came around to him.

He could almost see the bullet coming out of the barrel straight into his face.

The shot cracked loud.

Randollph caught Becky Palmquist's shoulders as she sagged.

Surprise was on her face, wonder.

"Norman? . . ." she whispered.

Blood oozed from both sides of her thin, pale-white neck.

Randollph lowered her gently to the floor as her grip on her gun loosened and it thumped on the carpet. Her eyes rolled upward as she died.

Another gun dropped, thumped the carpeted floor and bounced against the first.

"Becky!" sobbed Norman Palmquist in a cry of loss and

despair as he knelt next to his dead sister, "Becky! I had to—I couldn't let you . . .

He raised his head and brought his eyes to bear on Randollph's.

"The answer to your question is no."

Randollph nodded.

"Vengeance is a poisonous dish."

Samantha was in Randollph's arms, sobbing, "Oh, Chess!"

As he held and stroked and soothed his wife, he saw, over her shoulder, Clarence helping Casey to his feet.

"My apologies, Lieutenant. I greatly regret having treated your person with rude force. Unfortunately, I was unable to conceive of another stratagem for removing you from the line of fire while I attempted my crude diversionary maneuver."

Casey grinned, despite his obvious wounded weakness.

"Clarence, no apology is necessary. Any time. Any time at all."

"You are most gracious, Lieutenant." Clarence moved about the living room, picking up fallen pistols as if cleaning up after rambunctious children.

He returned to Casey with his handful of guns. "I'll take custody of these momentarily—if you've no objection."

"My pleasure, Clarence."

"Then, if you'll come to the kitchen, you can call for your subordinates. And I've first-aid materials at hand and a goodly amount of experience in dressing wounds and injuries, owing to a voyage on which the ship's surgeon was incapacitated and I was pressed into service."

Randollph thought, just the man I would have chosen in any such circumstance. He wondered if there would ever be a time or situation in which he would see the little Cockney lose his aplomb.

It was over.

Late now and quiet and dark in their bedroom.

Randollph held Sammy close and her trembling had stopped.

"Are you sure you want to keep talking about it?"

She nodded her head and it rubbed against his chest. "Talking helps keep the boogieman at bay."

"So it does," he laughed and mused that he loved her, perhaps most of all, when she was little-girl-afraid-of-the-dark-or-just-wants-to-be-held with him. Wondered if that made him a closet macho man or chauvinist.

"Well, to answer your question, I suspect that Mrs. Trent and Malcolm Jackson were afraid that Helga had done the murder of Trent because they knew she had a personal motive of uncommon power."

"Which was?"

"I'd guess the abuse they talked about to Casey wasn't against Mrs. Trent and wasn't physical violence. Remember that the Splendid Samaritan was an obsessive womanizer."

"Oh," she shivered. "Yuck! What a creep!"

Randollph nodded. "A reasonable assessment. And one that will, no doubt, replace the previous public perception of the not-so-splendid Samaritan now that the newspapers will print the background of the murder motivations."

"Good. Why was Warren Helperin so upset tonight?"

"Because, I believe, he is the one who brought pressure to have the police close the case with the burglar fantasy. He was the only one close enough to the situation to have what the boys call 'clout.'"

"Why would he want it shut down?"

"My hypothesis is that he was close to Trent, not because of BEFC, but because they had done business in the past. The sort of shady things Trent routinely did, which would ruin Helperin's political plans if they came out. So he had to have the investigation stopped before it went far enough into Trent's background to upset his gubernatorial ambitions."

"Sleazy."

"We won't vote for him."

She purred, "Definitely not. Now that I'm all safe and relaxed and we're wide awake and everything—can you think of something else to do?"

"Raid the refrigerator for one of Clarence's superb snacks?"

She bit his ear. "Chess darling, for a man so smart, you surely can play dumb."

Epilogue

The long blue breakers rocketed into the small back bay on Maui and slammed the sand with thousand-mile momentum, hurtled up the beach as they dissipated in size and force to a few foam-flecked inches of bubbling water clawing to cover an extra yard, foot, inch, and died, receded from the same highwater mark that had darkened the hot white sand for years. As if all the power and energy of any single wave's life focused on this tiny strip of land, dedicated to achieving an ocean claim on a tiny extra measure of earth and concluded at a spot, precise to a millimeter, preordained prior to the wave's wind-and-water birth.

The Reverend Doctor Cesare Paul Randollph stared at his sand-grained toes resting comfortably a meter beyond the surf line and reflected that that was probably as heavy a weight of philosophy as an ordinary tide could float.

Overhead, a ring of palm trees moved to the light breeze, serene in their life function, existence. Unconcerned. That's what I ought to be, thought Randollph. Unconcerned, serene. After all, it *is* a vacation.

He turned on his side and saw nearly five feet ten inches

of well-oiled, tanned, bikini-clad and artistically created, splendidly alive flesh topped by a dazzling head of long red hair blazing in the tropical sun.

"Restless, Chess?" asked Samantha without turning her head or moving her eyes behind her mirror-tint sunglasses.

"Not as much as yesterday."

"Good. It's only day two and we've got twelve more to go. By the time vacation's over, you will have forgotten all about it and the publicity will have died down."

"Perhaps. I just wish he hadn't done it."

"Mike apologized, Chess. And very handsomely, but he was in a box. He had to credit you for solving the murders."

"I know. I'm not holding a grudge—if he hadn't given me the credit, the police brass would have found a way to sabatoge his career."

She nodded. "That's right. I've been around Chicago longer than you have—believe me—those boys have long memories. They wouldn't do anything right now, but Mike would be a lieutenant in Homicide the rest of his working life."

"Yes. I wouldn't want that, but I hate being bandied about in the media as the Pastor Gumshoe, Preacher Sleuth, Deacon Detective, and what did the AP writer call me?"

"The Minister of Murder." Samantha laughed. "Poor Chess, you really cringe at your public persona, don't you? Football star, high-powered preacher, and now amateur detective."

"Yes."

She turned toward him and removed her sunglasses; she grinned impishly. "What reputation would you enjoy?"

He returned her grin, waggled his eyebrows and said, "Lover."

Her expression changed to mock-stern. "That well-deserved accolade will—if you know what's good for you —remain strictly private kudos."

"I definitely know what's good for me and it's you. That will remain our secret."

Samantha stared away at the bright-blue bay water. "Except . . . perhaps . . . one particular by-product."

"Come again?"

"I'm late."

Randollph's mind felt fuzzy. "For what? We're on a vacation . . ." His words ran out because an idea was insinuating itself.

"For my period, dummy. My last one was very heavy and, apparently, washed out my IUD. I went for the test the afternoon before we flew over. I'm expecting a call this afternoon. Concerning the mortality of the rabbit."

"How do you feel? Emotionally?"

She stared into his eyes. "A big piece of that answer depends on you."

Randollph sat up. "Sammy—I'm thrilled! I've wanted to . . . be a father for some time. I was afraid to bring it up because of . . . well, because of your career."

She smiled. "Career-schmareer. I can get maternity leave and when I go back—do only the talk show. You're really glad?"

"Ecstatic, but I had no idea you wanted to be a mother."

She stretched the muscles of her long, lithe body and grinned cat-content. "Neither did I. Until I realized I might be pregnant."

They kissed.

Held one another.

Lay back on the sand, holding hands.

"What will we name him?" Randollph asked.

"Or her?"

"Oh, that's no problem—Samantha would be the only acceptable name for our daughter."

She grinned. "We'll see. If it's a boy—shouldn't he have his father's name?"

Randollph shivered. "Would you really want to stick him with a name like Cesare? Not I. My father's name was

240

Charles, or my grandfather's name was Phillips—as is my uncle's."

"How about Charles Phillips Randollph—then he would have the same initials, C.P."

"Hmmm. That's not . . . bad . . . Charles Phillips Randollph. I . . . like it."

They lay in the hot sun and Randollph felt tension and irritation drain out of him. It was replaced by peace and the feeling of content spiced with the possibility of joy. Perhaps, he thought, perhaps, it is somewhat simpler after all. The meaning of life may just be—life.

The calming breakers sucked softly at the sand. Salt scented the air and palm leaves rustled in light breeze. The sky and sea were bluer than imagination and the red ball continued to heat the life-bubble of planet Earth from the safe distance of ninety-three million miles.

Afterword

On February 23, 1985, Charles Merrill Smith, my father and the author of the Reverend Randollph mystery series, died of a sudden heart attack. He was sixty-six years old and left behind a rich legacy. As a writer, he was the author of religious satires, such as the bestselling *How to Become a Bishop Without Being Religious*, several volumes of personal and spiritual reflection, including *Different Drums*, which we collaborated on, and the Randollph mysteries. He had a long and successful career as a Methodist minister. He was a renaissance man of wide interests, tastes, and appetites including a life-long love affair with baseball and other sports, travel, fine food and spirits, literature and the arts, theology, philosophy, and politics. He was a raconteur and wit, a steadfast friend, and a loving, challenging father. His full life would have taken most men eighty or ninety years to live.

When he died, he was in the process of writing *Reverend Randollph and the Splendid Samaritan*. I had begun publishing novels before Dad turned his hand to fiction and had encouraged him to undertake Randollph. I also had worked with him on plotting, characterization, and narrative ideas, so I was more than familiar with C.P. and friends. Upon the urging of relatives and friends, I undertook to complete the manuscript. I hope I have acquitted him honorably. Even more than most writing, this has been a labor of love.

I plan to continue the series, which will always be billed—Charles Merrill Smith's Reverend Randollph.

Terrence Lore Smith
Colorado Springs, Colorado
April 20, 1985

About the Author

CHARLES MERRILL SMITH died shortly before completing
this book, which was finished by his son, Terrence Lore
Smith. Reverend Smith was author of seven nonfiction
works and five previous Reverend Randollph novels. Terrence Lore Smith lives in Colorado Springs, Colorado.